This book kept me on the edge of my seat preventing me from wanting to put it down. I became so involved in the story, I found myself feeling the excitement and anticipation for Max, Sam, Peggy and Ann as they frequently waited for the next shoe to drop. I highly recommend this book to others

Freddy

Deadly Diamond is very moving, exciting and compelling from the beginning to the last page. I read it in one afternoon to see if the characters would survive all the vendettas that drew them in quite innocently.

Sue A.

Loved this book! It was very interesting and the guys characters are so real I feel like real people. I read this book in one day it was so interesting. I really enjoy Sam's crazy dreams and the descriptions of opulence.

Lynn H.

I found Deadly Diamond so interesting; I couldn't put it down once I started reading it. The plot involving the theft of a very valuable red diamond and many interesting twists was very believable. I especially enjoyed the surprised revelation at the séance. I highly recommend this book to everyone.

Billy D.

DEADLY DIAMOND

A DIAMOND TO DIE FOR!

By

Rob W. Davis

Evershine Press, Inc.

Copyright © 2018 by Rob W. Davis

Library of Congress Control Number: 2018959504

Published by Evershine Press, Inc.
1971 W Lumsden Rd #209
Brandon, FL 33511

ISBN: 978-0-9975108-2-9
eBook ISBN: 978-0-9975108-3-6

First Edition: Fall 2018
First Mass Market edition: Fall 2018

Printed in the United States of America

Dedication

This new tale is dedicated to some dear friends who insisted I continue the story of Max and Sam. With help from my publisher and editor and all the inspiration from my friends, I finally got this story told. Thanks to all of you for your support and encouragement!

Chapter One

It's late Friday night thirty years ago inside the Bellasetta estate along the River Fiume Petrace on the outskirts of the largest container port in Italy, Port of Gioia Tauro. Miggy/Miguel Bellasetta Junior checks his watch as he sits at his dark Mahogany desk in his home office. His six-foot tall frame and barrel chest seem to overpower his desk. *It is after ten, I should be sleeping!* His dark blue eyes admire the red diamond in his hand one more time before he drops it into the small black pouch he received today that he had made especially for it. He had it inscribed in gold letters *"MGB"* for Miguel G Bellasetta, his father's initials. He draws the gold strings securing the diamond in the pouch before locking it in the strong box in his desk. He thinks silently. *Such a beautiful diamond! This was a steal for five million at Christie's Auction House. On Monday after I give it to Papa for his birthday, he will transport it to the Bella Bank for safekeeping. My brothers Gustavo and Mario wonder why I bought this. It is perhaps a poor investment to them, but it will show Papa how profitable I have made his businesses. I cannot continue to keep this diamond here though.*

Miggy sips some coffee brought by his senior guard Salvatore Cresto. Miggy smiles knowing his younger brothers are still away at college in the USA. Another week will pass before they will arrive home for the Christmas holidays. This is his first year of running the huge shipping company and other multi-billion Euro businesses including the Bella Banks that were all crafted by his Papa, Miguel senior who can no longer hold the reins. Walking into the living room, he thinks about his first big deal.

In three days on Monday morning, he will deliver a signed huge government contract. He chuckles to himself as he again looks over the particulars of the contract on his desk as he runs a hand over his slick black hair. *Just one person goes missing for fifty thousand and presto we kill our strongest competition! Ruthless! I love it! Hah! My brothers would never approve! Gustavo would disapprove more than Mario, and surely Papa too! We will make millions and no one will find out. How can that be wrong?*

Miggy is excited playing the game and is not in bed as he usually would be. However, he is suddenly sleepy now after drinking the fresh coffee offered by Salvatore Cresto. His blue eyes give a questioning look at Cresto as Miggy staggers passed the other guard sleeping in the living room and aims for his bedroom. *I must go to sleep now...* Miggy barely makes it to his bedroom before collapsing on his bed.

The wind howls outside the Bellasetta estate whistling over the limestone and mortar walls, whipping about the well-manicured grounds and through the huge wrought iron gates. Just outside the massive entrance Salvatore's lifetime friend, Antonio Albero stares at the large gold B on the gates waiting for the gates to open. Tony already has his old gray Fiat turned away from the estate ready to make a quick retreat if necessary. The rugged six-foot tall Italian remains crammed in his car not wanting to stand outside in the wind. He keeps his eye on his rear view mirror waiting for the iron gates to move.

Inside the estate, Salvatore Cresto checks his companion guard slumped over in a chair. "Sleep well my friend," Sal says walking to the security control for the house. *Thank God, Miguel took my offer of coffee. We are out of time.* He enters the disarming code for the alarm and presses a control button to open the iron gates. After a moment, he opens the front door to let Antonio Albero come in.

"Are they all sleeping?" Antonio whispers pointing with a black crowbar as he nears Salvatore.

"Yes. I had to give Miguel some coffee too. Let's get the money and get out!"

"Miguel is knocked out? Why!"

"I had to. He just stayed up too late so..."

"Bah! Let's go!"

Salvatore and Tony hustle into Miggy's office. As Salvatore stands by the office door, Tony rips open desk drawers of Miggy's desk until he finds a strong box in a bottom drawer. The lock is no match for the crowbar and Tony lifts the lid to reveal a box full of cash and something else.

"Funny..." Tony says puzzled.

"What?"

"I see the thousands in cash you said would be here and all US Dollars - not Euros. There is more than enough for me to buy that brand new Cadillac in America! However, there is a black pouch on top of the cash."

"See what it is." Salvatore watches as Tony opens the pouch.

"It is a big red... Wow! It is a diamond!"

"Miggy mentioned to me he just bought a rare diamond at Christie's. He paid millions for it, but why is the diamond here? Do not take it! It is too valuable. We cannot sell it and live."

"If we get to the USA, I am sure we could find someone. They have a black market, no? The Bellasettas would have little influence in America to stop us." Tony crams the diamond in his pocket and starts stuffing cash in his money belt.

"Maybe, but I think it is a deadly diamond. I would leave it. Is the money not enough?"

"No. Miggy suffers more if I take it!"

Salvatore shrugs his shoulders as he stuffs the cash Tony hands him in his own money belt.

Emptying the last of the cash from the box for Salvatore, Tony checks the drawer again. He reaches out to Salvatore touching his shoulder. "One more thing Sal, show me where he is."

The bedroom light is on when Tony enters and Miggy is passed out on his bed. He shakes Miggy violently. "Wake up you evil one!"

"Wha..."

"I have your precious diamond." Tony flashes the black pouch in front of Miggy's face.

"You took my diamond?"

"Yes, I have your cash too!"

"Guards! Help!"

"They will not help you. This is Tony. Tony Albero! You remember my father!"

"Your father? Oh yeah Franco, too bad. Hey we paid

for a nice burial for him."

"You killed him! This is for my father!" Tony draws back the crowbar and Miggy raises a hand toward him. In a rage, Tony swings the crowbar, smashing it against Miggy's left knee. He swings again crushing Miggy's right knee crippling the man.

"Aah!" Miggy screams each time cursing at Tony.

"Good! Feel the pain!" Tony swings again crushing some ribs this time. He swings repeatedly battering Miggy's arms and ribs. After pausing to watch Miggy writhe in pain, Tony swings the crowbar one more time banging Miggy's forehead and spattering blood across the bedroom. He looks in awe at the limp body for a few seconds and nods approval before he rushes out of the room.

Miggy wakes up briefly after Tony leaves. He weeps in pain feeling his legs and arms seem to be broken. *I will survive. I will survive!* Miggy is thinking with too much pain to speak, when his world goes dark.

As Tony walks toward Salvatore, he sees the awakening guard reach for his gun. He swings the crowbar and the claw digs into the brain of the guard. Tony watches the guard slump down this time in a dead heap oozing blood from his head onto the blue marble floor.

"He was my friend Tony!" Salvatore raises his hands in disgust.

"I am sorry Sal. I think it is time we should leave now." Tony tosses the crowbar across the floor upset with killing the guard.

Chapter Two

Carefully closing the front door behind him, Tony rushes back to his Fiat with Sal. He races away from the estate. His hands are trembling as he zigzags through the outer streets of Port of Gioia Tauro and onto the North ramp for A3 highway. Leonardo da Vinci International Airport is over six hours away. A twinge of guilt creeps over him. *God forgive me I killed two people, but it had to be done!* He notices Sal looks distant as he speeds along A3.

Sal finally breaks the silence of the purring Fiat. "Okay I know you maybe had to kill the guard in self-defense. I heard Miggy screaming. Did you have to wake him to kill him?"

"We have both killed before in combat. I did not want to just kill him. Do you not understand? I wanted him to know who I was. Even if for just a moment I wanted him to suffer and fear for his life!"

"I know I know. And now they will be looking for a murderer as well as a thief."

"The family is better off with Miggy dead. No matter if they look, we will be out of reach."

"It's a long way to Rome." Sal says looking at his watch.

"We will be at least in New York by the time anyone sees what has happened."

"Pia will be waiting for us at da Vinci with tickets and the boys. Let's hope that's all that is waiting for us!" Sal says going silent again.

As the Fiat races along, Salvatore Cresto closes his eyes and begins recalling his evening meeting with

Tony nearly a week ago. He remembers removing his winter coat and hat as he nears his lifelong friend Antonio Albero. He looks around inside the small café located on the north side of the city. The dim lighting and the dark dank walls make it a fitting place for such a meeting. He sees Tony sitting at a small table. He orders a coffee and nods at Tony as he sits down at the small table.

"Boun wera, amico. Why this strange meeting place? What is on your mind Tony?"

"Thank you for coming here my friend. I need this secrecy, and revenge Sal! You know why. Miggy killed my father!"

"It does look that way Tony, but revenge can be very difficult. Especially since Miguel Junior is rich beyond your means. He pays me well as one of the estate guards. I can help some but..."

"I can't pay you Sal, but I need to avenge the death somehow. You have access. You can take him out!"

"You know Miggy has security wherever he goes. I would be shot immediately! Impossible!"

"There must be something I can do."

"Let me think." Sal remembers thumping the tabletop with his fingers as a girl sets a mug of coffee next to him. He remembers thinking just before Tony speaks, *Miguel treats everyone - and me too - like trash!*

"My father was a faithful Captain for the BTC, the Bella Transportation Company for over twenty years. Then Miggy takes over and starts smuggling drugs. Miggy even paid for that diamond at Christie's with drug money Sal! My Papa realized what he was doing.

He said to me he told Miggy to stop the illegal trafficking or he would turn him in to the authorities. Miggy offered him big money to go along with the illegal operations but he refused it. The next day after he told me this, just this morning, Papa is floating face down along the shoreline. Any proof about Miggy that Papa had died with him. They called it an accident, but I know it was no accident. Miggy the evil one did that!"

"There is no way we can prove that, but maybe we can do something. Did we not always talk about going to America?"

"Yes someday we go there and buy a Cadillac. I always want a new Cadillac, but just dreams Sal."

"Maybe not just dreams. Your wife is divorced and no kids from you."

"Yes."

"Okay. I know Miguel always keeps much money in his office at home. I think maybe a hundred thou in US dollars at times. He pays off some officials, bribery I think."

"But Sal I want to kill him!"

"Why kill him? What better way to punish him than to steal his money? You know the Bellasettas have their annual conglomerate holiday party next week at the Palace Hotel several kilometers from their estate."

"Yes, you told me about the party last night when we were all out for dinner. Oh, your woman Pia is beautiful Sal. Your boys too are so polite for five and six years old. After I hear about my Papa, I think about family and how you are the only friend I can trust. But what are you thinking, Sal?"

"I'm thinking all the local employees and many company officers will be at the party hotel as well as all the available guards. The family stays there the night before and after. Even the old man Miguel senior goes. The party lasts well into Saturday."

"So? We can't fight everyone to kill Miggy."

"Miggy told me he is not going. He rarely goes to these things. He will be home doing whatever he does there with minimum guards. Only one guard and I are on duty there that night. Miguel usually works in his office at home until maybe nine o'clock. The servants will be all gone or off that evening as well, and by ten Miggy will be asleep. If I can put knock out in the coffee for the other guard and shut off the alarm, you can come in while Miggy sleeps."

"I can wake him and kill him then! Yes!"

"No, my friend! We do not have to kill anyone. We take what he values the most - his money! We tie him up and the guard and fly to America before anyone discovers them. Simple!"

"Miggy will come after us if we don't kill him."

"Not if we get the cash and go to America, a hundred thousand or more! Would that not be enough revenge?"

The Fiat slowing down interrupts Sal's recalling. He looks around at the airport signs through the light fog.

"It will not take them long to figure out it was you and me Tony."

"Yes, but Saturday morning things will advance slower. Ah, I park over there. It will be harder to find the car." Tony rolls forward and backs into a corner parking space in the darkest parking area.

Sal checks his watch as he approaches the ticket counter at the airport seeing it's just six thirty in the morning. He sees his girlfriend Pia De Bacco in the American Airlines ticketing area waving tickets with one arm. She has her other arm around Sal's five and six year old sons Arturo and Don. He notices her coat is off and her tight red mini-skirt and flimsy white blouse reveal too much of her sensuous body. He shakes his head annoyed seeing Tony stare at her stunning body. Sal gives her a long kiss and embrace before rushing everyone to the check-in area for their flight out of Italy.

At seven thirty, they board the early morning plane for New York City, New York. During the long flight, Sal and Tony doze intermittently still overly excited about what has happened. Arriving in New York in the morning, they change planes and continue on to Fort Lauderdale, Florida. The robbery and escape is successful except for the murders. They estimate their money belts are carrying only fifty thousand dollars total. It is enough to live on for a long time. Tony knows the diamond will fetch a huge amount on the black market if he can sell it. Tony drifts into sleep again thinking, *Our troubles will be over!*

Chapter Three

In the early afternoon, a taxi delivers Sal and company at his father's house. The stark white older frame house of Angelo Cresto at 812 Clifton Street in Fort Lauderdale, Florida looks just as his father has described it. He knows his father is living alone. He knows the house has four large bedrooms so they should all be comfortable there. Sal walks across the porch and knocks on the front door.

"Hello Papa." Sal is in tears when his father opens the door.

"Dio Mio! Fialio Mio! Coma sta? I am so happy to see you my son." Angelo Cresto reaches out with both arms and hugs Sal.

"Bene, Papa." Sal says after hugging his father.

"Are these your sons? Who are this lady and this man?"

"Yes, these are my sons Donny and Arturo, my woman Pia, and my old friend Tony, Tony Albero. Remember him?" Sal pats Tony on the shoulder.

"Yes, Tony. You are so grown up now. Hello. What brings you all here?" Angelo shakes hands with Tony."

"Papa, we need a place to stay now. We come into a lot of money and always wanted to follow you here to America."

"How did you get a lot of money?"

"Just think maybe we won a lottery. Please Papa, let us settle in. We are tired. We can talk later if you will let us stay here."

"Of course my son welcome and welcome to your friends too. I just saw on the news about a robbery and murders right outside of Port Gioia Tauro. I am glad you are away from there. I only use the master bedroom. I have to stay near a toilet you know. You can choose whatever other rooms you want."

Tony took the isolated bedroom near the front of the house with a single bed. Don and Arturo took the smallest bedroom, and Sal and Pia the remaining room. They laid blankets on the floor for beds for the kids and for Sal and Pia until they could buy more beds. A short time later, everyone met in the living room.

"I was about to bring down the Christmas ornaments for the tree. Will you help me son?"

"Yes Papa. Tony and I will get it." Sal walks with Tony to the hallway. As he pulls down the attic ladder, Tony whispers to him.

"We should store our money belts in the attic. That seems like a safe place for the money."

"Indeed it is." Sal whispers as he removes his money belt. He stuffs his and Tony's belt behind a rafter atop some pink insulation. He hands the large box of ornaments to Tony.

"Tonight we decorate this tree and celebrate starting over in this new world!" Tony says setting the box next to the tree.

Sal and his children decorate the tree with lights, ornaments and tinsel.

"Just take one strand at a time Donny. It takes time to put all the tinsel on the right way."

Pia and Tony work in the kitchen. She stretches for a box of spaghetti strands on a top shelf but loses her balance. Tony grabs her waist helping her stay upright.

"Thank you Tony." Pia smiles at him.

"My pleasure, I can help you with that." Tony says. He holds on to her longer than necessary and then takes down the box of strands and a large jar of sauce to make the spaghetti. He rubs Pia's shoulders as she prepares a large pot of boiling water. Tony stays with Pia spreading garlic butter on some Cuban bread and helping Pia heat up the sauce.

After dinner the kids play, while the adults chat over glasses of Chianti.

"Pia, you make good spaghetti." Sal tells Pia with a smile.

"Tony was a big help." Pia says smiling at Tony.

"The house is happy with people. This will be a joyous Christmas. Now it is past my bed time." Papa says seeing the clock is pointing close to eleven. He waves goodbye as he goes to his bedroom and closes the door.

"We sleep too. Boys, go to bed. Maybe we go shopping tomorrow." Sal says taking Pia to his bedroom.
"Good idea! Good night." Tony replies.

Sal and Pia sleep like the dead from all the travel. At nine in the morning, they join Papa in the kitchen. Sal senior is wearing a faded orange and blue robe, frying some chopped up potatoes and onions. He smiles seeing his son enter the kitchen but his eyes are on Pia fidgeting with her robe.

"Where is Tony? Pia, tie the sash. Papa sees you!" Sal says.

"I'm still sleepy. Sorry." Pia flaps the robe shut and

ties the sash.

"Tony was gone when I got up son."

"Gone? How long have you been up?"

"Not long, maybe an hour. The kids are still sleeping. I heard you two stir so I decided to cook something."

"This is strange. I need to check on something Papa."

Sal goes to the hallway pulls down the ladder and climbs up to the edge of the attic. He sees the money belts are open and the cash is gone. He picks up the small black pouch next to the money belts noting the diamond is still there. Sal is confused as he descends the ladder, then he hears a horn blow outside. As he climbs down, the horn sounds several more times. He looks out the front window and sees Tony sitting in what looks like a brand new white Cadillac. As Sal opens the front door, he hears Tony beep the horn again.

"You know I always wanted a Cadillac. I had to have it!"

"This is a foolish thing you have done Tony! Did you pay cash?"

"Yes, I used most of the cash Sal, but we still have the other thing... I know we can get a lot for it!" Tony feels sorry seeing disappointment in Sal's face.

"Yes, the one thing we should not have taken!" Sal says.

"Talk to your father. He was a jeweler. Perhaps he knows of someone who can fence it."

"Let's get settled better before we do anything else."

"We have enough left for a few weeks, Sal. Do not

worry."

After many phone calls and frustrations, although his sons speak limited English, Sal enrolls Don and Arturo in a private school paying their tuition with most of the balance of the cash. Sal drives his sons to their first day of school the following Monday. When he returns his father confronts him and Tony.

"You and Tony have paid for many things with cash and no jobs yet. Maybe now you will stop stalling and tell me how you came upon so much money. A new Cadillac is not cheap!"

Sal rationalizes his actions. *My father was a jeweler I know he will appreciate the diamond. I want to show father the diamond. He can perhaps find a discreet buyer for it.*

"Okay Papa, we did not win a lottery. Tony, bring the diamond."

"I get it now." Tony retrieves the diamond handing it to Sal.

"Papa this is a unique diamond; a very rare red diamond. It is the Bellasetta Rose Diamond. They say it is over nine carats. I think a fence in Miami may pay a million or more for it. We can pay off your house and we can all live like kings!" Sal proudly opens the pouch and displays the diamond.

Angelo's face turns beet red looking at the diamond in horror. "My God Sal, the robbery! What have you done? I saw the TV news last week about the Bellasettas robbery in Italy. Two men were brutally murdered! Did you do that? This is a cursed diamond!" The look on Sal's face answers Angelo's question".

"No Papa! The Bellasettas are evil! We deserve to have this and the cash!"

"You are the robbers! You must! Ah, you must..." Angelo tries to speak but his eyes roll up. He grabs for his chest and melts onto the floor staring without seeing.

"Papa, are you okay? Tony! Pia! I do not know what to do! Find a phone. Call a hospital!"

An ambulance arrives, but Angelo Cresto is declared deceased at the house. After all the commotion of Angelo taken away to a morgue, Sal is alone with Tony and Pia. He weeps.

"We could have had such a beautiful life."

"I know Sal. You must live on now." Pia says.

Saddened by the loss of his father, Sal is determined to sell the diamond. *Papa could have lived comfortable too. At least I still have Pia and the kids and Tony.* Sal does not foresee what happens next.

Chapter Four

Thirty years later Don Cresto and his brother Arturo stand in a white infirmary room at Raiford Prison in Florida. Don is an athletic man with broad shoulders, a narrow waist and six-foot four. His brother Arturo is shorter and heavier with narrow shoulders. Don is a faithful Catholic law abiding citizen, unlike what he knows of his father and his brother. He feels uncomfortable being in a prison and being next to his sick father. He resents having to grow up with foster parents because his father is imprisoned. Seeing his father only reminds him once again of a terrible scene; the bloody bodies of Tony and Pia he and Arturo saw almost thirty years ago arriving home from school. Again, he thinks about his childhood friends in Italy. Now that his income is better than average, he telephones his friends at least once every month. He still misses them and his home land of Italy.

Don's gray pinstriped suit wilts in the dankness that surrounds him. Even the air feels heavy with death waiting to happen. His father lies gasping for air in a stark white bed beside Don. Don knows his brother Arturo is standing behind him looking as pale as his father and wheezing from his asthma.

"Come closer Donny, my voice is weak." Sal Cresto says gesturing with an even weaker hand. Reluctantly Don leans down and puts his ear to his father's lips. The odor of death grows stronger permeating his nostrils.

Sal barely whispers. "My son..." He turns away and coughs violently before he continues. "I have to tell you this. The doctor says I have only a few days. You are my oldest son I must tell you this before I die."

Don cries out to his father. "No Papa, do not die!"

"It is no use son. The cancer is eating a final meal. I could die today. You must listen now!"

"What is it Papa?"

"Remember what I told you when we all came here from Italy?"

"Yes Papa. I try to forget about all that."

"I know it brings you bad memories son. You were just six then, but you must hear this."

Sal begins coughing violently again accepting some tissues his son grabs from the tray table. After his cough calms down, he continues.

"You know that Tony and I stole a diamond, a valuable diamond, from a very rich and evil family!"

"Yes Papa, but you said it was lost..."

Sal lifted a weak arm. "It was not lost my son. I wanted everyone to believe that. I hid it and wanted to sell it when I got free of this prison and I could find a buyer. Remember we stayed with your grandpa in his old house on 812 Clifton Street. As you know, your grandpa died soon after we came here. We still had some cash from the robbery but we needed to sell the diamond. The Bellasettas knew Tony and I robbed them and they suspected we flew to the US so they alerted the American news. The robbery was in the American newspapers and television. We were waiting for the attention about the robbery to settle down so we could sell the diamond."

"In a short time, we were out of money, and we were using up what little your grandpa had in reserve. I heard of a buyer in Miami. We could have all lived a comfortable life!" Sal leans over quickly and retches dumping ugly slime and blood on the tissues in his hand. His heart saddens as he folds the tissues and tosses them onto the tray table.

"I was going to Miami to first meet the buyer before we sell. I drive our new car almost to I-95 when I see I need gas. I had no cash. I forgot my wallet. I had to go back to get money. Then I see Tony together with my woman Pia! I was only gone a few minutes and there they were in Papa's old bed! I grabbed my pistol from our dresser drawer. I made them get up but then I just went crazy son. I was blind with rage. When I came to my senses, I saw Pia and Tony crumpled onto the bed. Blood was everywhere and they were dead. The gun was empty so I tossed it at them."

"I had to leave the house, but I knew if they caught me they would find the diamond on me. I took the small pouch with the Bellasetta Rose diamond and I climbed into the attic. I crawled out on the rafters about three body-lengths east of the ladder opening in the attic. I lifted the pink insulation between the rafters and stuffed the pouch under it. I knew no one would find it there. You have to crawl on the open rafters to reach it but they are close enough together so you do not have to touch the insulation. Just follow along the right side beam. Then maybe with gloves, lift up the insulation to find it. I thought I would come back to get it later."

"The police tracked me down I think because I was still driving the Cadillac. They identified me with the robbery in Italy but they were more interested in prosecuting me here for murdering Tony and Pia. They had the gun with my fingerprints on it."

"I convinced them we lost the diamond in New York. They searched everywhere but never found the diamond. At least no one admitted finding it. If it is still there, you know where the diamond is now." He quickly turns his head away retching again but nothing comes out.

"Remember this. Lift up the insulation maybe twenty feet east of the ladder opening. That is where I buried it right where the dip in the roofline is so low. The attic is only maybe two feet high there."

"Papa, you are soon free, two months only..."

"The doctor says I have but a few days left at best son. That is why I called for you and Arturo to tell you this. You must also know the prosecutor was wrong! Killing Tony and Pia had nothing to do with wanting the diamond for myself as he proclaimed! My friend and that bit..." Sal raises his clenched fist. He coughs a few times before he is able to talk again.

"They had to die! It was a crime of passion son. Never the less, they sentenced me to thirty years for a double murder. All this time in prison - I waited to be free so I could hold that diamond in my hands again! It is so beautiful son!" He pauses cupping his hands together to catch his breath. He coughs and speaks again telling Don why he and Tony had to steal the diamond.

"I told Tony he should not take the diamond but he said it was the only right thing to do! I am sure there is a great reward for returning the diamond. Oh son, it is so unique and beautiful! You can get more on the black market, but if you prefer you can stay clean. Just claim you found it and return it to the owner. That reward is huge, but you must be careful! The Bellasettas are evil people! Better to sell it to some other buyer. Whatever you do, split the money with your brother and maybe Tony's relatives. I only ask you to ship my remains back to Italy and bury me in my homeland."

"We love you Papa!" Don can feel tears forming.

"I know son." Sal pauses to catch his breath again.

"Someone else lives in the house now. You must find a way to go into the attic and get the diamond. That beautiful stone must not remain lost forever. You must get that diamond!"

"Yes, Papa, I love you!" Don sobs.

"Yes, I love you and Arturo. Please son, be careful. I know you would rather return it to the Bellasettas but remember the Bellasettas are corrupt people! They will stop at nothing including murder to get what they want. They murdered Tony's father. They could murder you and just take the diamond from your dead body!"

"Papa, we must go now." Don whispers, seeing a guard tapping on the glass window of the door.

"We will find your diamond and find a way to sell it for you. You can have peace knowing we will do that Papa! I promise!" He kisses Sal's cheek and sees a calm smile form on Papa's face before he and Arturo leave the room.

Don pulls a handkerchief from his vest pocket and dabs at his eyes and nose as he and Arturo walk into the hallway of the infirmary. His mind is racing with clashing thoughts. *I am a successful broker. I have enough money already. I know Arturo always needs money. Yet this is evil money! However, I must do this thing for Papa. I promised!* As they walk, Don can still smell the odor of death mixed with antiseptics in the corridor. As he exits through the locking doors of the prison infirmary, he sighs with relief taking a deep breath of fresh air. Don knows he must get to the diamond but he does not know how. He turns to his brother.

"Arturo, we must talk."

Chapter Five

Don Cresto drives in silence to his small sun-faded blue and white house on the North edge of Fort Lauderdale. He is still shocked at the frailness of his father. He remembers that in his childhood years his papa played stickball with him and the other neighborhood kids. Back then, Papa was a rugged man. As he goes inside his rented house with Arturo, his brother breaks the silence trying to sound cheerful.

"I know you are sad about Papa and I am too, but to get that diamond and sell it will make us rich! This is a blessing Donny!"

"It's a cursed diamond Arty, remember how it was stolen. Nothing good comes from this I can tell you that now."

"That's easy for you to say big shot! You do not have my debts."

"Gambling debts Arty... why do you gamble?"

"Last year I made over ten thousand, damn asthma." He wheezes and gasps for air.

"Yeah, but now you owe what, twenty thousand?"

"I wish. Actually it's more brother."

"More! You know I cannot bail you out again. What were you thinking? Why..."

"I thought my luck was changing. I kept doubling up. Can you see now what a blessing this diamond is? I read about that diamond many years ago too. It is the biggest red diamond in existence. I think we can get two or three million or maybe even five million for it. My friend Zach knows a good fence."

"How do you know all these unsavory people? Sometimes I wonder what happened to you. Now that you must live in my house you will have to change Arty. Everything is by the law, no criminal activity."

"Oh yeah, you're mister prim and proper stock broker! Well you just lucked into a good job. I have all the bad luck for you."

"And you know all the bad people too."

"Okay, in the surveillance business you don't get to know the best people, I admit. Let's not argue Donny. Let us think of how we can get the diamond. We can set up a sale as soon as we have it. I need to see inside that house. I need to know if it is alarmed. I need to know when the people are away. I'll find out who lives there. Maybe they all go to work each day. I'll check that out."

"You want to break into someone's house?"

"No, I can pick the lock. No need to break anything."

"Oh no, I really didn't need this crap in my life Arty!" Don shakes his head, upset about this information about his father's stolen diamond. He worries about Arturo's big gambling debt too. His easy life is suddenly in turmoil and he feels dizzy. Staggering to the couch, he collapses into a limp body as he hears Arturo continue

"Think Donny. We are not the bad guys here. Papa and the Bellasettas are. We are just bringing a valuable diamond back to life, and getting a lot of money doing it. You promised Papa, remember? How can this be wrong?" Arturo waits. Don is silent for a moment.

"Oh, all right. You are the detective. Use your connections to see who owns the house now. Maybe we can buy it."

"Yeah right, just go up to the owner and say 'Sell me your house please', I don't think so. Oh wait, maybe we can look inside that way. Maybe look in the attic. I can print up a realtor card."

Don starts to reply when his phone rings.

"Mister Donald Cresto?"

"Yes."

"This is Officer Clarion at Raiford. I need to inform you that mister Salvatore Cresto is deceased."

"What! We just saw him a few hours ago."

"I'm sorry sir. We believe he passed at least an hour ago. He had no monitor on him. The nurse went in to check on him and he was already deceased. She did say he looked peaceful. You are listed as his next of kin, is that right?"

"Yes officer."

"We need you to sign some papers about what to do with his remains. Can you do that tomorrow?"

"Tomorrow you say? Yes."

"Visit us between eight and five."

"Thank you for calling." Don is in shock. He disconnects and stares at his phone not looking at Arturo.

"What is it?

"I must take some time off. Papa is dead."

Monday morning Don and Arturo drive to Raiford and sign the papers for the disposal of their father. They are both silent as they walk out of the office and get into Don's truck. As Don starts the engine, he breaks the silence.

"It's just you and me now, Arty." Don stares at Arturo.

"Yes. We must reverse the misery that diamond has caused us. We must use it to make our lives better. Papa could have had a wonderful life but we can Donny."

"You think we can get a million for that thing?"

"I read about it some time ago. It is worth millions to the right buyer."

"We only need thirty thousand to get you out of debt. Sell it cheap. Let someone else take the risks."

"Don with a million or two we could both quit working. We could live comfortably the rest of our lives!"

"It is stolen money Arty. I do this only because I promised Papa. Then I want nothing more from it."

"You will change your mind if we get two or three million. I looked up the current owner last night. He is Maximiliano Diego Merchado, what a name! He bought the house three years ago. I want to see inside the house. I must know if there is an alarm system. I want to check it out if he goes to work."

"What does he do?"

"He works at Silvan Enterprises as a salesman. I doubt if he ever looks in the attic."

"How do you know where he works?"

"Once I got his name, I looked him up on the internet and his name came up in an article from the company newsletter. It said he was their top salesman.

"Good. Let us try to buy the house then. Maybe he is ready to move to another house."

"That is so stupid Donny! We can go in when he is

not home and take the diamond. There is no need to expose ourselves to him. Unless he has upgraded with special security locks, I can easily open them to get us in."

"That would be breaking and entering and burglary. I want to do this legally if we can. What is the harm in asking? We were going to rush into this to show Papa. Now he is gone so we can take our time. Maybe if this Mister Merchado wants to sell, we can inspect the attic."

"Okay, if we go inside I can see if he has an alarm system and check out the locks. I still like my way better."

"Legal Arty, let's do it legally."

Chapter Six

The sun shines through a clear blue sky and a warm March wind gently blows Max Merchado's wavy black hair as he drives with the top down in his red Corvette. Heading east from Silvan Enterprises on Wednesday afternoon, Max drives to a Novelty shop on Andrews Avenue. Stepping out of his car a warm spring air surrounds him along with some exhaust fumes from the traffic. He walks to the shop entrance and stoops over to turn the unusually low doorknob on the bright red door. Max loves being the number one salesperson at Silvan Enterprises and he loves being a great prankster. Being the top sales rep gives him a considerable amount of discretionary money.

Inside, he searches the counters looking for that special something. He walks to the main counter covered with all sorts of novelties and assorted tricks and puzzles, but nothing appeals to him.

Max nods at the red haired boy behind the counter. The boy looks to Max barely old enough to be working as a clerk. He sees the boy nods back, recognizing Max as a regular customer.

"Archie my man, I'm looking for something really startling this time." Max gives the boy a high five.

"Ah yes Mister M! You want something that will shock and awe people!" Archie says smiling enthusiastically.

"Yes... exactly!"

"I think I have just what you want. We haven't put them on display yet. We just got these things in..."

Archie begins walking to the rear of the store. He

stands behind the last counter watching Max come to a stop in front of him. Archie smiles a sinister smile as Max leans over the counter top. *This will be fun!* Archie thinks as he looks under the counter. He separates one of the items and grabs on to it.

"I have what you want right here!" Archie says and flips a black rubber spider at the counter top.

"Aah!" Max shouts jerking his body back. The two beady red iridescent eyes of the spider bounce up and down and stare menacingly at him. A wave of anger comes over Max but then he feels a rush of excitement. Max guesses the spider is nearly a foot in diameter with three yellow stripes along its back. He picks up the spider. He feels it is flimsy enough to fold up, yet strong enough to toss like a Frisbee.

"Perfect Archie! Do you have any more?"

"Yeah, I've got five more."

"Just give me one more for now Archie."

Max follows Archie to the front counter, still flipping between being mad and chuckling about how Archie caught him off guard. He picks up a can labeled Deluxe Mixed Nuts along the way.

"Is this a new batch?"

"Yeah, the springy 'snake-in-a-can' gag. It has some rad colors now."

"You never know when you need these, and these spiders are awesome!" He hands a can of the snakes to the clerk before paying for the items.

"You really seem to enjoy pulling pranks on people Mister M. Do you ever get in trouble for that?"

"The main thing Archie is to never get caught. If you are careful, you can pull it off without getting in trouble."

"Well, good luck with the spiders. I don't see how you can use them and not tick off someone."

"I'll keep that in mind Archie. See ya next time."

Max exits the store and walks back to his car smiling. He now has a plan for the not so thrilling Friday event he agreed to go to with his girl Peggy, his friend Sam and Ann, Sam's girlfriend. Chet, a friend of Sam's gave Sam four complimentary tickets to a Danglebatts concert in the Sun Life Stadium in Miami for Friday night. Max feels obligated to go. He knows the hard rock band will not play his kind of Latino music.

He drops his purchase in the trunk before sliding back in his Corvette. He checks his expensive Jaeger-LeCoultre watch. It is after five o'clock, time to meet his friend Sam and the girls to play Hearts. With the spiders safely hidden, Max is ready to meet the rest of the gang at his house. Dark clouds are drifting overhead. Max chuckles as he puts the top up on the Vet.

"The concert will be so much better now!" He says driving home to 812 Clifton Street. Halfway home the sky bursts open with rain, washing a small dust accumulation from the shiny red Corvette. Max parks under his carport thankful for staying dry as he steps inside the rear door of his home.

A warm rainy wind whistles across Ann as she waits to get into Sam's minivan. In just a few minutes the sky has turned from sunny to cloud covered and rainy, a typical afternoon in Southeast Florida. Under her pale green raincoat, she is wearing light green shorts like Sam and a white blouse buttoned up to her throat.

Wednesday evening is the weeknight they play cards at Max's house. Sam likes a routine just because he likes routine things. He smiles thinking how his minivan has made so many trips there it almost drives itself. With windshield wipers flapping, Sam drives through the rain thinking how everything is normal. Nothing unusual is going on in his life and this is the way Sam likes it. He eventually parks in Max's three-car carport between the Vet and Peggy's pink Ford pickup truck.

Sam knows Max will have the rear door unlocked. He knows Max often forgets to keep all the doors locked. He and Ann enter the rear door after briefly knocking. He walks with Ann through the laundry room into the kitchen and into the living room.

"Hello!" Max shouts from his lounge chair.

Sam notes Max has on a colorful Hawaiian shirt but his eyes are drawn to Peggy. Sam notices Peggy is wearing only a long white shirt and apparently nothing else.

"Hey guys!" Sam gives Peggy a hug.

"Hello Sam." Peggy says giggling and swaying.

"She's had a lot of wine already, and forgot to put on some clothes." Max slurs his words seeming a little inebriated as well.

"Are you sure you want to play cards?" Ann asks accepting a hug from Max.

"Absolutely! I have a mug of red rose' wine at each place for you guys. Let's play some cards. What about strip poker?" Max says.

"Not tonight Max." Ann says smiling.

"Some night you'll be too tired to say no..."

"I don't think it would be fair. I don't have much to take off so..." Peggy says.

"I noticed. Why are you not dressed?" Sam asks.

"I want you and Max to be distracted and lose the games." Peggy giggles again.

"We'll see. Let's get started. Hearts it is." Max says, shaking his head. He shuffles the cards one more time and begins passing them around. Before he finishes dealing, the doorbell rings.

Chapter Seven

The evening sky is dark early and a warm rainy wind whistles across Don and Arturo as they step onto the porch of 812 Clifton Street. Don shakes off the rain. He stands still and stiff for a moment not wanting to walk to the front door.

"Ring the doorbell!" Arturo whispers and nudges Don forward. Arturo being the short heavy one, he feels awkward pushing on his much taller brother.

"Don't be so pushy!" Don gives Arturo a disgusted look before closing his eyes and mumbling a short prayer. He steps forward and rings the doorbell. Don fakes a nervous smile as he waits.

"Are you expecting someone else?" Sam asks.

"No, this is it. Peggy..."

"Do you want me to answer that like this?" Peggy wiggles her top for Max.

"Okay, I'll go." Max gets up and staggers a little grabbing the couch as he walks for the front door.

"Careful Max, don't break anything!" Sam warns.

Sam's chair faces the front of the house. He sips some wine as he sees two men when Max swings open the door.

First, Sam sees a tall athletic man standing in the doorway. The man is well dressed wearing a dark gray suit with a blue and gray striped tie. His tan leather shoes show beads of water from the rain. He has dark - nearly black hair but Sam cannot quite see his eyes. Another shorter stockier man stands behind him. The second man has an open shirt, no tie, and khaki pants on. Although they are standing all the way across the living room, within seconds Sam smells thick musky cologne.

"Hello can I help you?" Max holds on to the doorknob for support.

"Pardon this late call but maybe you can help. Are you Mister Merchado?"

"Yes I am."

"My name is Don Cresto, and this is my realtor and brother Arturo. We would like to buy your house. We can make an offer..." Don says but his brother interrupts him.

"This is an unusual situation Mister Merchado, but my brother insists we talk to you about this house. We are prepared to make a generous offer for it."

"Really? Yes...This is weird!" Max says looking at the two men.

"He is very interested in buying this house for two reasons. We want to move into this area and this house has sentimental value to us. A relative once lived here many years ago. Would you consider selling at a premium price?"

"You know I never thought about selling. I would have to do some research and get back with you. The answer is maybe."

"I love the openness of this house too. Do you mind if I look around? I would like to check the attic for water damage. It will only take a minute." As Arturo speaks, he steps inside next to the couch. He looks around for any sign of an alarm system. Seeing nothing, Arturo sneaks a tiny bug on the underside of the end table.

"Sorry, we're kind of busy right now as you can see." Max waves toward his friends sitting at the table.

Arturo looks beyond Max and raises his eyebrows giving Max a polite smile. He takes a business card from his shirt pocket and offers it to Max before speaking.

"Please think this over and call me if you consider selling. We will make it worth your while."

"Okay Mister ah... Cresto is it. " Max says after looking at the name on the card.

"Yes, just call me Arturo."

"I will get back with you."

"We will give you a few days to check things out. We can come back Friday evening if you like." Don offers stepping in front of Arturo.

"No, we're going to a concert then. I'll call you if I decide on this."

"I look forward to hearing from you Mister Merchado. Just call the number on my card." Arturo says stepping back in front of Don.

"Goodbye for now." Don says. He bows his head as he and Arturo back away from the door.

"Goodbye." Max says as he closes the door. He stands for a moment concentrating on his balance before stumbling back to the card table. He flops down in his seat.

"Those guys are really weird!" Max blurts.

"Max, why did you tell them we're going to a concert Friday night? I hope they're not burglars!" Peggy says.

"They seem honest enough to me."

"Yeah, but they really smell." Sam says to Ann.

"I think he bathed in cologne!" Ann pinches her nose.

"It's really strange that he knew your name Max."

"I have his realtor card. He probably just looked up who owns this place. The two of them are so different to be brothers though. Like the big man must be over six feet and lanky and the realtor is short and stocky. I think maybe they're a couple!" Max says lowering his voice as he finishes dealing cards.

"Would you consider selling this place?" Sam asks.

"Like I told him - maybe. I've thought about selling ever since that nutcase tried to burn down my house. According to the fire chief I talked to then, this is a bunch of kindling wood waiting to go up in smoke. This man claims my house has sentimental value to him. I can check for a price on the internet."

"You mean with your prized laptop - the ultimate laptop?"

"Yes Sam, the latest and greatest."

"His laptop has 'HiFi' and 'WiFi' and every extra thing one can have. It even has a built-in GPS thingy!" Sam says turning to Ann.

"Okay, let's play some Hearts." Max chuckles as he finishes dealing cards.

"Max, I don't want you to sell this house. It has sentimental value to me too!" Peggy is nearly in tears.

"Oh that." Max says remembering the first time Peggy stayed overnight at his house. It was only after a few dates. Peggy seemed to be special to Max. He remembers feeling comfortable about her staying with him, not like a stranger at all. He smiles and nods his head.

"Yes! You also said you would put a paddle fan in the little bedroom for me."

"Yes, I remember. I bought the fan the other day."

"I want to set up my sewing machine in that room."

"You are right Peg."

"So you agree not to sell?"

"Okay Peggy, now that I think about it, relocating everything is enough to kill the idea. I remember when I first moved in here. I didn't have as much stuff as I do now. The money is not worth the trouble."

"That's wonderful Max. I'll reward you later." Peggy goes from sad eyes to giggles. She winks at Max and sips more wine.

"I'll call him tomorrow to tell him no." Max says. He starts to put the business card in his pocket, but Peggy reaches across the table.

"We don't have to call him at all!" Peggy takes the card from Max, tears it up and tosses it into the air.

The Hearts games end with Ann and Peggy winning. Peggy slips into the bedroom and hears boos from Max and Sam as she comes out fully dressed. A few minutes later Sam and Ann give hugs to Peggy and Max at the door.

"I'll see you tomorrow at work. Maybe we can go fishing Saturday. I know Ann just loves to be on the ocean." Max smiles as he gives Ann a final hug.

"I tolerate it. I do like the fish though. Good night Max!" Ann returns the goodbye hug.

"Goodnight."

Sam and Ann cuddle briefly after they get into the minivan. Sam is puzzled as he starts the engine.

"It really seems strange."

"What?"

"That Max caved into Peggy so easily to not sell his house. It's not like him to agree that quickly. It's like she has a magic spell on him."

"I thought Max would jump at a chance to get out of that fire hazard house. Maybe Peggy is pregnant and Max may want a safer house."

"She sure doesn't look pregnant!" He hunches up as Ann slaps him on the shoulder.

"I saw you get a good look at Peggy in her flimsy outfit!"

"I think it distracted Max from the game just like Peggy said it would. I thought for a second you were going to strip down like Peggy."

"No way would I do that! What is crazy is I even thought about it. Something is happening to me Sam. I want some excitement in my life, like maybe go somewhere exotic. I do not want to be a boring wallflower anymore."

"I never ever thought of you as boring!"

"Believe me I'll never do what Peggy did! Any show I do would be just for you! You and Max played really stupid at Hearts. Were you guys excited?"

"I'm kind of excited now!" Sam grins placing his hand on her thigh.

"Oh, I think I'm getting a headache!" Ann says, lifting her hand to her forehead.

"You're kidding!"

After a brief pause, Ann flashes her eyes at him.

"Yes I am."

They smile at each other.

Arturo walks to his desk in his surveillance room he set up in Don's house. He pounds a fist on his desktop yelling as soon as Don enters.

"We did not look in the attic. We did not get the diamond!"

"There were four people there, too much company. We tried. I really don't like being deceitful like this Arty."

"It's bad to go when he has company. We must go when no one is home."

"Why don't we give him a couple days? If he says no, then we do something else."

"I know you do not want to cause a commotion. We are trying your way to go in the attic on the guise of buying the house. It appears that will fail or take a long time. We must force access and take the diamond. We have to get that diamond! I know Papa died, take our time and all that, but I need money now!"

"Can we wait until Friday? If I do not hear from him by then we will go there. I heard him say they would be at a concert Friday evening. We can get the diamond then."

Chapter Eight

Friday night at nearly eight o'clock, Sam is with Ann and his friends Max and Peggy looking for their preferred seating on the field in row two near the center. Sam is using the four tickets his friend and lead guitarist for the Danglebatts, Chet Hatter gave him for the concert in Miami. The sky is clear and the temperature is in the seventies, a perfect evening for a hard rock concert.

"Wow, Chet gave you great seats!" Peggy says impressed with how close to the stage they are as she sits down.

Max has mixed emotions seeing he is within twenty feet of the temporary stage that is set up on one end of the stadium field. That part is good but he wonders if his earplugs will be enough to mute the noise of the band. An unusually warm spring breeze blows across him as he watches his friends sit down. Looking around at all the people in the stands, he sees mostly summertime clothing and a lot of Danglebatt shirts. Max shrugs his shoulders before sliding into his seat.

As if they waited for Max to sit down, the Danglebatts start running on stage. Dressed in gold outfits with black bat symbols hanging from their shoulders they wave at the cheering crowd.

"Hey, Blair, John, Chet and Dan!" Peggy shouts.

"You know all their names?" Max asks in disbelief.

"Of course I know all of them. Blair Broker the drummer, John Fret is the Bass player, Chet Hatter lead guitar, and Dan Batts is the lead singer and rhythm guitar. The band name came from a joke the guys pulled on Dan. You know - Dangle-Batts?"

"A band after my own heart. Did they dangle Dan from a tree or something?"

"There is an obscene explanation for the name."

"I don't want to know. You got your earplugs in?"

"Yes sweetie!"

Max notices the giant screen is lit up with the Danglebatts logo of a gold guitar on a light blue background with a black bat hanging from the guitar neck. The crowd roars and waves their arms over their heads as the announcer welcomes the band. Before the crowd quiets down, the band begins playing their first song, 'Bats in the Night'. As the music roars, Peggy and Ann whoop, holler, and have a great time along with the crowd.

Near the end of the concert and the end of a song, Max smiles. He retrieves a large rubber spider from inside his shirt and hurls it toward the stage like a Frisbee aiming for Chet Hatter.

A strong breeze catches the spinning spider and it sails head-high curving toward the lead singer Dan Batts. It bounces off Dan's guitar before landing at his feet.

Having caught Dan by surprise he leaps backwards and stops singing. He looks furiously back and forth at the audience for a few seconds before reaching down and picking up the fake spider. Staring at its beady red eyes, he roars with laughter and waves the spider over his head.

"Hey Batt-fans, want a spider?" Dan shouts hurling the spider into the crowd. He laughs and turns away from the crowd.

Deadly Diamond: A Diamond to Die For!

The spider soars high landing deep into the crowd. The fans go nuts. A man wearing a blue and gold Danglebatts' T-shirt catches the spider and waves it about to the cheers and whistles of the crowd. He tosses the spider to his left and raises both his arms cheering with the audience. A red-haired girl catches the spider and tosses it again. After bantering around several more times, someone keeps the spider. The spider tossing ends.

While the crowd is tossing the spider around, Dan Batts converses with his band. As the cheering for the spider calms down, Dan turns back to the audience and shouts.

"In honor of the spider, and for the first time live, we're going to perform the lead song from our new album 'Black Spider Woman!'"

The audience goes crazy again as Chet Hatter plays the rhythmic lead-in to 'Black Spider Woman'. After the cheers settle down a little, Dan begins singing in his raspiest voice.

> *Black Spider Woman, You're crawling all over me*
> *You strutting your hot body woman, so everyone can see*
> *Then you wrap your web around me, I can never get free*
> *Yeah woman!*

Chet rips a short instrumental before Dan continues.

> *Black Spider Woman, You make sweet*

> *love to your man*
> *I got arachnophobia; I do the best I can*
> *When you wrap your legs around me,*
> *We make sweet love again!*
> *And again - yeah!*

Chet starts a long guitar solo as the fans are deafening. Peggy cups her hand to Max's ear.

"Your spider made Dan miss the last word of his song."

"Hah, you would too if a big black thing came flying at you! I was really aiming at Chet just for fun."

"I hope Sam's friend didn't see you!"

"He was looking the other way when I tossed it. I aimed for Chet but the wind caught it."

"You and your pranks, we could have been thrown out of here. Dan could have had an accident!"

"Sorry. I didn't think it would drift off that much." Max raises his hands apologetically but cannot resist smiling.

"Well it did. I hope you're not planning to toss one of those things at our wedding!"

"Did you see how much fun the people had with it? I wish I had brought my other one too. I say enjoy the journey!"

"You have another one?"

"Not with me."

After the show, they wait for the main crowd to dissipate. They walk across the open grass field and through the grandstands. As they are walking to the parking lot, Sam's phone rings.

"Hello... Chet! Great concert! Thanks for the invite!" Sam shouts over the crowd noises. He pauses before turning to Max.

"Chet says cool way to segue into their Black Spider Woman song. Dan loves it!"

"He saw me throw the spider?"

"Their manager was standing on stage left. He saw the toss. He says it's a great idea. They'll do that at their next concert in LA. I guess you got caught!" Sam says after covering his phone.

"It's okay if it's part of the show! They loved it!" Max says.

"Let's face it Max you're losing your touch. And you promised not to prank anymore, remember?" Peggy waves a hand at him.

"I only promised not to prank you my love."

"Forget it! I can't believe this! Once again you stepped in it and came out smelling like a rose!"

"That's what I do best!"

"Go figure!"

"Yes! Now they have a great act to segue into their new album! You should tell them I planned it that way!"

Sam interrupts. "Chet says they want us to come back stage. Say hi and maybe tip some booze."

"Come on Peggy!" Max grabs Peggy's arm as he turns around. "My spider paid off! We get to drink free booze with the band! Enjoy the journey!"

Chapter Nine

The windows are down and the engine is off as Don and Arturo wait patiently a block away from 812 Clifton Street. Don is sitting in his older gray Ford F150 truck. Even though he is dressed down with a cotton shirt and denim trousers on, and there is a gentle breeze flowing through the open windows, he sweats profusely. Sweat oozes out all over him as he mops his forehead with a hanky.

"Look! They are finally leaving for the concert." Arturo says seeing the foursome exit the house and load into the minivan.

"I don't like this. This is illegal. I just go with you because I promised Papa and to pay off your debt to the Boss-man. After this I want no part of what you do with the money." Don is sopping wet. He slides his flashlight inside his shirt hoping he does not look suspicious.

"Don it is Friday and he has not called. I need the money and this is the only way left. I know he has no alarm system and they will be gone for hours. The neighbors have the shades drawn and running air conditioners. No one will even notice us go in there. We need the money. I need the money!"

"I don't need the money. I don't like doing this. If we are caught, I will be embarrassed beyond belief. I'll lose my job!" Don says as he and Arturo get out of the truck and walk toward the house.

"Just walk naturally and stop looking around! You look like a crook when you do that. We're doing nothing wrong yet." Arturo mumbles at Don.

Don is six-foot four and close to three hundred pounds with very little fat, but he looks like a scalded dog following his shorter heavy-set brother. His breathing is heavy and he can feel his heart pumping faster and faster. He follows Arturo up the three gray steps onto the porch and to the front door. His custom leather shoes make a tapping noise that worries Don thinking someone might hear him.

Arturo rings the doorbell and waits for a few seconds, knowing no one is home. He works his picking tools on the simple door lock.

"We're in!" Arturo says and opens the door.

Don follows his brother inside closing the door as Arturo walks across the living room and turns on the hallway light. Don can see a short rope hanging from the ceiling.

"Remember the rope pulls down the ladder Donny. I can't reach it but you can. Let's do this." Arturo motions Don to get busy.

Don stands frozen. This is the first time he has been inside this house since the tragic murders thirty years ago.

"This place brings back terrible memories Arty! You remember what we saw here. The last time we were here, I remember the blood and the bodies. This is too creepy and horrible!"

"Yes, Donny I remember. That was thirty years ago. Get over it! We need to do this. Now come over here and pull down the ladder."

"I still picture Tony and Pia in a bloody bed. We covered them up. Our Papa killed them!" Don clutches his stomach thinking he may throw up.

Arturo steps back into the living room. He rests a hand on Don's shoulder and feels the tension in Don's body.

"You don't have to go in that bedroom Donny. Just go pull down the ladder. I will go up and look for the diamond." Even though Arturo is the younger brother, his touch has a calming effect on Don.

Don shakes his head and walks to the hallway. He pulls the cord and hears the creaking noises as he unfolds the old wooden ladder.

Arturo climbs up the ladder hearing it snap and moan with each step of his heavy body. He shines the flashlight around the attic not seeing what he wants.

"The beams are all covered with fiberglass! They're supposed to be bare! I can't crawl out on this."

Not any of the beams Arturo wanted to crawl on are exposed. He punches an old box of Christmas decorations sitting atop a lot of gray fiberglass insulation. The jarring sends a cloud of dust around him and he sneezes. He climbs up as tall as he can, away from the dust, and without touching any insulation he fans the light beam around the East end of the attic.

"Can you get to it?" Don calls from below.

"I see nothing but a lot of insulation everywhere. The man must have had extra insulation blown in. It is all over everything. Maybe you should look. Papa said it is out about twenty feet to the East." Arturo carefully backs down the ladder.

"Why should I look?"

"That gray insulation is covering all the beams and everything. Maybe you can think of a way to get to the diamond."

Don climbs to the top of the ladder; his head is near the peak of the attic roof. Panning the light beam to the East, he sees nothing but insulation.

"I don't see how we can get out there. All the beams are covered. That stuff will get all over us."

"We must get the diamond! You have to crawl out there."

"No way! I'd be lying on my belly with that insulation all over me! We need a blanket, or something. I am not sure I could even fit out there. That is one of the lowest places of the roof too. Either of us will barely fit there. I can't do it Arty!"

"We should have been better prepared! We need blankets or something, look around." Arturo walks into the living room and sees Max's laptop on a table. His surveillance mind kicks in.

"I'm going to put a bug on his laptop, too."

"Why do that? What kind of bug?" Don comes down the ladder.

"We may need to hear what they say later." Arturo shouts. He plugs in a thumb drive from his pocket, boots up the laptop, and starts installing his malware because he can.

"This will send me via the internet everything they say even when he thinks it is off. If we cannot get the diamond now we may need to come back and I want to hear what goes on. I did not count on the fiberglass all over the rafters and everywhere. Look around. Maybe you can find something."

"Like what, the sheets from his bed?"

"Yes, that would work."

"Arty, I can't do that!"

"I'll see if he has a linen closet." Arturo walks to the guest bathroom.

"I'll look for some gloves."

"Try not to disturb anything. They mustn't know we've been here."

Don starts opening drawers in the desk of the office bedroom. When he pulls open the bottom drawer, three springy snakes fly out.

"Good Geese!" Don shouts jumping away from the flying snakes.

"What did you find?"

"It's a gag. Someone is a real prankster!" Don gathers the snakes and stuffs them in the drawer again.

"Keep looking."

After searching everywhere, all Don comes up with is a giant salad fork to dig into the insulation.

"We'll need some blankets and some gloves." Arturo removes his thumb drive, seeing the malware install is complete.

"Gloves with a twenty foot reach?"

"I don't know. Maybe some grippers with a two or three foot reach. Like what people use who can't bend over to pick up things. We can use these blankets to cover the fiberglass stuff to get close to it." Arturo pulls some wool blankets from the hallway closet.

"Yeah heavy blankets, you know it's hot up there."

Arturo looks around the whole house too but cannot find anything more suitable. "There's nothing else here."

"What do we do now?"

"This is the perfect time to do this. You have to lay

out the blankets and dig into that insulation with your hands." As Arturo utters the last word, he gasps for air and clutches his chest.

"This asthma..." Arturo whispers.

"Just go sit on the couch. It's probably all that dust from the attic triggering that." Don helps his brother to the couch.

Arturo uses his inhaler. He feels a dull pain in his chest and he starts sweating when he looks up at Don.

"Our fortune is a short distance away and we can't get it!" Arturo says gasping for air and clutching his chest.

"Arty, what's wrong? Are you okay?"

Arturo says nothing. He slumps back on the couch clutching his chest and makes a rasping sound as he struggles for air.

Don stuffs the blankets in the closet and closes the attic ladder. He checks around making sure everything is as they found it before he grabs Arturo by the arms to help him up and toward the door.

"Maybe I take you to a hospital!"

"But the diamond - we need the diamond!" Arturo collapses in Don's arms.

"Not now Arty." Don holds up Arturo as they stagger across the living room and out the front door.

"Oh, yeah... Be sure to lock the door." Arturo gasps as Don helps him walk. He feels his chest tighten as he reaches the truck.

"The diamond will have to wait." Don says. He cranks up the truck and races to Broward General Hospital.

Chapter Ten

Don Cresto paces the floor in the waiting room at the hospital. He looks at his watch. It is nearly midnight. His brother has been with the staff for what seems like an eternity. Finally, a doctor walks from behind a door followed by a nurse pushing Arturo in a wheel chair. When they stop, Arturo stands up.

"How is he doctor?"

"I'm fine!" Arturo shouts somewhat disgusted.

"Mister Cresto is doing very well. He had a mild heart attack. We wanted to keep him here for a few days but he insists on leaving. It is very lucky you brought him here so fast. We medicated him and he has a prescription to take now. No signs of memory loss or anything, but I suggest he lose some weight."

"That's good news! Does he need bed rest or anything?"

"Yes, maybe a couple days until he gets all his strength back. He can do just normal routine stuff, no strenuous work or lifting. Are there any other questions?"

"No, thank you. Can we go now?" Don sees the doctor nod.

"Let's go, Don. I don't like being in a hospital." Arturo grabs Don's arm and pulls him toward the exit. Outside Don leads him to the truck. As he slides in the driver's seat, Don talks.

"I have a solution for retrieving the item. We have some rubber gloves, and those old blue tarps. I can lay a tarp over the rafters and work my way out there. Then I use the gloves to dig down to the diamond. It should work."

"Is there room enough for you?"

"I think so. Do you have a better idea?"

"No, I think that will work. Maybe if Mister Merchado goes out somewhere we can get in there tomorrow. I'm glad I put that bug on his computer."

"No, we can go there Monday after he goes to work. I want to get this over with quickly but you need to rest a couple days. The diamond is no good if you are dead."

"Yeah okay, let's go home. I am very tired."

It is after midnight when Max unlocks his door and asks Sam and Ann in for a nightcap. He immediately sees the hall light is on. He smells a hint of muskiness but does not recognize the odor. He looks around and nothing seems disturbed.

"Peggy, did you leave that light on?" Max is sure she did not.

"No I don't think I did, Max. It was still daylight when we left. Maybe we didn't notice it was on."

"Check everything Peg." He starts looking around as Peggy goes into their bedroom. Max hears a small scream and Peggy storms into the living room carrying one of the springy snakes.

"Oops! I forgot about that. Sorry!" Max ducks as Peggy hurls the springy snake at him.

"Well, everything is okay. I'll get some wine for us." Max says.

Max pours four glasses of Rose'. He smiles as he toasts to his good friends and the evening.

"The music wasn't bad. I had a great time with that

spider too. Here's thanks to the Danglebatts."

"You liked them Max?" Peggy asks raising an eyebrow.

"They're not as bad as I thought."

The small talk continues until the glasses are empty.

"Well, I think we should go home now." Ann says.

"Are we still shopping in the morning?" Peggy asks Ann.

"Yes. I haven't been to the Sawgrass Mall for a while."

"Oh Sam, can you help me install a paddle fan?" Max asks.

"You need help with that?"

"Well, yes I will. It will be fun to do on a Saturday."

"Yeah, okay. See you about nine?"

"Nine is great! We'll take our time and drink some beer. It will be a nice relaxing day."

"Sure Max, putting up a paddle fan is relaxing - not!"

"You'll see it will be fun." Max says, not foreseeing the future.

Saturday morning Sam and Ann drive over to Max's house. They open the door and step into the living room not bothering to ring the doorbell, knowing Max will leave the door unlocked for them. Wearing shorts and T-shirts like Max and Peggy, Sam and Ann wave hello.

"Hey guys!" Max says sitting on the floor next to the open paddle fan box.

"Hello!" Sam replies and sees Peggy come to him.

"Hug time." She says wrapping her arms around

Sam.

"Okay, Peggy. Let's get going. I want to look at some clothes." Ann gives Max and Peggy a small hug.

"Sawgrass here we come." Peggy follows Ann out the door.

"Hello friend! Want a drink?" Max says in a happy voice.

"Just a bottle of water is fine."

"No problem! I'll get it. Take a look at that paddle fan stuff." Max gets off the floor and heads for the kitchen.

"You've got parts scattered on the floor. Why did you do that? Why did you open all the little bags of screws and stuff?"

"I got bored waiting for you so I prepared everything. I just haven't put it all together." Max shouts from the kitchen and retrieves two bottles of water from the refrigerator.

"I asked you not to open everything! Well at least you left the stuff in the bags this time. Remember that model ship you ended up throwing away?" Sam shakes his head.

"There were too many little pieces. That was different."

"This green matches the wall colors. How did you do that? The motor looks like it could propel a small car. But you haven't put together anything yet!"

"I opened all the stuff. I waited for you to get here."

"Well let's get started. Is there an instruction sheet?"

"Yes I have it over here." Max hands Sam the paper.

"Thanks Max. This doesn't look very complicated."

"Exactly, I think I can assemble most of this. The hard part is the wiring in the attic. I brought in some tarps from the Vet I bought a few days ago and put them up there this morning. You can spread them out on the rafters so you will not get the insulation on you. I am not agile enough to crawl along on them as you are. I figure you could easily do that. Just tap into a junction box, the one near the access hole. Run a wire over to the spot where the paddle fan goes. You'll have to dig up the insulation and drill a hole where the wire will come through the ceiling..."

"What! You want me to crawl around in your attic? There could be anything up there." Sam blurts, not knowing how right he is.

Chapter Eleven

You know there are probably spiders up in your attic. I hate spiders!"

"Not as much as I do! You are so much more agile than I am. You know, brown belt in Judo and all. And you owe me!" Max hands Sam a bottle of water.

"I owe you, what for?"

"For my spider... You got to meet the Danglebatts last night!"

"Yeah great, I already met the Danglebatts, and Chet gave me the tickets! I figure we're even!"

"Okay, I tried... I'll owe you big time if you would just do this... please!" Max clasps his hands together as if praying.

"Oh all right. Let me borrow a long sleeve shirt and some long pants. I want to keep the creatures in the attic from biting my goose bumps!"

"It's not that bad." Max assures him. "I was up there a couple days ago. That's why I bought some tarps to lay on the insulation. I started to spread the first one, but you'll have to finish spreading them. I swear I did not see anything moving. The attic ladder has been hanging open all morning and nothing has crept down here yet. What could live up there anyhow? I'm just not as flexible as Mister Judo-man. I might get stuck up there." While Max talks, he retrieves a long sleeve shirt and a pair of stretch long pants from his bedroom.

"This should fit you just fine." Max hands the clothes to Sam.

"You don't really know if there is anything up there do you?" Sam grunts as he slips off his shorts and slides into the pants. He finishes dressing and follows Max toward the hallway.

"No, no I don't. However, there shouldn't be anything up there. Trust me. When they tented this house for termites a couple years ago they killed everything."

"Nearly three years ago! Anything could be up there now!"

"There's nothing Sam, trust me. You know how religious I am about keeping up pest control living in a wood framed house, you'll be fine."

"So this is the fun time we will have installing a paddle fan? Oh never mind, where do I have to put the hole?"

"I already measured the distance to the center of the room. The wire should come out exactly twenty feet east of the edge of the opening along the right side rafter." Max says.

Sam looks at the creaky wooden ladder Max has swung down from the attic. He smells a dusty odor coming from the opening. After a silent prayer, he starts climbing. Each step he takes brings a squeak or groan from the ladder. Sam grabs a pair of gloves, a tape measure, a roll of wire and some electrical tools from Max. He sets everything at the edge of the attic before slipping on the gloves.

Thinking about what he has to do Sam lifts himself into the attic. He finishes spreading out the first tarp and measures out twenty feet from the edge of the attic hole with a stretched out tape measure. After grabbing the tools, he looks out to the end of the tape. The heat is closing in on Sam as well as the roof just above his head. He sees where he needs to put the wire up against a rafter.

Max shouts up at him. "Hey I really appreciate this Sam. I'll take us all out to Nick's tonight - my treat! Okay... I'll start putting the fan together. Holler if you need anything!" He pauses and then heads back to the living room.

Sam shines the flashlight around and looks at all the dark brown wood surrounding him in the huge attic. He never realized how big the house is. He guesses the attic is eighty feet long and fifty feet wide. He could stand upright at the tallest part of the attic. The old attic is dark warm and musky with no cross-braces, unlike what many new attics have. He sees the only ventilation is from two small louvered vents at each end of the attic. The old pine wood roof and rafters are dark and even black in some areas. Fortunately, the ductwork for the air conditioning is not in his way.

He thinks as he looks. *At least it's not brutally hot like in July or August, but it still feels creepy.* He stoops slightly as he moves further into the attic. He sees gray fiberglass insulation all over the rafters and remembers how fiberglass feels like little knives sticking him if he touches it. He knows even taking a hot shower will not remove all the itching.

He finishes spreading the second tarp on the joists. The tarps are just long enough to reach out the twenty feet he needs covered. Apparently, Max bought the tarps especially for the attic. He kneels down crawling back and forth across the gray ocean of insulation keeping his hands and feet atop the tarp covered rafters. Sam swings the flashlight around, always checking the ceiling and the floor as he shuffles along. He sweeps away hands full of cobwebs as he eases deeper into the attic, but he sees nothing moving.

Sweat breaks out on his face as he finally approaches the end of the measuring tape. Then sweat oozes out all over Sam making his clothes sticky. He feels sweat run down his forehead as he pants loudly. *If something jumps out at me right now, I'll have a heart attack and die! How will they get me out of here?*

Hunching down on all fours with his head inches from the roof, Sam swings the light around the attic one more time. He scrapes away insulation with his glove, pushing it away from the spot to drill a hole. When he reaches down to lift up the bottom pink insulation pad, his hand hits something hard and out of place. Lifting up the pad, Sam shines the light on a black object very close to his face! He jerks his head up bumping it on a rafter and shouts. "Ah!"

The black object is lying against a rafter hidden under the insulation until now. After shining the flashlight on it for a moment, his eyes focus. He sees a small black pouch with a gold drawstring top. He nudges the pouch with his flashlight to be sure nothing alive is on it. Sam stares at the pouch and then lifts it from its resting place.

He feels a grape sized lump inside the pouch, but the pouch does not feel as heavy as he expects it to be. The initials *MGB* in gold lettering are on the outside of the pouch. Out of curiosity, he opens the pouch, removes a large stone, and shines the flashlight on it. Sam stares at the large red brilliant cut diamond.

"Well I'll be..." Sam whispers.

The light hitting it makes an eerie red glow displaying a thousand multi-colored sparkles around it. Mesmerized Sam stares at the diamond for a minute rotating it to see the amazing patterns it displays on his surroundings. *If this is real, it's the biggest diamond I've ever seen!*

"Hey Max!" "I found something up here. You gotta see this!" He shouts toward the attic opening. He hears a muffled response as he puts the stone back in the pouch and stuffs it in his shirt pocket. Sam shuffles backward a few feet before he manages to turn around in the cramped space. He ignores the possible spiders and creepy things as he rushes across the tarps and speeds down the ladder.

Max is kneeling on the living room floor screwing the last paddle blade onto the motor. He looks up at Sam puzzled.

"Hey Max! I guess you didn't hear me tell you I found something up there!" He shouts as he walks into the living room.

"Look I can't help it if something moves up there. I think I got this all done." Max tightens the last screw on a paddle.

"No Max, forget the fan. Look what I found in your attic!" Max looks up at Sam confused.

"There's nothing there except a box of Christmas lights. I was up there already."

"Trust me there was this!" Sam takes the pouch out of his shirt pocket and dangles it at Max.

"What's that?"

Max opens the pouch and removes the contents. He

looks stunned as the red diamond sparkles and a thousand colors flash at him in the bright living room light. The diamond seems alive. It has the same mesmerizing effect on Max as it did on Sam. After a moment, he looks at the initials on the pouch. *MGB*

"Wow! Sam this actually looks like a real diamond! What is this doing in my attic? Where was it?" Max is stunned.

"It was under the insulation in the attic, right where I was going to drill a hole for the wire."

Max stands up in the living room admiring the awesome stone. He is quite sure it is a real diamond and he has never seen a red diamond this big, ever. Still focusing on the stone, he hears Sam.

"I'm guessing it must be at least five or six carats."

"Yeah, and I happen to know this deep red is rare in a diamond. If it's real it's worth a fortune!" Max puts the diamond back into the pouch and slips it in his pants pocket. He walks to his front door and puts the dead bolt on.

"I don't know why it's here Sam. It must have been here when I bought this house. Nobody has been in the attic that I know of except to blow in the extra insulation. Someone must have hidden it here before that. I bet this thing is worth millions!"

"That means someone will want it back." Sam says.

"I did lock the door, Sam. Hey, there must be a reward for it."

"It would be a big one Max. Just hypothetically, why hasn't someone tried to get this already? You've been here for three years."

"It's been there at least three years. I am guessing

something happened to whoever put this here. Maybe he or she died before coming back for it. That makes more sense. Otherwise, yeah, someone would have come back and got it. I just don't know what to do. I think I'll call Mark."

"You mean Mark Goodman our boss at Silvan Enterprises?"

"Yes, our boss. Since our wild and crazy event in Jamaica, Mark is like a second father to me. He is older and maybe wiser, and you know we can trust him."

"Yes, maybe he knows a trustworthy jeweler. We're not totally sure this is the real deal."

"Right Sam, but I'd bet my money it is real! I am sure Mark has a jeweler friend. We need a professional opinion."

"Assuming this is real, why would someone hide it in your attic?"

"Good question Sam. I'm going to make sure it's real and find out why it's here!"

Chapter Twelve

"Hello Mark. I need help."

"Calling me on a Saturday, are you in trouble?"

"No, I don't think so."

"That sounds questionable Max."

"No, I am fine. Do you know a trustworthy jeweler?"

"Yes. Ogden Bunford is an old high school friend of mine. He designed wedding rings for Martha and me. Why?"

"I know this will be hard to believe Mark, but Sam found a very large diamond hidden in my attic. I need a trustworthy person to tell me if it is real and what it's worth."

"This is hard to believe Max. You know not to pull a prank on the boss. Are you sure about this?"

"Yes boss, this is not a prank. Sam was running a wire for a paddle fan. He lifted the insulation and there it was. Is your jeweler friend an honest person? Would you trust him with a million dollars?"

"I can only say that he has been fine with me. Think Max, if you found a real diamond hidden in your attic, it is most likely a stolen diamond. No one would hide a diamond in the attic."

"Oh, yeah, Sam mentioned that. If it is real, maybe we should call the police. Anyway, can you give me his number? I'd like to check this out."

"Sure, I'll get it. Do you want me to call him first?"

"No, I'll call."

"I know he's on Power line Road near Commercial Boulevard. Here's his number." Mark gives Max the number and rings off.

"Come on Sam, I can call him on the way."

Max pulls off Powerline Road and parks his red Vet under a large 'Bunford Jewelers' sign. The front of the faded yellow building has thick iron bars over large tinted glass windows. Max and Sam ring the doorbell outside and wait for the buzz to go in. They are the only customers in the well-lit reception area. A short stocky man in a white shirt comes from a back room to greet them.

"May I help you?" The man asks.

"Hello, Mister Bunford?"

"Yes and you must be Max, Mark's friend. Here take my card."

"Right, I need you to tell me if this is a real diamond." Max pockets Ogden's business card, and opens the black pouch. He hands the diamond to Ogden feeling nervous as he sees Ogden grab the diamond by its edges. Max watches him rub the stone with a yellow cloth before examining the diamond with an eye loop.

"Wow! This is a beautiful diamond Max. I've never seen a red diamond this big. It has an IGI serial number on the girdle." Ogden sets the diamond on a soft cloth, grabs a tablet and pen and scribbles down the serial number.

"You say it's real? The girdle is the edge?"

"Yes, the edge around this top and oh yes, it's registered with the International Gemological Institute! It's real and traceable too. Give me some research time and I can tell you where it came from. As you said, if it was in your attic, it is probably stolen from somewhere. Maybe you should take it to the police. Here, I give it back to you. It's too tempting for me to run away with it! I have the serial number I can look up." Ogden admires the sparkling diamond again before he hands it back to Max.

"Just curious, what do you think it's worth?" Max slips the diamond back in the pouch and pulls the golden drawstrings tight.

"Max, you guys be careful. If I were a crook, I'd take out my gun and rob you right now. I read about a deep red diamond that was smaller than this one. It sold for ten million dollars!"

"Ten... that much?" Max is in shock but finally thanks Ogden and leaves the store with Sam.

"We were right Sam. It is real and has a serial number Ogden can trace. I just hope he doesn't tell anyone we have it. I want to know who the real owner is before I do anything."

"I agree with Mark, it has to be hot. We should call the cops."

"No cops yet, we need to know more about it. Let's hope there is a big reward. I'm going to hide this somewhere until we find out more about it."

Max walks to his car and glances around before sliding in his seat. He speeds home, walks inside his house after Sam and bolts the door. Before he can hide the stone, his phone rings.

"Hello Max, this is Ogden Bunford."

"Yes, hello Ogden. Did you find out anything?"

"Oh yes, I got some interesting information for you."

"What did you find out?"

"It is indeed registered as a 9.2 carat red diamond..."

"Wow! Nine carats has to be the biggest red diamond ever!"

"Yes Max, the biggest brilliant cut red diamond known to exist. As we suspected, it is a stolen diamond, stolen thirty years ago from the Bellasetta family in Italy. There are two brutal murders connected to the diamond so the media nicknamed it the 'deadly diamond' instead of its original intended name of 'The Bellasetta Rose' diamond. It is highly newsworthy since the Bellasettas are worth billions!"

"Billions, not millions?"

"Yes Max, billions! The Bellasettas own all kinds of businesses; shipping, hauling, manufacturing plants, they even own an entire bank franchise."

"What happened thirty years ago in Italy? How could this diamond wind up in Fort Lauderdale, Florida?"

"I called my friend Paul Zimmer at the newspaper. He remembered the story behind the Bellasetta Rose diamond and was able to dredge up the information from the archives for me. I can forward it to you via email, and you can do a search for the 'Bellasetta Rose' on Google, Max. You will see what happened. It is interesting to say the least. There is also a substantial reward for returning the diamond. As I told you, please put that diamond in a safe deposit box or somewhere very safe. I do have a big safe here you can use. Maybe you should contact the police too."

"Thanks Ogden let me look at the article before I do anything. A big reward sounds great! Thanks a lot. I owe you!" Max gives his email address to Ogden.

"You guys be safe. Mark says you are good men. I'd hate to see anything happen to you."

"Why should anything happen? Thirty years and nothing has happened."

"I'm just saying; Read the article, check it all out."

"Okay, thanks again for calling."

Max rings off. *I have to check that.* He fires up his laptop and goes to the kitchen to hide the diamond. Ogden's email pops up and Max immediately reads the article.

"Holy cow, remember our visit by the Cresto brothers?"

"Yeah, I remember the cologne."

"A man named Salvatore Cresto is one of the diamond thieves!"

"So those guys may be related?"

"Yes. He had two sons, raised in various foster homes."

"So what do we do now?"

"I found an old phone number for the Bellasettas. I wonder if it is still good. Sam, let's find out how to call Italy. I want to talk to the Bellasettas!"

Chapter Thirteen

Just after two in the afternoon, and after more research on the internet, Max dials the number for the Bellasetta estate and turns on the phone speaker. After two rings, a man answers the phone.

"Pronto!" a man says.

"Do you speak English?" Max asks.

"Who is calling?"

"This is Max Merchado in Fort Lauderdale, Florida, USA. I want to speak to Miguel Bellasetta."

"He is not taking calls. I am Henri. May I help you?"

"Please tell Mister Bellasetta we have found the Bellasetta Rose Diamond and want to return it for the reward." A long pause follows before the man speaks.

"I will tell him." Max waits a whole minute before a different voice comes on the phone.

"This is Gustavo Bellasetta. Papa cannot come to the phone. I interpret for him. You claim you have found the Rose diamond?"

"Yes. It is in a black pouch..."

"Are you related to the Cresto or Albero family?"

"No, not at all. We found the diamond hidden under some insulation in my attic."

"How is it you looked for it?"

"We were not looking for it. My friend was trying to install a paddle fan. He had to lift the insulation away from the attic floor to drill a hole for a wire. There it was under that exact section of insulation."

"You say he only lifted one section and found it?"

"Yes. I guess it is dumb luck."

"I... Well, I am shocked at this time. You again

bring memories of thirty years ago and not so pleasant ones."

"I am sorry for your loss. I have read about it. We want to return the diamond to the rightful owners. Should I take it to the police?"

"No, please do not do that. You must know we have heard many false claims to have the Rose Diamond."

"I am sure you have, but we checked with a reputable jeweler. This is the real diamond Mister Bellasetta."

"Please call me Gustavo. You must send a picture of the diamond today. Close pictures. We have had many fake diamonds presented before. There is a small mark after the serial number that we never revealed in the newspapers. Tell me what that is and the serial number."

"I will need a strong eyeglass to check that."

"Send it to my email with your pictures, phone number and name. Write down my email now." Gustavo tells Max his email address and repeats what details he wants to be convinced Max has the real diamond.

"Will you send a courier to the US to retrieve the diamond?" The phone goes dead again. Max waits another minute and then Gustavo comes back on the line.

"You will send the proof and I will determine what to do next. I want to conclude this as soon as possible. My people will check on you too. You say you are not related to Cresto family or Albero's?"

"We are absolutely not related to them, but I believe the sons of the original thief some way know the diamond is in this house."

"We know who killed my brother and stole from us Max." Gustavo's voice sounds bitter.

"Yes, this is the house Salvatore Cresto's father owned when your diamond was stolen. We are very sure it was Sal Cresto or Tony Albero who hid the diamond in the attic."

"I will personally come to America for the diamond if this proves to be real."

"You are the son of Miguel Bellasetta?" Max pauses for a second. He feels sweat forming on his scalp.

"Yes, I am one of three sons. Just Mario and I are left. Our concern is that Papa may die soon. He will want to see this beloved rose diamond before he dies. Miguel junior told us about the purchase of that gift for Papa and its pouch. It is the last memento Papa will have of his oldest son. We must conclude the exchange rapidly before Papa's health fails further."

"We want to do the deal quickly too. How soon will you be here?" He hears muffled voices from the phone for a moment. Then Gustavo talks again.

"My brother wants to know if you agree to the reward of one million dollars."

"Yes, that is very acceptable." Max says after pausing for a few seconds. He feels sweat trickle down his forehead on to his brow. He wipes his face.

"Then we have a gentleman's agreement. The million is not a problem. You send the proof and we will come within two days."

"Two days?"

"Yes, we will need time to transfer the money to an American bank to conclude this exchange."

"Okay Gustavo. I will send the email within the

hour."

"That concludes our talk for now. I am looking forward to seeing your email, Max. Goodbye." Gustavo rings off.

Max sits in his office chair his mind racing. *Wow! A million dollar reward!* He turns on a bright desk lamp and opens a 10X magnifying glass. He examines the diamond writing down the serial number and he sees an infinity symbol a few spaces after the serial number.

"Gustavo was right. There is a mark after the number."

"We knew we had the right diamond. That just further confirms it."

Placing the diamond on the current newspaper, he takes several pictures of it. After sending the pictures and his note about the symbol to Gustavo, he stashes the diamond back in its pouch.

"I think you should treat us all at Nick's tonight Max."

"Absolutely! After the girls come back. I will make reservations for six o'clock. It's Saturday so they will be crowded. In the meantime, I'll get some beer and hide this rock. Tonight we celebrate our find!"

Chapter Fourteen

After a great meal at Nick's restaurant, Sam drives to Max's house. Back at 812 Clifton Street, Sam accepts a beer from Max. The girls go off to Peggy's sewing room while Sam chats with Max mostly about work. After eleven o'clock, they gather in the living room.

"Well, I think it's time to go home Max." Sam takes his last sip of beer. He hands the news article printed from the email back to Max.

"Some story eh Sam?"

"Yes, it's hard to believe that diamond is worth millions of dollars and it has been lying up there in your attic so long." Sam shakes his head.

"Yes, and you deserve the reward money Sam, not me."

"No, it was in your attic, in your house."

"But you found it. I would have never found that diamond. No one would have ever found it! I don't need all that money anyhow Sam."

"You imply that I do?"

"Well, you... Okay, why don't we split the reward?"

"Split the reward? Yeah, okay. I can always use a half million."

"Don't be so flippant about it. A half million is a lot of money. I think the sons of Salvatore Cresto, Don and Arturo know about the diamond. They did offer to buy my house just last week."

"Yes, according to the dates in that article, Sal Cresto will be released from prison in less than two months. This cannot be a coincidence that suddenly the Cresto's want to buy your house."

"That fellow Ogden said to be careful. I guess he is right. I thought whoever put the diamond there was dead. Why would they leave it there for thirty years! I didn't think about someone being locked up in prison."

"The article says Salvatore claimed he lost the diamond in New York. I think he just did not want anyone looking too hard for it. Originally, there was a ten thousand dollar reward for its return. The reward has gone up by two decimal points now."

"I am sure the value has gone up too. The Cresto boys seem benign, and Ogden got his info from Paul Zimmer who has been with the newspaper for decades. I don't see any threat there. He wants to write up an article about how we found it, and bring up all that old hype about the world's biggest red diamond"

"Good grief, half the crazies will be after you if he publishes that now! Let's tell him to wait until we return it and get the reward!"

"It's okay Sam. Ogden talked to Zimmer and asked him to keep the story under wraps until we get the reward. Ogden says he felt confident telling Zimmer about the diamond because the man has been with the paper forever. So I don't see anything wrong with that."

"Well that's another person knowing about our diamond. Now I have to worry about Bunford, Zimmer and the Cresto's. Great Max, I was enjoying our nice peaceful life until now!"

"Stop worrying so much Sam. We just have to be cautious. I know it's a million dollar reward but this will be over in a few days."

"I've heard that before and then we trekked to Jamaica Max. We are not just talking about a million-dollar reward here. This diamond is worth ten million dollars or more. It is the biggest red diamond known to exist. It's the Bellasetta Rose diamond!" The doorbell rings.

"Yes I know Sam. I suppose we should be very cautious. Just hang for a minute. Someone is at the door."

Paul Zimmer lurches up the three steps of the porch barely staying upright as he staggers to the front door of 812 Clifton Street. He leans against the door and presses the doorbell. When he hears motion inside, he waves at the peephole with his unarmed hand, waiting for the door to open.

"Hello, can I help you?" Max says but he sees the gun.

"Get back! Don't give me any trouble!" Zimmer slurs his words as he pushes his way inside forcing Max back.

"What is this, a holdup?"

"Yes. I want the diamond!" Zimmer grabs the edge of the couch to steady himself.

"What diamond? Who are you anyhow?" Max asks.

"Just call me the bandit. You need to give me the diamond. I have nothing to lose. I'll start shooting your pretty girlfriends!"

"No don't shoot anyone. It's in a safe place in the kitchen."

"I thought it would be here. Bring it to me!"

"I have to go to the kitchen. Is that alright?"

"Don't do anything funny or you lose these pretty

girls!" Paul points the gun at Peggy's face.

"Okay." Max slowly backs out of sight into the kitchen.

Sam watches the man standing less than ten feet away and hopes for any opportunity to disarm him. He thinks about the empty bottle in his hand. *If the man aims the gun away from Peggy, I can jump him.*

"Here it is." Max walks back in the room carrying the black pouch. He starts to hand the pouch to Zimmer.

Paul Zimmer staggers backwards swinging his gun straight up and away from Peggy.

Sam heaves the bottle hitting Zimmer's forearm. He leaps onto Paul and crashes to the floor with him. The gun flies across the living room as Max steps back. Sam wrestles with Paul pinning his right arm behind him.

"I'm calling 9-1-1 now." Max says picking up the gun.

An hour later with lights still flashing outside, Officer McMasters wraps up his report with Max. Paul Zimmer is already in a squad car and rides away in cuffs.

"You were all lucky. I think the man is crazy. He thought you all had a million-dollar diamond and he was going to steal it. Can you believe that?"

"He has a wild imagination. He smells like he's been drinking." Max manages to stay calm.

"Yeah, he is drunk as a skunk! I am amazed he was able to drive over here without hitting anything."

"Thanks for everything officer."

"John's Towing Service will be by to tow away his

car. You take care now, and watch who you open the door for."

"I will." Max closes and bolts the door.

"And the trouble starts. Another fine mess you've got us into Ollie." Sam says, but Max ignores the comment.

"Well it seems you saved us all Mister Judo Sam. I'm glad it's over. Imagine Paul Zimmer the reporter guy going nuts."

"Not much of a struggle Max, but he can get another gun. Do you remember what he said? He has nothing to lose!"

"Quit worrying Sam. By the time he gets out of jail, we will have the reward money, not the diamond, and he will be sober. If he can't post bail he will be in the pokey a long time."

"Let's hope he comes to his senses in jail. I think Ann and I will go home now. Thanks for the dinner, and the entertainment Max."

"You're welcome. You two have a nice night what's left of it. Sam, please don't have nightmares about this now. Ann, keep him from having nightmares."

"I haven't figured out how to do that yet."

Max waves goodbye to Sam and Ann. He checks all the locks and gets his newly bought .45 semi-automatic pistol from the nightstand. Max bought the gun after his adventure in Jamaica.

"It's bedtime Max. Are you going to sleep with that thing?" Peggy asks as they walk to the bedroom.

"Yes, under my pillow. I hid the diamond again before the police got here. If I die, that diamond will never be found!"

"You put it in the kitchen, right?"

"Yeah, I can't keep a secret from you. It's in the false electric socket."

"I knew that already. You didn't totally snap on the cover."

"Cripes!"

Chapter Fifteen

Late Sunday morning Don Cresto stands in his living room holding two large blue tarps he found in his shed. *I am sure I can get to that diamond now, but I'm not going to that house alone.* He flattens the tarps with his hand and the commotion wakes Arturo.

"I see you found them."

"Yes, I am ready to go."

"Come here. Max is away now I think he went to church with his girlfriend. I will tell you how to pick that lock."

"No Arty. You must go with me."

"I'm too weak."

"Then, we wait one more day. The diamond isn't going anywhere is it?"

"No brother, but..."

"Your health is most important. We can wait..."

Don hears a noise at the front door and starts to go there but the door swings open and two muscle goons barge into the house.

"You should lock your door Cresto. Don't try anything!" One man says as he pushes Don toward the kitchen. Don drops the tarps and stands rigid, numbed with fear.

"Arturo! Boss-man wants you to pay up!" The taller man shouts.

"I need just one more week. You will have all of it with interest. I promise!" Arturo says sitting up in bed. He recognizes the man called Scarface from the long cicatrix on his left cheek.

Scarface grabs Arturo by his shirt and lifts him out

of bed. He pushes Arturo against the bedroom wall banging his head hard. Arturo doubles over in pain when the man punches him in the belly.

"That's from the Boss-man. You have until Wednesday, after that we take the money in blood!"

Arturo groans watching the two men back out of the house. He sees his brother close and bolt the door with shaky hands.

"This is foolishness Arturo. We cannot go on like this. I cannot get another loan. This Boss-man must be paid or he will send those thugs back and worse will happen!" Don helps Arturo back into bed.

"Just let me rest now Donny. I feel awful, but I think he will wait if I can convince the Boss-man we will get their money. I'll call him."

"You want to call him now?"

"Yes Donny. I want to reassure him we will pay the money."

"You will get better. We have to get that diamond. It is the only way we can pay off your debt."

"We will get that diamond Monday after Mister Merchado goes to work. My friend Carl knows a major fence. He can come up with big cash for us."

"Carl is one of your low-life friends. I've met him before."

"My friends are just different from what you are used to Donny. Let me call Carl first to give the buyer time to get cash."

"How will we protect the diamond from them stealing it?"

"Carl will know how to do that."

"Here's the phone. Let's get this over."

"Please believe me. We will have cash by Tuesday and I have learned my lesson, no more gambling. I promise!" Arturo dials his friend and lies down on his side.

"I've heard that before Arturo."

"But this time I mean it. All our problems are over when we get that diamond. I promise no more gambling!" Arturo's promise is more correct than he knows.

Monday morning Arturo starts to get out of bed but he feels very weak. He sits back down on the bed. He can feel his heart pulsing out of sync sometimes. He checks his blood pressure and it is down very low. His brother walks into the bedroom just as Arturo lies down.

"I called in sick because of you Arty. I just tend to you for now."

"Donny, you must go get the diamond by yourself. I am still too weak. The house will be empty now."

"No I cannot do it by myself."

"I show you how to pick the lock. What's the matter?"

"I am afraid something will go wrong."

"It is an easy thing to do. Nothing can go wrong. I know we can bargain for time if we have the diamond."

"No, we wait until tomorrow. You should have more strength by then."

Max strolls to his boss' office late Monday morning. He knocks on the open door of Mark Goodman the CEO of

Silvan Enterprises. Mark motions him to come in and says a few words into his phone before hanging up. He shuffles some papers into a neat pile before speaking.

"Hello Max. What do you want?"

"As you know, I talked to a man named Gustavo Bellasetta. Gustavo and Mario are the two Bellasetta brothers. Anyway, Gustavo needs a day or maybe two to move the reward money into an American bank here in Fort Lauderdale. He will meet us at our bank with his gemologist to verify the diamond. Then he will transfer the funds to my account."

"So how are you holding up Max?"

"I'm okay, but Sam is a basket case. I am keeping the diamond in my safe deposit box. I just wanted to say we would have to take more time off whenever they are ready to do the deal. I did not notify the police since the owner is in Italy and doesn't want the police involved."

"I am glad you put the diamond in your safe deposit. Does the bank know about the diamond?"

"Yes, when I put it in this morning, I talked with John Thurman the bank manager."

"Putting it there is the smartest thing you did today."

"Yeah, apparently my secret hiding place at home is no good."

"So we're through here. Let me know when you need to leave."

"Right, boss." Max salutes Mark and exits the office.

Tuesday morning Arturo feels better. His blood pressure is almost normal. Aside from the wheezing with the asthma, he is good to go. He feels a wave of elation knowing his debt problem is about to end.

Arturo and Don sit in their truck parked near the house on Clifton Street. At seven thirty, they see Max and Peggy leaving. After watching them drive away, Arturo waits a few minutes before speaking.

"Okay, it is time to go!" Arturo sees a frown on Don's face.

"I hate this!"

"We have to do this Donny and remember, just look casual. Don't keep looking around like you're guilty of something!"

Even though Don is the stronger taller and usually more confident of the two, he is already sweating buckets and jumpy with nerves. He carries the tarps for the attic and though Arturo tells him not to keep looking around, he still does it and he looks more suspicious than ever. By the time he stands with Arturo at the front door, his nerves are shot and his shirt is soaking wet.

The standard locks are easy for Arturo to pick. He opens the door and goes inside with Don. Arturo hears Don exhale noisily as he closes the door.

"I saw a man watering his yard only two houses down the street. I think he looked at us going in here." Don says.

"Relax, Donny. He didn't give us a second look. Let's get busy. Get that ladder down and go get our fortune!"

"Oh you're the boss now just because I am so nervous. You had better hope I find that pouch. Please let me get this over. I wish I had not promised Papa I would do this! I hate to be in the house where Tony and

Pia were murdered! I want things back to normal!"

"I am sorry, Donny. Remember my deadline, tomorrow night!" Arturo winces and rubs his rib cage.

"Hand up the tarps when I ask for them." Don says accepting his fate as he pulls down the ladder and climbs up.

Don takes the tarps and gloves from Arturo. He flashes the light where the pouch should be about twenty feet away from the east edge of the ladder opening. He sees bunched up insulation there and blue tarps already on the beams from the opening. *This is all wrong! Who put tarps here already?* Suddenly he feels a rush of more sweat pouring out of his body. He sets his tarps aside and shuffles out on the rafters to the rumpled insulation, the exact place where the diamond should be. He sees a bare area with the pink insulation pulled back. *How is this possible? Someone found the diamond!* Don has no explanation for this.

"It's gone!" Don shouts after shuffling back to the attic hole.

"What? That can't be!" Arturo's legs weaken. He leans against the ladder feeling his heart palpitating.

"I tell you it's gone! Someone already laid tarps up here and the insulation is all tossed aside where it should be. It was not that way before! One of those Raiford guards must have overheard Papa talking. They got to it before we did!" Don looks down and sees Arturo slumping against the ladder. He rushes down to keep Arturo from hitting his head on the floor.

"I think... another heart attack!" Arturo gasps grabbing his chest.

"No Arty, not here!" Don lifts Arturo to his feet but

Arturo barely makes it to the couch before collapsing again. With no other choice, Don lifts his brother over his shoulder. He hears Arturo groan as he opens the front door and peeks out. The street is bare. Adjusting Arturo's heavy body to better balance him, he carries Arturo's limp frame out of the house closing the door as he leaves. *I can't believe I am carrying a body down Clifton Street in broad daylight and nobody cares!* Don is sweating even more profusely. He worries he might have a heart attack too.

He swings open the passenger door and drops Arturo on the front seat of his truck. Behind the steering wheel, Don gasps several times for air before he is able to start the engine. He drives directly to Broward General Hospital in time to save his brother's life again.

Chapter Sixteen

At work Tuesday, Max knocks on his boss' door. Mark motions him to come in as he piles up some papers.

"Hello Max. What do you want?"

"Hello boss. I talked to Gustavo Bellasetta again this morning. He said he has the funds available. He wants us to meet with his people at eleven this morning. Just a reminder, I have to meet them at the bank in an hour. They have their own gemologist and guards and…"

"The bank is ten minutes from here but go ahead Max. Get it over with and get back to work."

"Thanks boss. Do you mind, I want to take Sam with me?"

"Yes, okay. Just get it done." Mark shakes his head and motions for Max to get out.

Max leaves Silvan Enterprises with Sam heading for his house on Clifton Street. As the red Corvette purrs along Max smiles thinking about the reward money. He knows Sam is still worrying that something bad will happen before they actually get the reward. Max drives south toward Clifton Street.

"Hey, where are you going? The bank is north on Commercial."

"This morning I was thinking about the diamond and I think I left the coffee pot on at home. It'd be just my luck to get the reward and burn down my house in the same day. Peg always wants it unplugged after hearing about a Mister Coffee pot catching fire."

Max steers the Vet into his carport. He walks to the

front door with Sam. When he puts in his key, he feels no resistance in his lock.

"Hey, my door is unlocked!" Max shouts.

"I knew something would happen!" Sam tenses.

"I know I locked this myself when we left this morning, or did I?"

"Let me go in first." Sam's body stiffens, like when he was taking Judo lessons. He goes inside, glances around the living room but sees no one. However, he sees the attic ladder down in the hallway.

"Max did you leave the ladder down?"

"No! Someone's been here!"

Sam on high alert goes from room to room looking for an intruder. He comes back into the living room.

"All is clear but someone left a flashlight in the hallway." Sam says.

"What?"

"Okay, someone must have come here to retrieve the diamond, but why did they leave all this behind? Did they see the diamond is gone? Let me call 9-1-1. What say Max?"

"No! We have to be at the bank in forty minutes. The cops will have us here for an hour or more. I want to get this exchange done!" Max taps Sam on the shoulder and starts for the door.

"Are you serious Max? You're just leaving everything to go to the bank?"

"Yes! I have to be there Sam. If you want, you can stay and talk to the police but I have to go."

"No way! Just leave everything as is I guess."

"Yeah, let's go." Max starts for the door again and turns around.

"What now?"

"I have to check the coffee pot. Then we go. The Bellasetta people are going to give us a whole lot of money!"

Max and Sam arrive at the Atlantis Bank in Fort Lauderdale. They go inside and see a small group gathered in a private glass-walled room. Max meets Carlo Nesa the gemologist and Bianco Nacci the authorizing agent. The bank manager John Thurman and a reporter for the Sun Sentinel Joan Canova are present too. Max notices two men standing off to the side. Last to introduce himself is Gustavo Bellasetta, the man Max talked to on the phone and his strong-arm man Henri Blanco.

After the introductions are over, a clerk escorts Max to his safe deposit box. He takes out the small black pouch. All eyes focus on the pouch as Max comes back into the room. He smiles as he gives the black pouch to the gemologist.

"It is agreed the diamond stays here until the funds are verified." John Thurman reminds them. Gustavo nods in agreement.

"The funds are from an American bank. This will not take long. You will be checking the account Mister Thurman." Bianco says.

Max watches Carlo Nesa as he wipes the diamond clean with a special cloth. He weighs it, measures the dimensions and examines it with a strong eye loop for several minutes. Carlo smiles as he looks at his audience.

"Gentlemen and lady, what was lost thirty years

ago is now found. This is indeed the Bellasetta Rose Diamond. The color, the weight and the dimensions are correct as well as the serial number and the symbol."

"Very good sir. I will commence the wire transfer according to the agreement of one million dollars to Mister Merchado's account." Bianco says seeing Gustavo nod toward him.

"Max, I need to speak with you privately." Gustavo says motioning everyone else out of the room except Henri. He sees Max lift his hand toward him as the door closes.

"First of all, thank you Mister Bellasetta. I am sure Sam and I will be doing some charity work with a lot of the money."

"Thank you for finding the diamond. Just call me Gustavo please. We have had a development since we came here. Our Papa passed yesterday. We originally intended to give the diamond to Papa, as our late brother would have wanted. Now in the home with us it would be a reminder every day of the tragic murders in the past."

"I am so sorry for the loss of your brother and now your father."

"At least he knew we will once again have the diamond his son was to give him. It brings back sad memories for Mario and me though. We will not have it close to us. Mario and I decided to donate it to the Bella Museum in Reggio Calabria. The diamond will stay there permanently for other people to enjoy. I am inviting you and Sam to the ceremony to see this magnificent diamond placed in the museum. You can stay at our estate in Italy."

"You want us to travel to Italy?"

"Yes. You can stay with us until the ceremony next week. You can tour Italy sightseeing until then. It is a wonderful country Max. It will be a rewarding experience for you and Sam."

"So just pack up and fly to Italy?"

"If you can leave now, you can go with us in our private jet. The jet can hold two more people comfortably."

"As good as that sounds, let me talk it over with my girlfriend Peggy. Sam will have to decide what to do too."

"As you wish, call me if you decide to come to Italy."

"Also, there is one thing that we will do if you come there."

"A thing? What kind of a thing?"

"Just something Mario and I want to clear up - a good thing. I think the ceremony will be better if you are both there when the diamond is shown."

"We already have the reward. What else is there?"

"Ah when you come to Italy, you find out." Gustavo smiles at Max.

Gustavo tells Max his version of how the diamond came to be in Fort Lauderdale. He wants Max to say little about the diamond details until he returns to Italy. Then seeing Mister Thurman staring into the room, Gustavo motions everyone to come back in.

"Sam we need to go to Italy." Max blurts as the men come in.

"You are kidding, Max." Sam has been quiet until now.

"No Sam, Gustavo wants us to come to the ceremony

when the diamond is placed in their museum. I think we should go. What a great vacation! We can spend a few days in Rome or Naples before the ceremony."

"Fly to Italy just like that?"

"Yes. I feel somehow drawn to Italy and the diamond. We must go to the ceremony. Hey, the girls will have a ball in Italy. What's the problem?"

Sam stares at Max dumbfounded.

Sitting at the edge of the group, reporter Joan Canova keeps track of the names of the players, the bank and the time. Bianco agrees to let her take some pictures of the diamond itself. As she snaps pictures, Bianco reminds her of what to do.

"You will not publish any of this for forty-eight hours. We need time to return anonymously to Italy with the diamond before the news is out. You will email your text to Mister Gustavo Bellasetta at least twelve hours before it is published?"

"Agreed, and it will be a favorable story sir. Anything else you want to tell me about the Bellasettas?"

"No more than what you may already know. The Bellasetta's estimated worth is six billion Euros, more or less. The diamond was to be a gift from the late Miguel Bellasetta Junior to his Papa thirty years ago. It was stolen before that happened. Now in his honor, the two remaining brothers Gustavo and Mario were to present the diamond to their Papa when we return but Mister Bellasetta Senior passed away yesterday. On Monday, they will donate the diamond to the Bella Museum in Reggio Calabria, Italy. Gustavo invited Max and Sam to come to Italy for the presentation, thus the secondary... You may want to wait and include pictures from that event in your article. The international press will have pictures and Gustavo can also send pictures to you."

"I may do that if Mister Merchado and Mister Stormen actually go to Italy as requested. You mentioned a second, a second what?"

Chapter Seventeen

There is no second thing that is incorrect. Forget I said that Miss Canova. I am sure Max will go there." Bianco says. He turns to Max and Sam.

"You can return with us now. The Bellasettas want to return to Italy forthwith. As soon as all are on board, we will leave for Italy in the Bella-Jet."

"The Bella-Jet?"

"It is a private jet, property of Bella Industries, Max. We will fly non-stop to Reggio Calabria Airport. From there we travel just eighty kilometers to the Bellasetta estate in Gioia Tauro."

"I thank you for the offer but I want to bring my girlfriend and fly to Rome if I can convince Sam to go. I want to sightsee around Rome a couple of days."

"Very well, the ceremony is Monday. The sons will present the diamond to the museum then. Please make contact at least a day before so you can stay at the estate. They will honor you at the ceremony as well." Bianco says.

"We will call Gustavo when we are in Italy. I have Gustavo's phone number here, correct?"

"Yes. Call when you are in Italy. The Bellasettas will make arrangements for you at the estate."

"We will go to Rome first. I want to do some touring. I will call when we get there."

Max and Sam chat with the men until John Thurman makes his announcement.

"The transfer is complete. Max, you are now officially a millionaire. Congratulations!"

"Wow and thank you!" Max says shaking hands

with Bianco and Gustavo. He says goodbye to the Bellasetta group as they leave the room with the diamond. Max shakes hands with John Thurman.

"You are transferring a half mil to Sam's account?"

"Yes Max, you are only a millionaire for a few minutes. Is there anything else we can do for you Max?

"No, just do the transfer to Sam Stormen's account. I think we are done. Now if you will excuse us, someone was inside my house. I'm going to call the cops and an alarm company!"

Tuesday afternoon Don Cresto arrives home later than his usual time from work. He has drawn all of his money from his savings account. He opens a can of beer and plops on his couch to watch the last half of the six o'clock news. After dumping all the money on the couch, he loosens his tie and counts it again. He has a little more than seven thousand dollars, just a third of what Arturo needs to pay his debt. As he wonders what to do next his phone rings.

"Donny I want you to bring my laptop tonight."

"Why? You have it set up with all the wires and everything."

"I want to listen to the recordings. I must know what happened to the diamond. I must also show you how to listen to the recordings, just in case. Disconnect all the wires and bring the computer and the charger." Arturo rings off leaving Don hearing a dial tone.

"Just in case, he says. Does he think he is going to die?" Don mumbles to himself as he goes into Arturo's office. After unplugging all the wires, he puts the laptop in his truck and drives to the hospital.

Don walks swiftly as usual to the elevators. He adjusts the laptop under his arm as he enters Arturo's hospital room 425. Arturo is sitting up in bed.

"You look weak brother." Don says.

"Yeah, well I did have another heart attack. Bring the laptop here. I want you to know how to access the recordings."

"You're not going to die Arty."

"Doc says I will be fine. I just want you to know this."

Arturo tells Don about his pride and joy malware as he shows his brother how to play the recordings of the conversations.

"Now we start all over Donny. Let me see you play the rest of the recordings from Max's house. Maybe we find out what happened to our diamond. Is the diamond still hiding under the fiberglass somewhere? Did a guard find it or did Max find it? I want to know!" Arturo watches as Don fumbles with the computer and plays back the recordings. Each one is voice activated so there are many separate files to hear. Eventually they hear about the paddle fan and Max persuading Sam to go in the attic. Then they hear about Sam finding the diamond.

"This is terrible! Of all the stupid things to happen, this has to be the worst luck! Papa should have told us sooner about the diamond! I should have shown you these recordings sooner too. Maybe you could have taken the diamond from them." Arturo stares in disgust at the computer after he hears Max planning to put the diamond in a safe deposit box and return it to the Bellasettas.

"Well, it's over Arty. He has returned it and received the reward by now. There is nothing left to do."

"No Donny, it cannot be over! I still need the money by tomorrow night!" Arturo wheezes and reaches for his inhaler.

"I have seven thousand. I think I can raise a few more thousand from my credit card tomorrow..."

"No, I need it all tomorrow!"

"They will have to be happy with maybe ten Arty. You must stay here and rest for several days now. I don't think they will do anything while you are in the hospital. It gives me some time to find more money."

"Please help me this one more time Donny. I know you want to be so honest and law-abiding but I need you to get the money somehow and the diamond money is the only option. I promise I will never gamble again!"

"I'll see what I can do Arty. Try to rest. I'll see you tomorrow."

Wednesday evening Don feels nervous seeing a black sedan with dark windows stopped along the curb when he parks his truck in his carport. It is after five and he could only raise another three thousand dollars in cash that his boss generously gave him on loan. He stashes the envelope filled with ten thousand dollars under his truck seat and hurries inside his house. Before he can relax the doorbell rings. Don opens the door and two men force their way inside.

"Where be Arturo?" Scarface, the taller man asks.

"He is not here." Don focuses on the large scar on the left side of the man's face. He can tell the wound is old and deep into the cheek.

"Last chance... Where he be?" Scarface grabs Don by his shirt and backs him across the living room bashing his head against the wall. Don winces in pain.

"I don't know! Oww!" Don shouts and feels pain as Scarface jabs him in the stomach. Don tries to defend himself, but he is no match for the two men beating on him relentlessly.

Finally Scarface stops. "I ask again, where he be!"

"In the hospital. Broward General room 425!" Don cries. Scarface gives Don two more punches to the gut.

"In a hospital, you be sure Cresto?"

"Yes, I told you what you want! Aww, why keep hitting me?"

"I like to hit. Thanks for the info Cresto." Scarface and his pal back out the open front door.
Don slides down to the floor weeping and passes out in pain.

Chapter Eighteen

Abe Balaster aka Scarface walks through the lobby at Broward General Hospital with his companion Zeke. He and his pal are wearing dark sports jackets and open shirts. They smile for the receptionist as they show their fake ID's before walking to the elevators. No one pays much attention to the two men.

"Poke four." Scarface says.

"For sure." Zeke pushes the elevator number four.

 Scarface looks around as he exits the elevator on the fourth floor. The hallway is quiet. He can smell the faint odor of disinfectant in the air. He sees the directions for the room numbers on the wall across from the elevator doors. Just as he figures out which way to go, a nurse stops in front of him.

"Hello, may I help you?" Nurse Julie asks.

"Yes miss. You sure look lovely."

"Thank you but what are you doing here?"

"Excuse me miss, I didn't mean to offend you. We are looking for our cousin Arturo Cresto in room 425. Can you direct us to him?" Abe asks.

"No problem. It is just down the hall this way. I'll take you there." She motions Scarface to follow her.

"Thank you so much." Abe nods and walks behind her with Zeke.

"You are smiling again man." Zeke whispers.

"I always like it when Boss-man says take 'em out!"

"Yeah, and you look good in dat wig. Here come the room. Be quiet." Zeke says.

"Is he expecting you?" Nurse Julie asks.

"No, we want to surprise him. We're his cousins from New Orleans." Scarface knows he has a slight accent from his childhood days in New Orleans.

"Great! I'm sure he will love to see you. What are your names?"

"I'm Abe and this is Zeke." Scarface says and then sees Nurse Julie motion to shush with her finger.

Scarface looks up and sees 425 a few feet away as the nurse leads the way into the room. Both Scarface and Zeke smile as they follow her in.

Arturo sits up in his bed startled at seeing the two men come into his private room behind a smiling nurse. He recognizes Scarface and panics. Arturo gives the nurse a surprised look as she smiles at him and introduces the men.

"Mister Cresto, these are your relatives from New Orleans Abe and Zeke..."

"Hello Nurse Julie, maybe you should..."

"You look so happy to see your cousins." She says.

"Arturo! Good to see you looking so well." Scarface walks to the bedside and pats Arturo on the shoulder.

"Well, I'll leave you with him." Nurse Julie turns to leave the room.

"No! I need some medicine now, don't I?"

"Not until eleven Mister Cresto. Have a good visit. I'm sure you have a lot to talk about. I must tend to the other patients. See you at eleven. Goodbye."

Arturo is speechless as he watches her leave. He wants to yell out to her but Zeke closes the door behind her and he feels pain from his head.

Scarface watches the nurse exit. After the door

closes, he grabs a handful of Arturo's hair, pulling up. He smiles into Arturo's face hearing him grunt in pain.

"I know I don't have the money now but as soon as I get out of here I can get it." Arturo tries reaching for his panic button but Zeke quickly pulls it away.

"Like why should I believe you?" Scarface asks.

"It's true! Listen, someone I know just got a huge payoff. I can get the money from him in a few days."

"I don't believe you. It's curtain time now." Scarface drops Arturo back onto the bed.

"Wait! Trust me. He got big money returning a diamond. I can get all the cash from him. Just give me some time."

"You know some rich friend. Just how dumb you think I be?"

"No! I don't say you're dumb!"

"Is he a big friend of you? The Boss-man says he just take the loss, and lose you. You be example for others. He don't care no more."

"Ask him. Really, I give you his name. He has the money! I know I can get the money. Give me another week. You won't be sorry."

"You still try to cheat the Boss-man."

"No, I'm not trying to..."

Arturo sees a smile come on Scarface just before a pillow presses over his face. He tries to scream but the pillow muffles his voice. *This is wrong! They know I'll get the money. He's just scaring me!* Arturo screams but the scream leaves him with no more air in his lungs. He squirms flailing his arms.

Scarface loves his job, especially when he gets to

snuff someone. He watches Arturo wriggle and slap his fists trying to get free, but Scarface is too strong for him. He smiles big and watches Arturo heave and try twisting away but with no blood to the brain, Arturo finally goes limp. Scarface smiles like a child finding a wonderful toy at Christmas. The job for Scarface is over.

"He be dead." Scarface sets the pillow next to Arturo's head and folds Arturo's arms across his chest. He looks at Arturo for a short time admiring his work before he leaves the room with Zeke.

"The Boss-man says no more time."

"You be right Abe. You done good man." Zeke says.

The two men casually walk out of the room. They see a different Nurse smile at them as they pass her on the way to the elevator. They smile back and disappear behind the elevator doors. Within minutes they are out of the hospital and drive away unnoticed.

Nurse Julie feels exhausted by eleven o'clock. She had to tend to several patients but especially a Mister Donnelly in room 411. The man kept ringing his panic button asking for more pain medicine. Julie finally gave in, calling his doctor to authorize the additional pills. Now at eleven o'clock, Mister Donnelly finally is asleep. The only good part about the night is it passed quickly. Her twelve-hour shift will end at midnight. Nurse Julie selects Arturo's pain pills, putting them in a cup to take to his room. This is her last duty before writing up the paperwork for the night.

She sighs as she walks down the hallway to room

425. She senses something is wrong not hearing Arturo greet her. He is apparently sleeping. As she reaches his bed to wake him, she realizes he is not breathing.

"Oh my God!" Julie shouts. She hits Arturo's panic button and within seconds, another nurse rushes in the room.

"What's the problem Julie?"

"It's a code blue!"

Chapter Nineteen

Don feels the morning sun burning on his face through the open front door. He winces in pain from several areas of his body. His left cheek is swollen and he feels some teeth are loose in his bone-dry mouth. He realizes he spent the night lying on the floor. His gut and his rib cage ache as he gets up and closes the door. A little panic hits him as he remembers the thugs from last night. He hopes his brother was able to strike a deal with the Boss-man. Don only has ten thousand available to pay off Arturo's debt. He staggers into the bathroom, and turns the sink faucet on. After splashing on some cold water, he stares at his bruised face in the mirror.

"I don't deserve this!" He shouts in anger.

Don is angry mixed with worry over his brother. He ignores his pain as he hurries to his truck and drives to the hospital. After a quick check-in with the receptionist, he goes directly to room 425 expecting to blast Arturo. Don gasps seeing a different man is in Arturo's bed. He rushes out to find a nurse.

"Where is Mister Cresto?"

"Are you related to Mister Cresto?"

"Yes! I'm his brother Don. Where is he?"

"I am so sorry Mister Cresto. We left a message to call the hospital. Doctor Manning will see you. Wait here for a minute."

Don pacing in the hallway sees Arturo's doctor walk toward the nurse's station. Don is confused and anxious wanting to find his brother.

"Doctor I'm Arturo's brother, Don Cresto. Where is

Arturo?"

"Holy cow, what happened to you?" Doctor Manning says seeing the bruises on Don's face. He reaches out to touch a lump on Don.

"I had an accident last night... Where is Arturo?" Don asks brushing away the doctor's hand.

"I am sorry to tell you this but Arturo Cresto passed last night."

"No! You said his heart was okay!" Don can't believe his ears.

"Two cousins visited him last night, and we think they murdered your brother. Does he have a problem with these cousins?"

"Two cousins?"

"Yes, we believe someone suffocated Mister Cresto with a pillow. By the estimated time of death, the police are sure it was when the cousins were there. Do you know where either of them lives?"

Don is in shock. "We have no cousins!"

"Come with me. You can verify it is your brother and maybe give the police some details."

"Okay." Don walks in a daze. He feels like his head is detached as he follows the doctor to the morgue area of the hospital.

After seeing his dead brother and answering questions with the police he leaves the hospital. His mind is going crazy with sadness and resentment. *I have avoided illegal activity all my life. I always try to be just the opposite of my brother and my father. Now my job is in jeopardy, my brother and father dead, and I fear for my own life. I must fix this crisis somehow!* Don takes a deep breath and exhales as he slides into his truck. Lost in thoughts he barely recognizes his phone ringing. He cranks up the engine before answering his phone.

"Hello. Who is this?"

"I'm Arturo's friend Carl Salano. Is this Don Cresto?"

"Yes, what do you want?"

"Arturo called me yesterday and we came up with a plan. He gave me your phone number. He was to call me today after he talked with you. Did he tell you about our plan yet? He hasn't called me."

"My brother is dead!" Don feels tears welling up in his eyes as he realizes the meaning of his words. He swipes at his eyes before shifting into reverse and backing out of his parking space.

"Oh no! Did he have another heart attack?"

"No. One of the Boss-man's goons suffocated him."

"Wow, Arturo is dead. Let me think for a minute..."

"I don't know what I am going to do, Carl. I tried to save him. His gambling was like a disease."

"Okay Don, let's regroup. He told me about the diamond and everything. Max Merchado got a million clams for it. That money should be yours!"

"No... Well, I don't know. He returned the diamond, it all seems hopeless now." Don has listened to the recorded conversations, he knows Max and his friends are going to Italy.

"Just think about it Don. I know Arturo says you're a law abiding citizen, but this Max took away what is rightfully... well yours now."

"Just what did you and Art think of?" His voice reflects a deep resentment stirring in his mind for Max and Sam.

"The plan is to kidnap Merchado's girlfriend."

"You want to kidnap his girlfriend? What for, money?"

"Yes and we want all of it Don, we want the whole million!"

"You want to do a million dollar kidnaping?"

"Yes! We agreed I would get a third. You can have two thirds. We agreed to a third to you, a third to Arturo and a third to me."

"Kidnap someone, have you gone nuts? Oh, Max is booked to leave for Rome, Italy tomorrow so he won't even be here. He wants to sightsee and then see the donation ceremony in Italy."

"He's going to Rome on your money, even better!"

"How is that better? According to what I got from Arturo's laptop, Max and his friends are all leaving. There is nothing else I can do."

"Yes there is! The plan works better in Italy. If they fly to Rome, they must travel to Gioia Tauro. I have friends there. We must go there!"

"Are you crazy?"

"I will talk this over with Bruno Nero."

"I know Bruno. Didn't he do spy work with Arturo?"

"Yes, he's our associate. He knows everything about this."

"Another person knows about the diamond?"

"Well, I trust him. He can handle anything we need."

Don Cresto goes silent, thinking. *There really isn't anything left for me here. I've kept in contact with my childhood friends for many years now. I've been good all my life. What has it got for me? Now Arty is dead because of Max.*

"What's the matter Don? Are you okay?" Carl asks.

"I'm just thinking. Is there any Italian blood in you Carl?"

"My last name is Salano, what do you think? We are friends because my father is from Gioia Tauro like yours."

"It's a small world Carl. Desperate times require desperate actions. I know what flights Max and his friends are taking. Maybe we can get on a same flight just to intimidate them. Here is a new plan. I have friends in Italy too. Maybe we stop Max there and just steal both women. As you say, this will be easier in Italy than here."

"Steal both girls?"

"Max gave half the money to Sam."

"Wow, what a friend! Are you sure?"

"Of course I am sure. I heard Sam thank him again before he went home. They were checking their bank accounts."

"Oh yeah, the laptop thing. Okay, we hold both of them until they hand over all of the money. I want my cash in Euros though. I plan to stay in Italy."

"Me too, I have nothing left here. Arturo is dead and my Papa died last week. I want to be with my old friends in Italy now."

"I know. Arturo told me about your Papa. Such a shame, he had two months only left on his sentence."

"So we should meet. I have cash. I think I can pay the plane fares if you cannot pay for your own."

"I can do mine. Let's meet now for lunch."

"De Augustine Place on Federal highway, are you close?"

"I will be there by noon."

"Look for me with a swollen jaw and a black eye."

"What happened to you?"

"The Boss-man's goons got to me too. More reason to go to Italy." Don rings off. All his pent up evilness is taking over his mind. He feels euphoric about the kidnapping, and especially about kidnapping the enemy's women!

Chapter Twenty

Friday morning Max, Peggy, Sam and Ann go through the screening and luggage checks at Fort Lauderdale International Airport. At eleven o'clock, their American Airlines plane taxis away from the terminal ready to take off.

Max sees Sam grip the armrests as the plane bolts down the runway and soars into the firmament. He watches Sam grip the armrests until the plane levels off at thirty thousand feet. Two hours later, Max feels the plane touch down in Charlotte, North Carolina.

After hustling to the next plane, Max barely scans the passengers as he boards the plane for Europe. He sees many new faces and strange odors but he pays little attention to them. He finds his seat and waits impatiently. Finally, the doors shut and the engines start up. The huge 737 plane starts taxiing toward the runway getting in line behind a few other planes. Max thumps his hands waiting for the plane to take off.

"Charlotte must be a busy airport." Max says. He looks at Peggy and starts fidgeting with the booklet in the seat pouch.

"It won't be long now Max."

"Do you have a firm grip on the armrests Sam?"

"Hey it works so far."

Max hails the flight attendant passing by.

"Hi Miss! What's your name?"

"I'm Donna, sir."

"Pretty name Donna. I'm Max. How long is it to Rome?"

"About nine hours, sir."

"Just call me Max. What time zone will we be in?"

"Rome is six hours later than here Max."

"Thank you!" Max smiles and watches Donna stroll down the aisle before he advances his slim Jaeger-LeCoultre watch six hours.

"Thank you for no pranks Max. I saw that rubber spider in your carryon." Peggy says, happy having kept Max under control.

"I'm too excited to think up anything right now Peg."

"Good. Let's enjoy this trip." She hugs Max as the speaker blares.

"Welcome aboard American airlines flight 1289 to Rome, Italy. For you clock watchers, the time in Rome is six hours ahead of Charlotte." The attendant continues to explain the life jackets and safety procedures.

Ten minutes pass before the plane swings onto the runway and catapults into the warm North Carolina sky. Sam clamps down on the armrests until the plane reaches several thousand feet in altitude. He sees Max full of excitement clap his hands and speak.

"Well, we're on the way to Rome. I love it! This is a trip of a lifetime." Although Max could easily afford the trip, the reward money is paying for everything courtesy of the freak finding of that diamond. He even smiles when he hears a nervous Sam talk.

"I'll be happy when we land in Rome. You know the middle of the ocean is several miles deep. If this thing goes down out there no one will ever find us."

"Relax Sam. Planes make dozens of trips across the Atlantic Ocean every day. The chances our plane will go down are slim and none."

"I wonder if someone will try to get our money. Don't you worry about that?"

"Again Sam, the chances of someone even knowing we are going to Italy are next to zero until we go to the ceremony."

"I think we should have a secret code word for emergencies though."

"What emergencies?" Max asks.

"Well, like if one of us gets in a bind and can't tell the others in front of their enemy, one could say the code word in a sentence and we would know that person is in trouble."

"You expect us to have trouble?"

"No, I hope not but just in case, we ought to have a code word. That's all I'm saying Max."

"You mean like code red, or something?"

"Let's be more subtle."

"I'm thinking this is a dumb ass idea, Sam."

"Perfect! Let's use dumb ass. It's a word we would not normally use and easy to work into a sentence."

"I'm thinking about using those words now."

"Does anyone object to that code word?" Sam sees them shake their heads. "Then dumb ass it is. No matter if it's ten years from now, we can still use this code word. I feel better now. I'll be even happier when we land safely in Rome, and even happier still when we land back in Fort Lauderdale."

"Okay worry wart. Worry all you want. I'm going to enjoy some of American Airline's finest adult beverages. Oh Donna!" Max waves seeing the same stewardess approaching in the aisle.

"Yes, Max is it?"

"Excellent Donna. What kind of booze do you have?" Max smiles and chats a little before placing his order.

Sam's nerves are on edge ever since the attempted robbery. At least now, on the plane he feels a little safer knowing there are no guns. Even worrying about the trip to Rome, he knows he needs sleep to be alert later. Ann looks tired too.

"I think I'll make a pit stop and then take a nap." Sam turns looking toward the restrooms. He joins the line behind two people at the rear of the plane

The restroom door finally opens in front of Sam and a dark haired woman rubs by smiling at Sam as she heads back to her seat. Sam smiles back before he steps into the restroom and locks the door. He looks into the small mirror over the sink shaking his head as he opens his fly. *Why in the world am I flying to Italy?*

Sam finishes in the restroom and as he walks down the aisle, he catches a whiff of cologne. *Where did I smell that before?* Sam slips back in his seat and looks at Ann.

"You still dazzle me with those eyes!"

"Thank you, handsome devil." Ann says.

"I think I'll try to nap."

"Me too, you kept me awake twisting about all night."

"Sorry honey. I've had a lot on my mind this week."

"Yes, let's rest up for Rome. Maybe we can avoid jet lag."

"Okay, let's try."

"You guys, I'm wide awake. I need a pit stop, too." Max gets up seeing Sam and Ann leaning back. He sees

Peggy smile as she leans back and closes her eyes too.

"Are you all going to nap?" Max says. Peggy smiles at Max as he stands up. He walks to the rear rest room.

The plane is droning on steadily as Max exits the restroom. Feeling good as he walks down the aisle, he is shocked when he sees Don Cresto raise a hand and speak.

"Mister Merchado!"

"My God what are you doing on this flight? You were in my house too!"

"More important, people have died because of the Bellasettas! They are the real bandits! They will kill you and..."

"Why don't I believe you?" Max raises his hands defensively. He hustles past Don Cresto not hearing anything else Don says. As he flops into his seat, he nudges Sam.

"What's up? You look a little pale."

"Uh... Did you see who spoke to me?"

"No I just closed my eyes and sat in my seat with no talking to anyone. I like normal remember?"

"Do you remember the dumb-ass who stole the diamond and his dumb-ass sons?"

"Well, yeah, Salvatore Cresto stole it with his friend that he killed. His sons broke into your house. Hey you used dumb-ass."

"Yes I did. Don Cresto is on this plane!"

Chapter Twenty-One

"That's the cologne I smelled!" Sam whispers to Max but Ann hears.

"How can Don Cresto be here?" Ann asks.

"I don't know, but from what he said to me, he hates the Bellasettas. I wonder if he will seek revenge on them. He called me by name too. I should have asked him some things but I was too shocked seeing him." Max says.

"We need to stay together when we get there. It's another mess we're into Max, but this time we have the girls in it too!" Sam shakes his head.

"Let's hope we lose him in Rome. We have a day to spend there before we go to Gioia Tauro. I think we can ditch him in Rome before we go to the hotel. Then Sunday we drive to Gioia Tauro. That's what we'll do."

"He could follow us and see where we are staying in Rome. He knows where we are eventually going. He seems to know everything else. There is one main highway from Rome to Gioia Tauro. All he has to do is follow us and stop us along the way. We have to think of something else."

"I wish I had my gun. We should buy a gun!"

"Let's not go crazy, Max. Let's think on that." Peggy says.

"Try not to worry so much love. We'll get through this just fine." Sam says to Ann trying to sound confident but he is not sure he believes his own words. He faces forward and leans his seat back as far as it will go and closes his eyes.

"I need rest. We all need to rest to prepare for Italy.

We have many hours before we reach Rome." Sam remembers an awful dream he had once about a small plane going down and sharks circling around the sinking plane. He thinks about the Atlantic Ocean being several miles deep in the middle. *I know if the plane goes down out here, we will never be found! A great thought to have when I'm trying to take a nap!* His head is full of the danger and excitement but the drone of the engines and the hiss of the cool air from the vents help him doze off into a restless sleep.

In his sleep, Sam awakens to see Don Cresto reaching over the seat behind Ann. Don is holding a long jagged knife blade to Ann's throat. Some blood is oozing onto her chest from a cut on her neck.

"What are you doing?" Sam shouts.

"Give me the diamond or I kill her!" Don is pressing the blade against Ann's throat lengthening the cut. Sam sees her eyes wide open with fear and her lower lip is trembling. She seems to be praying too.

"I don't have it!"

"You have it, don't lie to me!"

"No I don't, honest!"

"You must have the diamond. Max says you have it."

"He would not say that. How do you expect to get away with killing someone on this plane?"

"I want the diamond. That is all that matters! Give it to me. I am counting to ten and then I kill her. One, two, three, four..."

Bang! Sam's ears hurt from the blast and he sees Don Cresto's head rip open. Blood splatters everywhere. Don Cresto slumps out of sight dropping the knife. A loud wind whistles through a broken out window. Sam jerks his head around and sees Max holding a smoking gun.

"I told you I need my gun with us!" Max shouts over the noise.

Sam feels the cabin air pressure dropping and sees the hole in a window. The bullet ripped through Cresto's head and took out a large area of a window. The plane tilts down at an extreme angle.

"Cover that hole!" Sam shouts aloud. He immediately feels someone nudge him on his shoulder.

"Hey, I was trying to sleep. What hole?" Ann asks.

Sam shakes his head and looks around. Max and Peggy turn sleepy eyes toward him. Ann is staring at him, too. Sam sees no blood and no knife or any whistling wind from a hole in a window.

"Um... Did I mention a hole?"

"I think you said 'Cover that hole!'"

"Were you having some kind of erotic dream?" Max chuckles.

"You don't have a gun Max?"

"Max does not have a gun on the plane" Ann shakes her head.

"I'll tell you about the dream later." Sam sees her concerned look, smiles at her and kisses her on the lips. He leans back in his seat, closes his eyes and soon falls asleep fighting not to think about Cresto again. Sam tosses and turns and it seems like just seconds later once again he feels someone nudging him on his shoulder.

"We're about to land Sam! Look out the windows. It's daytime here." Max says patting Sam's shoulder.

Sam rubs his eyes, yawns and looks at his watch. It shows nearly nine thirty. Glancing out the window, he sees buildings and trees getting larger as the plane starts to make its final approach to Leonardo da Vinci International Airport. He whispers, "What's Don Cresto doing?"

"He was staring at us for a while. Now he's ignoring us."

"Let's stick together when we get off and keep an eye on him!" Sam feels Ann grabbing his arm. Her face is pale like she may be sick as the seatbelt sign comes on with a bong. She buckles up preparing for the landing and the next phase of the mission.

Sam feels the plane touchdown and seconds later, the air brakes come on. He looks at his watch - it is 9:45 in the morning Italian time. He feels the gentle lurch when the plane comes to a stop at the terminal. His heart is thumping.

The usual hustle and bustle ensues as people begin gathering their belongings to get off the plane. The people in the row in front of Sam have a large bag stuck in the overhead compartment. He waits until they manage to haul it out and move on. Sam follows his friends off the plane.

"Chilly!" Max says and puts on his coat.

Sam sees Ann already has her coat on. He feels a chill in the air even though he is inside the building. A feeling of apprehension comes over Sam. He speaks as he puts his coat on.

"Here we are. Where do we go now?"

Chapter Twenty-Two

"First we go to the baggage claim." Max grabs Peggy's hand and rushes down the corridor.

"Max, there's no need to rush. We have to wait for our luggage anyhow. Cresto will get there before we can get our stuff and leave." Sam feels Ann grab his arm as he follows Max and Peggy.

"I know. I just want to get going."

Sam peeks behind but sees no sign of Don Cresto. His image of Don Cresto is somewhat vague anyhow mainly remembering the musky cologne odor. Even on the plane he could smell it when he walked by Cresto. When he saw Don Cresto at Max's house the man seemed like a very nice man. However, the impression etched in Sam's mind now is Don grinning at him on the plane. A creepy feeling comes over Sam and as he walks, he wonders. *How did Don Cresto get on the same flight as we did? It can't be a coincidence!*

Max gets his luggage without seeing Don Cresto. However as Max orders a rental car he sees Don Cresto appear from nowhere watching him from across the baggage claim area. He can see another man with his back toward Max standing with Don Cresto and Don looks over his shoulder to stare at Max off and on. Cresto looks like he has on that same dark gray suit with a different yellow and gray striped tie. The other man with his back to Max is wearing a dark overcoat and neither man is carrying luggage. They are standing fifty feet away and occasionally glance in Max's direction.

Before Max turns back to the counter, he sees two

more men walk up to Don Cresto. They appear to know Don and both are much shorter than Don is. Both are wearing black jackets and blue jeans. They shake hands and hug briefly. The men stay with Don and his friend. Max watches from the corner of his eye not wanting to stare at the men. The strangers talk a lot and use a lot of hand gestures before they all walk away. Max completes the paperwork for the car and smiles at the woman behind the counter.

"Okay now where is a nice Italian restaurant around here?" Max asks her.

"Most all the good restaurants open at seven or seven thirty tonight. I only know the McDonalds on via Portuense is open at this time."

"How do I get there?" Max listens to her directions.

Max walks outside and helps Sam stash the luggage in the trunk of a red Ford Focus.

"Yeah I know it's another red Focus." Max waves off Sam and helps Peggy get in the front seat before getting in to drive.

"I like having you drive Max." Sam says cuddling on Ann in the back seat, but Ann is tense and worried.

"Sam! We have to watch out for that creep! We don't know what he is doing here."

"We haven't even got on the road yet."

"Well, keep an eye out for him and those guys." Ann leans into Sam. She feels his comforting arm wrap around her.

"We have all day to sight-see after we check in to the hotel. The rental girl gave me good directions to of all places a McDonalds. It seems all the main restaurants close until about seven at night. She also told me how to get to the hotel and how to go Sunday when we head for Gioia Tauro. She printed them in English from Google maps. We work our way to A3 highway and it's a straight shot south. The girl said it will take six or seven hours to get there, but it's a no-brainer. The hotel for tonight is only ten kilometers away."

"You're not worried those guys will follow us?" Sam asks.

"Not yet. Maybe they just want to intimidate us."

"You think Don Cresto flew all the way to Italy just to intimidate us? I don't think so. I want to know what he's up to."

"What can he do? He's not going to kill us is he?"

"I think they want the money. It's always about the money."

"So how can he get the money from us?"

"I don't know but let's find that McDonalds. I'm starving." Sam can feel his stomach growling and knotting up.

"Roger and aye-aye sir!" Max aims a salute toward Sam, as he pulls out of the rental car area. He turns onto via Portuense and sees a familiar sign.

"Hey I see the small pair of arches on that building. It has to be a McDonald's restaurant. McDonalds is everywhere! It's not a luxury diner but it beats going hungry." Max pulls in to the parking lot next to a police car.

Max sees a blue Mercedes sedan and a black Citroen pull into McDonalds after he does. They park a few slots away from him, one on each side of the Focus. *I hope this is just a coincidence.* Max thinks as he joins the others inside and orders a hearty lunch. Max watches who comes and goes. He sees two police officers leave and many people come and go but no one who looks like Don Cresto. Max chomps on his last fry when a tall skinny man stops at his table with a carryout bag in his hand.

"Hello Max. I am Carl. My friend Don is outside." Carl has a noticeable gun pointing from inside his trench coat.

"What do you want?"

"I want all of you to come with me. You must know the Bellasettas are evil people. They gave you money, but they will take it back when you get to Gioia Tauro in exchange for your lives! You must give the money to us before they take it from you."

"You're crazy! Why would we do that?"

"Are you staying here in Rome?"

"Well yes, no... I don't know."

"It is a long drive to Port of Gioia Tauro Max. We have friends here in Italy and you are the strangers. Bad things happen if you do not cooperate now. You come to the bank and draw out money."

"There is a bank with a million in cash?"

"We take your girls with us in the Mercedes. You go in the Citroen."

"You know I don't have it all even if I wanted to give it all to you."

"Yes, that complicates things. You should have kept it all. We deal with both you and Sam now. You give us what we want and I promise no one will be harmed."

"Why should I trust you? How do you know all about us?"

"Never mind how or why, you and Sam just go to the

Citroen. I will take your women with us." Carl waves toward the door.

Max follows Carl's motion to go outside with the others. As he steps outside, he sees two policia getting out of their car next to the Focus.

"Good morning officers!" Max shouts. He directs Sam and the girls to the Focus.

"Boun giorno!" One of the men says and tips his hat.

"Everyone get in the car!" Max mumbles. He seizes the moment knowing Carl would be foolish to shoot. Max nods toward the officer as he and the others hustle into the Focus. Carl backs off and rushes to the Mercedes as Max starts the car.

"Okay, what do we do now? Do we get out and hail the officers or just try to lose them?" Max asks.

"The police are already in the restaurant." Sam says.

"I think we take off then. If we get out of the car without the police, Carl may come back for us. He's getting back out of his car now!" Max shifts into reverse and guns the engine backing out before Carl can get to the car.

Max starts forward but the Mercedes backs out in front of him and the Citroen backs out behind him. The Mercedes moves forward in the parking lot exiting to the right motioning Max to follow him. Max turns left and speeds down a narrow lane. The Citroen is soon on his tail. He zigzags through a maze of narrow streets, but the Citroen stays with him.

"Start praying guys!" Max says as he takes a sharp turn onto another side street, but the Citroen easily stays with him.

"We can't lose him Max. If we loop around too much the Mercedes will find us!" Sam says.

"What are we going to do?" Peggy asks.

"I'm calling Gustavo. Maybe he can help us." Max shouts.

"Go ahead and call him, dumb ass."

"Hey that's for when you're captured or something dumb ass!"

"It's appropriate right now."

Chapter Twenty-Three

Max frowns as he takes out his phone to dial Gustavo. After dialing, he puts his phone on speaker mode. The car is not too quiet inside so they all lean closer to the phone. After two rings, a man answers.

"Ciao!"

"Hello, Mister Bellasetta?"

"No, who is calling please?"

"This is Max. Is Gustavo Bellasetta there?" Max waits.

"A moment." The phone goes silent for a few seconds.

"This is Gustavo. How are you Max? You must be in Italy now. Did you have a nice flight to Rome?"

"Well, we made it to Rome okay but I think we have some bad company following us."

"Someone is following you?"

"It is Don Cresto and some of his friends. I am trying to lose the black car behind us. I got away from the Mercedes with Cresto."

"Donald Cresto from America is here, you say?"

"Yes! He and his friends are following us. They want the reward money. They tried to kidnap us already at a McDonalds. We escaped because there happened to be some police around. We are concerned he will stop us eventually."

"Yes and I am sure he is dangerous."

"We thought maybe we should call the police."

"No policia please. We can handle everything here Max. You must come directly here. Forget about Rome, Max. We will take care of the problem if you can come here now."

"We are still in Rome many hours away. We can go directly there but it will be late afternoon, if we can keep Cresto and his men from stopping us."

"Please just call me Gustavo. I cannot help you where you are. If you can stay ahead of them, then go directly to Gioia Tauro and Banc Bella. I am at the bank now on other business, and I will be here."

"Will the bank be open that late?"

"We have guards here and that is not too late. Also, the bank will be open if I say so." Gustavo hints of arrogance in his tone.

"Okay, I will call again when we are closer."

"Thank you, be careful Max. When you see Rosarno exit, get off and go to Via Vallamena." Gustavo continues to give directions but Max focuses on getting Peggy's attention.

"We will be on the right side of the road at 100 Via Provinciale. Look for Banc Bella on the front of a powder blue building. It is a very distinguished looking bank. You should have no problem finding us."

"Would you repeat the directions for Peggy?" Max motions to Peggy to write down information. Gustavo repeats the directions and then continues talking.

"I have done some research since we last talked Max. Salvatore Cresto is due to get out of prison in two months but he is a very sick man - Cancer I suspect... too bad." Now Max detects hatred in Gustavo's voice.

"We tried to extradite him to stand trial for the murders here. We have requested extradition for him if he lives and gets out of prison. He betrayed us. Cresto was a trusted sentry before the robbery and murders. We do know what made him take such terrible action."

"I read about the robbery and murders. I am sorry for your family's loss Gustavo. Why did Cresto snap?" Max asks.

"The reason is better left untold. It was a long time ago but I still miss my brother. It is bad for Don Cresto to come here. He reminds us of what his father did."

"I think Don is only after the money."

"You know Cresto's sons Donald and Arturo were born here in Gioia Tauro. I am sure they have friends. Cresto and his partner Albero are the murderers and thieves. You say Don and Arturo are aware you have returned the diamond, so they are after the money. How do they know this?"

"I don't know. They want all the reward money though."

"They are as evil as their father and his friend! I will have extra guards at the bank. You should come directly to the bank. We can protect you here. I look forward to seeing you again. Be careful my friend and good luck!" Gustavo rings off.

"I say we forget Rome like he said, and go straight to Gioia Tauro! I am sure the Bellasettas are not evil as Carl said. I also think Gustavo can help us. Anyone got another idea?" Max asks speeding along a narrow road with the Citroen inches away from his bumper.

"You think the highway will be safer my love?" Peggy asks.

"It can't be worse than this. I think we need help from the Bellasettas now. I think we have to drive to Gioia Tauro."

"Gustavo seemed nice enough, but then so did Cresto."

"Yeah but I have an uneasy feeling about Cresto, not so with Gustavo. He seems genuine to me. Can I get an okay from you guys?" Max asks and sees them nod. Ahead he sees a sign for the A3 highway and maneuvers around to the southbound on ramp.

"The Citroen is still with us, Max." Sam says looking behind.

"I know, I know. Let's see if this Focus can outrun it!" Max floors the gas pedal racing along the four-lane highway but the Citroen stays on his tail.

"I see cameras along the road Max. Maybe you shouldn't speed."

"That must be why they are just following us for now."

"What are they doing, just staying on our tail all the way to Gioia Tauro? I'm sorry that you and Peggy are in this mess now. I never thought Don Cresto would be after us." Sam holds Ann close feeling her tremble against his side.

She separates from Sam and leans forward. "I think I'm going to be ill. I hope we live to see tomorrow!" She leans forward raising her hands to her head.

"You're thinking he may try to kill us?" Sam asks.

"Yes! We took away a lot from him. What do you think?"

"Unfortunately he might. Max, keep up the good driving!"

"I'm on it Sam but whatever I do, he stays behind us."

"We are right to forget Rome for now. Let's go straight to Gioia Tauro and hope we get some help from Gustavo. We can cancel the hotel in Rome later."

Sam does a silent prayer as he looks forward. He remembers a quote from Satchel Paige. *"Don't look back. Something might be gaining on you." What kind of plan do we have for this?* Sam gives an involuntary shiver.

"Next stop is Gioia Tauro, Sam!"

"And what do we do when we get there?" Sam asks.

"Gustavo will help us. I am sure of it."

"Is there a 9-1-1 number for Italy?"

"I don't know. I saw something about that when I was browsing for this trip but I cannot remember the number. I'll call information. Does anyone know how to do that?" Max hears nothing.

"Just concentrate on keeping away from the bad guys Max. I remember Mister Carl saying it is a long way to Gioia Tauro. Let's hope we make it there."

"We will Sam, you'll see." Max sounds confident but his heart is pounding. He keeps eyeing the Citroen. His mind keeps nagging, *what will we do if the Mercedes catches up with us? What will we do?* As if on cue, he looks back and shouts out. "Sam, we have more trouble! The Mercedes is back and it's passing the Citroen!"

Chapter Twenty-Four

"That's not good, and we're still far away from Gioia Tauro." Max says.

"Yeah and what if Cresto is right? What if the Bellasettas really are bad guys? We're stuck between a rock and a hard place!"

"I don't think so Sam. I'm good at sensing people. I don't feel the evil in them that Carl said. I think they will be on our side. Besides, we have no choice. We can't get away from that big bad Mercedes or the Citroen."

"You're handling the Citroen okay so far."

"The Mercedes is bigger and faster, and we're hours away from Gioia Tauro. Did I tell Gustavo that Cresto was on the plane with us?" Max says staring at his phone.

Everyone is silent. Ann bends over putting her hands on her head as Sam pats her on the back before breaking the silence.

"Cresto and his sons were born here. They know the language and their friends know how to get around here. They have friends helping them and we don't."

"Let's hope Gustavo really is our friend!" Sam says.

"I know we can trust him." Max feels a sixth sense about him. He is usually right in pegging people as good or bad and Gustavo is good to Max.

"I believe Cresto will do anything to stop us."

"We're on a major highway. What can they do?"

"We are bound to hit an unpopulated area at one of these exits. That's when they'll try to force us off the road. Then they could do what they want. Watch closely Max!"

"If that Mercedes pushes us off the road we have a major problem!" Max grips the steering wheel tighter.

"There's a guardrail along this highway so he can't force you off the road. He cannot do much. If he bumps us at this speed, we might crash. I think he wants the money so he won't crash us."

Max tries to ignore the situation for a moment. He glances over the countryside of Italy full of blooms and greenery passing by the window. Plants are starting to flourish to life in spring. He sees lush greenery, trees and open fields of various crops flash by along the roadside but he cannot enjoy any of it. His thoughts always go back to the mad men following him. He continues to stay close to another car or alongside of one as the two cars stay with him relentlessly. Max keeps glancing at the rear view mirror as he drives through little townships and farmlands heading south.

The blue Mercedes starts to pass on a long semi-deserted part of roadway. Max jams the accelerator to the floor and blocks the car. He hears the Focus engine's laborious groan as he keeps just ahead of the blue car. He shifts lanes with the Mercedes keeping it at bay. As he approaches some cars, the Mercedes backs off.

Max is near panic mode as he drives. He feels the sweat on his head and body. The scenery flip-flops from small towns to open undeveloped areas and farmlands along the fenced-in highway. He sees a sign for the town of Pizzo ahead and notices how thin the traffic is now. The Mercedes and the Citroen keep pace with Max but he still manages to avoid being overtaken. Time passes and the countryside rolls by along with the other cars. Max is able to keep the blue Mercedes behind but he knows. *They are waiting to pounce!* Then just when he sees relief, his fears come true.

"Hey look! We get off here. We're almost there Sam!" Max ignores the Mercedes briefly, excited seeing a sign for Goioa Tauro ahead."

Max veers onto the exit and turns right onto SP1 roadway. The two cars follow him along the straight road. Max accelerates but the Mercedes out-guns him pulling alongside Max catching him off guard. Max feels the big car bump his side forcing him to swerve off the road. He slams on the brakes but in the soft dirt, he slides too far. He slams the Focus into a large tree on the side of the road. The Mercedes stops in front of him.

"What do we do now?" Sam shouts.

"Oh no!" Ann shrieks and sinks down in her seat.

"Is everyone alright?" Max shouts and sees the seatbelts apparently held.

As his air bag deflates, Max pans back forward. He sees steam gushing from the crumpled hood of the Focus. Then through the mist, he sees the passenger door of the Mercedes open and Carl jumps out and rushes toward them pointing his gun.

"Get out!" He says waving his gun at Max.

The man is small but holds a big gun aimed at Max's head. Max gets out of the hissing Focus with the others. He can feel his knees are unsteady as he helps Peggy out.

"You girls go to the car!" The man shouts pointing to the Mercedes.

Sam helps Ann out of the car. His body goes on full alert and tense. He can see Ann shaking as she stands up and stumbles toward the Mercedes. Another car slows down as it approaches the wreck, but the driver sees the gunman and speeds off.

"Just girls go! Men go there!" Carl shouts pointing to the Citroen.

"Okay, but we must help them to the car." Sam says "Then you go back."

Sam and Ann stagger along toward the Mercedes following Max and Peggy. He sees the side of the four door Mercedes has virtually no visible damage from bumping the Ford off the road. The man waves his gun motioning the girls into the back of the car. Sam waits as Max opens the rear door and Peggy and Ann crawl in.

Sam watches the door close and is about to turn around when suddenly he high kicks the gun from Carl's hand. Before the man can react Sam throws a right cross to his jaw and watches him fold like an accordion crumpling to the ground. With super speed, he leaps inside the open front door. He sees Don Cresto behind the wheel reaching for his gun. Sam leans over and fist hammers him. Don Cresto slumps down onto the steering wheel sounding the horn.

"Max! Dump him and drive this thing!" Sam shouts over the horn blasting as he undoes Cresto's seat belt.

Max opens the driver's door and tumbles Cresto onto the road. He slides behind the wheel as Sam hops into the front seat. Max sees a man from the Citroen hustle toward them as he spins the tires taking off. A dust cloud fills the air around the man and the Citroen.

As Max accelerates down the road, he feels the rush

of his adrenalin. Finally up to speed, he is able to speak.

"My God Sam, I think you just saved our lives or at least our money!" Max shakes his head as he checks his rear mirror.

"Something snapped. I guess all those Judo lessons paid off! And we have a better car now."

"Yeah, I hope we can lose the black car now!"

Sam just nods with a blank expression at Max. Coming off the high of his attack, he begins shaking violently out of control. Finally settling down he exhales noisily. The painful knot in his stomach returns and he groans.

"Are you okay?" Max says after a quick glance at Sam.

"I will be. I think we should get to Bella Banc as quick as possible. I was hoping those guys would give up the chase."

"No worries. Even if they don't, we have the better car now."

"Yeah! I want to swap places with Peggy."

"Okay, just climb over the seat. I don't think it's wise to stop before we get there."

"Right, just climb over the seat."

"Yes, Sam. Just hop over the seat! Peggy can climb up here."

"Okay." He feels awkward but Sam climbs into the rear seat.

"I'm glad I didn't wear a dress." Peggy says. She rubs against Sam and smiles as she slides into the front seat.

For a moment, all is well again. Ann leans against

Sam.

"You did it! I thought we were dead!"

"I did it!" Sam smiles as he peers out the rear window. "I did it..." Sam mumbles to himself exhaling noisily again. He feels the knot in his stomach tighten.

Chapter Twenty-Five

Albert starts to rush toward the Mercedes but it accelerates away. He pounds the hood of the Citroen. His heart is pounding and he takes several deep breaths. Don and Carl are lying on the ground and the Mercedes is gone.

"We must get Don and Carl." Albert shouts at Angelino as he runs to his friends. He and Angelino help the men back on their feet.

"Where is my gun?" Carl asks. Still groggy from the punch, he looks around and rushes to get his gun about ten feet away.

"Pronto Carl. Why were you so careless with your gun? We must now catch up to them!" Albert says helping everyone back to the car.

"Let me drive!" Don barely is over the pain from the thug's attack and now he feels his jaw swelling. His anger now splits equally between Max and Sam.

When the last door closes, Don floors the Citroen. He can no longer see the Mercedes in the distance but he knows where it is going. Don races the Citroen back onto the SP1 roadway.

"Be careful Don. Remember this car. We must not get caught for speeding. You still have a few pain pills?"

"Yes, from home."

"Give to me please. My jaw is aching." Carl says.

"We must catch them Carl. We must get the money from them! Here, just take one." Don hands his bottle of pills to Carl.

"You look worse Don. Now you will have two black

eyes. Maybe you take one of these too." Carl says as he drops two pills in his mouth. The bruise on Don's face is rapidly swelling.

"No but when we catch them, I will have my revenge. I see the Mercedes maybe a half kilometer ahead." Don says but he wonders. *How can we stop them when we catch up with them?*

"If you get closer maybe I can shoot out the tires." Carl says.

"Good Carl. We cannot outrun them in this."

Continuing toward Goioa Tauro, Max sees the Citroen catch up with him. He can see all four men in the car with Don Cresto driving.

"For sure that's Don Cresto and all his friends..." Max stops talking when the rear window of the Mercedes shatters with a gunshot.

"Everyone duck down! Max, do the best you can!" Sam shouts.

"I can't duck much!"

"This thing has a lot of metal in it. I don't think they can shoot through it with a handgun and I don't think the Citroen has enough guts to get around us." Sam says.

"He won't have a chance!" Max stomps on the gas pedal but he sees a roundabout ahead and has to slow down. The Citroen is on his tail now.

"Where's a cop when you want one!" Max ducks down hearing more bullets thump into the Mercedes as the Citroen moves closer again.

Sam lies gently on top of Ann in the back seat. Even as the bullets are hitting the car, he feels the heat from her body against him stirring his passion for her. *It is great just lying here! If we die, at least we will die together!*

Peggy leans onto Max's side as he hunches down just above the steering wheel. She feels sorry for herself. She tastes her salty tears that start oozing down her face. *I want to go back to work at the flower shop. I just want to go back home! We are going to die. We are all going to die!* She keeps weeping with her head leaning against Max's side as he drives on toward Gioia Tauro. The gunshots eventually stop. She feels the car slowing down. *What is happening now? Is the car dying?*

Max slows down and glances at his Jaeger-LeCoultre watch seeing it is almost six o'clock. The populace of the city and the road filling up with other cars ends the gunfire as Max enters a roundabout circle.

"Our journey is almost over! Peggy, where do I go now?"

"I am sorry about this. I'm just scared. Oh yes, turn right there onto SS-18." Peggy remembers as she wipes her eyes and unfolds her paper.

"Gustavo is our friend. I know I am right. I have a feeling that I must see his family too. We will go directly to the bank." Max says turning onto the new road. The black Citroen stays a block behind him now. The whole situation seems surreal to him.

"Yes, we just have to trust Gustavo." Sam says as he tilts up.

"Let me call him to let him know we're here." Max takes out his phone turns on the speaker before dialing.

After two rings, Gustavo answers. "Hello Max."

"Hello Gustavo. We took the Goioa Tauro exit SP-1 and SS-18. We are now in the blue Mercedes that was following us."

"How are you in the Mercedes?"

"There was an incident. I will explain later. I would like to go directly to the bank but I am concerned about the other car that is now behind us. Four men in a black Citroen shot at us several times along the way."

"I will have guards outside the building to escort you inside. They are prepared for any trouble. They will protect you Max and all of your friends."

"Oh, I just went passed Vallamena!"

"Then you must turn around. You were not watching for that?"

"I was watching the Citroen. I will find a place to turn around."

"Follow Via Vallamena to the round-about and go onto Via Roma. You will see us a half kilometer past the loop on Via Roma."

"We'll be there soon. Thank you Gustavo." Max rings off.

"We made it!" Peggy leans across to hug Max just as he finds a wide area of a main road branching to the left to turn around. She feels her body roll forward as Max stomps on the brakes and turns sharply to the left. Max manages to make a complete U-turn in the intersection. Unable to catch herself, Peggy rolls onto the front floor. She waits until the Mercedes straightens after the U-turn before she can get up from the floor.

"You should have warned me!" She swats Max's

arm.

"Where's your seatbelt?"

"In all this excitement I forgot to put it on."

"I didn't see the turning area until I was right there. I had to act fast. I am sorry. I had to make a quick decision."

"You still could have warned me!" Peggy sits upright in the seat and tries smoothing her hair back in place.

Max looks in his rear view mirror and sees the Citroen making a U-turn behind him. He looks at Peggy and smiles.

"Sorry Peg. Maybe put on your seatbelt now."

Max turns onto Via Vallamena. The street is narrower than he expects. Some of the buildings extend nearly into the street. The buildings are mostly pastel shades of blue and tan while some are stark white. Some have trash piled alongside and some are clean looking. Max slows down approaching a circle.

"Here's the circle Gustavo talked about. Loop around and onto the second Via Roma to go south. Gustavo says the bank is a half kilometer on the right." Peggy says buckling her seat belt.

Max loops on to Via Roma. The road looks like a typical inner city street to Max except it looks clean. It is void of clutter as if a street washer has just cleaned it. Buildings rise on both sides of the street and only a couple cars are on the dark paved road. A sidewalk runs with the street on both sides. The shops have an old yet fresh look about them, as if they were recently painted. An occasional blue trashcan hangs on a post along the sidewalk. He can tell most shops are closed or closing as he drives along.

The pleasantness of the scenery causes Max to forget about his problem for a moment. *I like to see new places like this. Such a lovely quiet street, but I'd still rather be going on a cruise. I've sailed to the Bahamas several times with my own boat and so far, I've been to Jamaica and now Italy. I still have not been on a nice relaxing cruise ship.* His daydream snaps as Sam taps his shoulder.

"There it is, Banc Bella! Cripes, the Bellasettas even own a Bank!"

"Well, duh...Bella, Bellasetta makes sense. I see the guards are out front waiting for us just like Gustavo said." Max slows down as he approaches the bank. He sees the light blue building ahead. The large gold letters BANC BELLA seem to emerge from the building as if they oozed out of the front wall. The angled parking places directly in front of the bank are all empty. Two guards in khaki uniforms are standing on the sidewalk in front of the bank holding black machine guns. Max feels sweat form on his brow as he approaches the bank.

Gunshots break out and Max ducks down again but nothing hits the Mercedes. He peeks at his rear view mirror and sees a gun battle going on between a dark van and the black Citroen. He pulls into a parking slot at the bank and kills the engine.

Max sees one of the guards knock on his door and then opens the passenger door.

"Come inside the bank please." The guard speaks

perfect English as he helps everyone out of the car.

Max notices the gunshots from the Citroen have ceased. He gives a quick look back toward the Citroen and sees men standing around it. A nervous smile forms on his face aimed at the two escorts holding machine guns. Max shakes his head and whispers, "Welcome to Gioia Tauro!"

Chapter Twenty-Six

Franco, in his combat uniform, on orders from Gustavo pulls his black van behind the Citroen. He steps out behind his door and points a megaphone at the parked Citroen.

"Get out of the car!" Franco shouts in Italian.

Instead of obeying, Carl opens his door and fires at Franco. The bullet just misses Franco lodging in the megaphone. Men spring out of the Citroen and the van with guns firing.

Carl and Albert use the car doors for cover. Bullets hit Don in the side and shoulder. He drops his gun and sprints away from the Citroen behind Angelino. Don copies Angelino's zigzag pattern to avoid any more hits. They dash behind a faded gray building next to the Citroen and out of gunshot range.

Franco sees the two men running away are bloody. He lets them go concentrating on the remaining two men shooting at him and his crew. Seconds later the gunfight is over. Franco's men win the battle.

"Okay men! Check them out!" Franco shouts. He enjoys the smell of the spent gunpowder that is slowly dissipating.

"This one's dead. This one is too." One of Franco's men says.

"Too bad. We cannot ask them who was with them! I report to the boss now. Luis, take Jose and search the area. Find the others." Franco dials Gustavo. He relates what happened.

"You were to detain them not kill them!"

"We had no choice sir. They fired at us first."

"Have you found the others?"

"No, they have eluded us but I saw blood from each man. I am sure we hit them. They will need medical attention. We will find them."

"Were any of your men hit?"

"Just two flesh wounds, nothing serious."

"Good. I am disappointed with what happened, but you did good Franco. Our new friends are much safer now."

Don Cresto feels the searing pain in his side and his shoulder as he runs for his life away from the gunfire. He keeps pace with his friend Angelino running behind him and seeing his friend gripping his bloody left arm. He follows Angelino around a brick building into an overgrown forest area. Don feels thorny spikes jab into his ankles as he runs. The sound from guns firing no longer pierces his eardrums. With the silence of the guns, he can hear mashing of weeds with each pounding foot and his heart pounding as he races along. He stumbles and collapses in the underbrush wreathing with pain.

"Get up Donny! We cannot stop here!" Angelino backs up to Don and helps him to his feet with his good arm. He grabs his left arm again putting pressure on his wound as he pushes Don to continue.

"What are we going to do? Where can we go?" Don is exhausted and sick with fear.

"We make it to my house. Camilla will fix us. Come on Donny it's just a few kilometers from here."

"What about Carl and Albert? I do not see them behind us."

"There is nothing we can do Donny."

"We should wait here in the forest. I am weak. Maybe we will see Carl. I am afraid the police will be searching now."

"Perhaps you are right. Let me clear a spot so we can rest. We are both losing blood. Perhaps now we bind our wounds."

Angelino and Don flatten some of the underbrush with their shoes before squatting down. Angelino tears a sleeve off his shirt and wraps it around his arm. Don takes off his shirt to wrap around his middle just below the rib cage. The two men clear enough brush to lie down until the darkness of night engulfs them.

"I've never been shot before!" Don says.

"I am sure it looks worse than it is Don."

"The car, they will trace the car to you."

"No, Albert borrowed it."

"He stole the car?"

"Yes Don, both cars. Now stay calm. Camilla will fix our wounds."

"I know and then what? Max will be with the Bellasettas now. I fear Albert and Carl are dead or prisoners."

"I am sorry for my friends too. We did the best we could. Your plan should have worked but for the policia. Bad timing Don."

Don is abuzz with thoughts about what to do next. He keeps some pressure on his side and shoulder wounds and lies in the weeds with Angelino until dark. He is weak but travels on foot to Angelino's home. As he nears the front door, he sees three small children scatter away from the small house.

Camilla screams seeing Angelino and Don staggering through the front door. She rushes to Angelino terrified seeing all the blood on his arm. Then she looks at Don, his shirt covered in blood and she has to grab on to Angelino for support.

"What has happened Angie? You were only to help Don."

"We met some policia. Carl tried to shoot them and then gunfight started. Donny and I managed to get away. I think Albert and Carl may be dead!"

"Oh no! Why did he shoot? You don't shoot!"

"I don't know about Carl, I think he was high on something, maybe those pills Don gave him. He just acted nuts."

"Now he is possibly dead and Al too." Camilla says.

"I saw Carl hit by a bullet to his head. I am sure he is dead. I must have revenge." Don says and collapses into a chair.

"Oh Don, your shirt is soaked in blood. I must bandage Angie's wound, then I will help you. Please rest now." Camilla goes to work cleaning up Angelino's wound. She sees the bullet went through his muscle just missing his arm bones. She dabs the gashes with alcohol and puts on Band-Aids.

Don winces lifting his arms as Camilla removes his bloody shirt from around his waist. He grunts in pain feeling the sting of the alcohol as she wipes his side. He sees tears form in her eyes.

"This looks like the bullet went through your side Don. Lucky it was not a few inches over. You would be dead now." Camilla says. She tapes a large makeshift bandage on his side. She examines the shoulder wound next and sees only an entry point.

"The bullet must be in your shoulder. You will need to go to hospital."

"No hospital! You must do it Cam." Angelino says.

"No il mio amore!"

"Yes!" Angelino insists.

Camilla drapes a cloth across Don's chest as he downs another gulp of Puni Nova whiskey. She places a folded washcloth in Don's mouth before pouring some alcohol on his wound. Grabbing a pair of thin-nosed pliers she boiled sterile, she jabs into the bullet hole moving the tines around until she feels the bullet. She blocks out the muffled screams from Don as she squeezes onto it and pulls the bullet out. Blood immediately gushes out of the wound as Don screams in pain. Camilla presses clean gauze onto the hole and tapes it in place. Wiping sweat from her brow, she sits down and bows her head.

"I must have revenge!" Don says slurring his speech as he begins to recover from the pain.

"Who are you going to fight?" Angelino asks.

"It is Max who caused all this trouble, Max and Sam too. They have the money that we should have. Now Arturo is dead and two of my dear friends are most likely also dead."

"You need rest Donny, rest now. We will talk later."

"I must think of a plan. All my life I never do anything illegal. I had many chances considering my brother and my father but I never did." Don is bitter.

"I know. Arturo has complained to me before. I was surprised to hear you would come here for this." Angelino says.

"So what have I to show for being the good guy? Nothing! I want to avenge their deaths. I will get that money for us Angie, but most importantly I want to see Max and Sam die!"

Chapter Twenty-Seven

The massive pillars alongside the huge front doors of Banc Bella exude strength and confidence. The building image is of trust and safety. A spray of colors from trays of flowers along the walkway, enhance the view of the area. Guards with ready machine guns offset the peacefulness of the scene.

Max stands outside the Mercedes for a moment catching his breath from all the excitement as he examines the building. He begins to follow the guards, but notices the smell of gasoline. Looking back at the rear of the Mercedes, he sees gas leaking onto the asphalt.

"Wow! They punctured the gas tank! Much further and we would be out of gas or on fire! We'd be dead either way!" Max says stopping to look. He exhales with a loud whistle.

Max gets a nudge from Sam and walks toward the front door. He grins as he walks with the others through the doors of the bank. *At least the guards aren't pointing the guns at us!* He sees a young woman at the reception desk and walks up to her. Before Max can ask her anything, Gustavo appears from one of the private offices. Max again notices the tall man in a trim gray suit and tie, jet black hair swept straight back, a slightly dark complexion and dark blue eyes. To Max the man looks like a middle-aged Italian movie star.

"Hello Max and everyone. I am Gustavo Bellasetta. I welcome you to Gioia Tauro, Italy and our Banc Bella." He says shaking hands with everyone.

Max once again notes the well-manicured fingers and smooth palm. He sees the gentle dark blue eyes stare at him. Then Gustavo pats Max on the shoulder.

"Max I need to see you in private. Peggy, Ann and Sam, Miss Fiora will make you comfortable please, we will only be a moment." Gustavo ushers Max into a private office.

"What is this about?" Max asks as the door closes.

"First I am curious. Tell me how you came to be in the Mercedes. The car with the people you were afraid would hurt you."

Max describes in detail what happened including his confusion of how Don Cresto was on the same flight with him.

"I am impressed with what you have done." Gustavo nods.

"Okay, why did you want me to tell you this in private?"

"Oh, the privacy is for me Max. First I am taking care of the problem with the men who chased you."

"What happened? I heard gunshots. Was anyone hurt?"

"Yes. My men were only to detain them so they would not bother you anymore. Perhaps something went wrong. However, I know my men prevailed."

"You said two things. What else?"

"This is the crazy thing Max." Gustavo quits talking and raises his hands, obviously having difficulty finding words to say. He silently claps his hands together raising them to his face as if to pray.

"This whole trip has been crazy, Gustavo. No offense, but I will be glad when we are all back home."

"Yes Max. I know this is a strain on you and the others and I hope this doesn't strain you even more. To be perfectly frank, well the thing is I wired an additional four million dollars to your account."

"Holy cow, you did what? What's the catch?"

"No catch, an explanation is in order, I know."

"Yes please tell me. You just give away four million dollars?"

"Mario and I feel like all of you are decent people and will do some awesome good things with the money. I want you to be the one who tells the rest. Well, you do not have to tell them at all. I want you to do what you want with it." Gustavo continues before Max can talk.

"Papa had a stroke and Miggy took over running everything back then. You see we know that our brother Miguel dealt in drugs and stolen goods. There was no need for him to do this as Papa's businesses were doing great. Miggy just liked being as you may say dirty. Mario and I even suspect Miggy had Mister Tony Albero's father killed because he refused to cooperate with the drug dealing. Salvatore was a blood friend of Tony. Tony must have asked for help and maybe things went wrong. We know that the five million Miggy paid for the diamond was with profits from his drug deals, not honest money."

"So Miguel was like a bad apple?"

"Yes, the worst, and Papa never knew this. We want to put the diamond on display in the Bella Museum. Do you understand now?"

"No. It is hard to understand what your brother did."

Robert W. Davis

"Mario and I came back to Italy immediately when we heard Miggy was murdered. We took over all the family businesses. We had to squelch the drug business and the stolen goods business Miggy was running. It was not an easy task. Some men went to prison before we were clean again. Papa was content to do painting. He has over a hundred paintings now. We never told Papa about Miggy's drug dealing and fencing of stolen goods. It would have killed him. The newspapers portrayed Miguel as a wonderful son who was to gift Papa that diamond, but murderers stole it. They coined a phrase the Deadly Diamond. I would have been happy if it remained missing forever. Nonetheless, if the public now finds out the truth of our brother it would be bad publicity for our businesses."

"Okay, I know you want to get this off your chest and you are telling me about your brother Miguel. I am not complaining, but why give me four million dollars more? You have the diamond and rightly so. I know the diamond is worth much more maybe ten mil but we are happy with what we got."

"Actually Max, because of its rarity the diamond is priceless. That is why we donate it to a museum so others may see its beauty. Mario and I do not want to acquire the diamond because it was bought with illegal money. It would always be the 'Deadly Diamond' instead of the 'Bellasetta Rose Diamond' in our minds. We are happier to pay the full amount Miggy paid only now with honest money, otherwise this will always hang over us. Do you see now?"

Max is about to answer when a uniformed man knocks and enters to room. He whispers a few words into Gustavo's ear. Gustavo nods and the man leaves.

"Of the two men who are dead, neither man is Don Cresto. He and one other man escaped on foot. They have wounds and will need medical attention. Now, before we go back, you will not talk about Miguel to anyone. You can tell your friends what I said after you return home."

"Yes Gustavo. I will keep your secret." Max follows Gustavo back into the main reception area in a daze. *Four more million, good grief!* Max thinks to himself.

Chapter Twenty-Eight

"Two of the men chasing you got away. I am glad you are safe. You must stay as our guests in our home." Gustavo tells the others.

"We are here a day early. Will that be a burden on you?"

"Not at all Max. We have a new wing added to our house a few years ago with four bedrooms and four bathrooms. You can double up or all sleep separately."

"We have no luggage. It is all in the wrecked Focus."

"Tell Henri where the Focus is and he will get your things."

Max has hardly noticed Henri again in dark clothes always standing in the shadow of Gustavo. Max examines Henri noting his mulatto arms are as big around as Max's legs and the man has no visible fat. Henri has dark brown eyes and looks to be in his late twenties. To Max he looks strong enough to bench press a horse. Max explains as best he can where he crashed the Focus. He watches Henri bow and turn to talk to one of the guards.

"Well we certainly appreciate this."

"Henri! Bring the Qubo here!" Gustavo says. His shadow nods and immediately walks away.

"Our bank just repossessed this car. It is ugly lime green but is only a few months old. We will need it to transport you to the house. You cannot all fit in my car."

"We will have to cancel our hotel reservations Gustavo."

"Yes, our accommodations will be safer. The diamond brought life back to Papa but alas, it brought sad memories of Junior too. I think that is what caused Papa to pass. I had no idea this would affect him in such a way."

Gustavo's phone rings as Max is about to speak. Gustavo answers and begins speaking in Italian. A minute later, he smiles and nods his head at Max as he ends his call.

"Henri is bringing the Qubo around front. He sent a man to find your car. The man will load your luggage in the Qubo when he returns. We wait for that and then we go. You say the Ford is only a few kilometers from here?"

"Yes, near the Goioa Tauro exit as I explained. Again we appreciate all you are doing."

"I think everything will work out fine." Gustavo smiles at Max.

"You say you studied at Emory University?" Max asks.

"Actually Mario and I both went there. Our cousin Antonio lives in Atlanta, Georgia. He has connections with the University. I went there first and a year later Mario came to America."

"What did you major in?"

"We both studied business and business law. Now tell me about yourself, Max. What do you do? Did you attend college?"

"Well, I did go to University of Florida in Gainesville for a year. Then I went to a trade school, but my real love is in sales."

Deadly Diamond: A Diamond to Die For!

Max tells his story and listens as one by one Gustavo hears what his friends do, and how they all met. He can tell Gustavo is genuinely interested in everyone. He sees Miss Fiora bring out a round of cookies and ice-cold water bottles. Max suddenly realizes his mouth is dry. He grabs a bottle of water, snaps the cap and takes a long delicious drink.

A half hour passes before Gustavo receives another phone call. "Bene!" He says a moment later before ending the call.

"My man has found your crippled Ford and has your luggage. He will place it in the back of the ugly Qubo now. I will walk with you to the car out front."

Max stops. "Excuse me, why do you call it an ugly Qubo?" Gustavo laughs a little before speaking.

"It is a small car made by Fiat. You will see it is just big enough to fit four. I hate the lime green color so I call it the ugly Qubo. Even if you hate the color, please do not wreck it. We will have to auction it off later. Henri and I will come around in a dark blue Ferrari. You will follow us to the estate. No more worries Max. Our home is the safest place in Italy." He pats Max on the back as he walks him to the door.

Max cautiously steps outside with his friends through the huge glass doors. He sees the iridescent green Qubo shining like a beacon in the early evening street light. One guard is in front and one is behind Max as he walks to the car with his friends. After a final wave to Gustavo Max slides into the driver's seat and the others climb in the car. They turn to wave goodbye again but Gustavo is already out of sight.

"The bank must have a rear door. He said he will be

in a Ferrari and we follow him. Here comes Gustavo now."

Max floors the Qubo to catch up to Gustavo as the pristine blue Ferrari pulls onto the road in front of the bank. He follows the tail of the Ferrari turning north winding along several streets and into an elevated area of the city. After driving for about two minutes, Gustavo turns onto a side street and up a long winding road.

Max continues to follow watching the early evening streetlights coming on and the late sunlight casting long sprays of amber across the road and onto the trees and buildings along the way. He follows Gustavo onto a newly paved road with almost no bumps or potholes. Gustavo turns onto another winding and narrow tree-lined road. Max feels this is the entrance to the Bellasetta Estate and he is right. As he rounds a long curve, he sees massive black iron gates ahead. As he approaches the twin gates, he sees a large gold 'B' split across the wrought iron. Gustavo drives closer and the gates open to let the Ferrari and the Qubo drive through and into a perfectly manicured yard leading to the house. Max looks around enjoying all the hedges, potted flowers, and the elegance of his surroundings.

Large stone stanchions are all around the front of the house. A guard with a machine-gun in a Khaki uniform stands at ease next to each of the two stanchions by the front door. The entire exterior of the two-story house looks like river rock; inter-mixed rust colored flat stones. Tan colored columns support the wide overhang in front. The guards apparently are aware of them coming, and do not seem alarmed to see a strange car behind the Ferrari. He sees Gustavo park in the circular drive under the overhang. Max stops just behind the Ferrari. One of the guards moves to the large front door of the house as Gustavo and Henri get out of the Ferrari. Max sees Henri get back in the driver's side of the Ferrari and drive it out of sight behind the house. He looks back to see the large iron gates clank shut. A six-foot high stone and rock wall surrounds the estate from each side of the gates. Atop the wall, he sees what looks like razor coils just like what is atop US prison fences.

Gustavo comes to the Qubo and motions everyone out. "Come with me my friends. Let us go inside."

Chapter Twenty-Nine

Max steps out of the Qubo first and looks around at the oversized two-story house. All the windows are equipped with black bars. He stands next to Gustavo and waits until everyone is out of the car.

"This is a magnificent home! Beautiful gate too!"

"Thank you. We had the gate motorized many years ago just before the robbery. You leave the car here. Erik will park it in the garage near the back."

"We have all our stuff in the back."

"Yes. Erik will bring your luggage in for you."

"Okay I left the key in the car. Is that alright?"

"Yes Max. No worries, Erik will handle everything."

Max and his friends follow Gustavo up the walkway toward the giant front door. Max mentally guesses the wooden door to be eight feet tall as he walks to the front of the house. The door is various shades of diagonal wood planks ranging from dark brown to light tan. The colors are mostly in a pattern. A small window with decorative trim is at eye level in the middle of the door.

A guard opens the massive door and Gustavo motions them inside. Max sees a young dark haired woman standing inside the doorway wearing an obviously expensive black dress open in a V-shape from her shoulders to her waistline. Her black hair flows across her pearl-white shoulders. For a second Max stares into her dark purple eyes until he notices she is holding a black cat in her arms.

The cat seems to stare into Max's skull making him

feel uneasy at first. He sees the cat stretch its front paws out almost inviting Max to shake hands with the creature. He watches the cat stare at each of his friends and then stare back at him. Max hears the soothing purr of the cat, and he looks for a flaw in the solid black fur. There is none. Then Gustavo interrupts his train of thought.

"Everyone, this is Hera, Mario's wife. Hera, these people are here about the diamond. This is Max, Sam, Peggy, and Ann. They will be staying for a few days."

"I am so glad to see you." Hera extends a hand to Max. "I see Zeus likes you. He tends to stare at people he likes."

"My pleasure," Max says feeling her warm smooth hand grip his for longer than he expects. He sees her cat look into his eyes again and purr loud enough to hear. A strange feeling comes over Max as if the cat is telling him, *I am the reason you came here!* Hera slips her hand away to greet the others. Max stares at Hera and then slightly dazed at the cat.

Two more women enter the room breaking Max's trance. The older woman is wearing a gray dress with a white apron over it and a white cap atop her black hair. Behind her, an even younger woman stands in similar dress. Another older man dressed in black joins the women. Max can smell the faint aroma of meat cooking. Suddenly he feels hungry. Other than a couple of chocolate chip cookies, he has not eaten since the McDonalds many hours ago.

"Carla and Sophie, these are our guests, Max, Sam, Peggy and Ann. We will have four guests for dinner. Can you manage?"

"Grazie." Carla nods and smiles at Max before she scurries off with Sophie through a door on the left side of the entrance area.

"Carla understands English but will not speak it. Lastly, this is Sergio our head of staff. He is the most valuable man to us."

Max watches with curiosity as Sergio just bows his head and backs away as if embarrassed by Gustavo's comment. *Something is wrong.* Max thinks.

"He has been with us since before I was born." Gustavo makes sure everyone greets each other before moving on.

Max looks around. He walks passed the foyer into a large open area with a huge glass and gold chandelier hanging from the open two-story ceiling. On the left side near the back of the room, he sees a spiral stairway all made of blue tinted marble posts and steps. Even the floor is the same shade of marble as the stairs. There are large tan couches on each side of the room with dark wood armrests and dark Mahogany coffee tables and end tables with the same blue tinted marble on top.

On the far side of the room opposite the front door, he sees a large bay window that goes halfway up the rear wall to meet what looks like a walkway above it. Behind the bay window, he sees a massive garden with lights illuminating a multitude of colored flowers and shrubs. The walls are a light tan and all the furniture dark brown, tan, gold, or blue tinted marble. On the right side, he sees what looks like dark wood elevator doors. Gustavo sees him looking curiously at the doors.

"It is an elevator, Max. We had it put in for Papa.

His bedroom is on the second floor. He could no longer climb stairs. Miggy had that installed over thirty years ago. I do not like the way it looks. It takes away the beauty of the home."

"I think it looks very elegant with those beautiful doors." Max looks around for Hera but she has vanished.

"Thank you, Max. Without those wooden doors it would be intolerable." He pauses for a moment. Then he gestures toward the elevator.

"First let us go to the guest rooms." Gustavo moves to the elevator and reaches for the singular elevator button. The faint blue light of the button turns bright blue when Gustavo presses it.

"We use the elevator now."

The massive doors open to reveal the giant elevator large enough to accommodate all of them plus Gustavo without squeezing together. He presses the number 2. The massive doors close and the elevator starts its journey to the second story area. Max sees a button marked three.

"What is the 3 for?"

"It is for the roof." Gustavo says.

"The elevator goes to the roof?"

"Yes it does. We have a small observatory up there originally for Miggy. Now Mario likes to telescope the stars on clear nights. Hera goes there often as well. We are only 20 meters above sea level here but the views are spectacular on clear nights because there are so few lights at night in the area. The sky is black except for the stars. You may go up there later if you like."

The elevator stops and the massive doors open

showing Max a walkway. He moves a few paces and sees a panoramic view of the receiving room below. The walkway has a baluster made of the same blue tinted marble. The rail goes around the second story to meet the spiral stairs on the other side of the open area. Max stands still impressed by what he sees until Gustavo prompts him to move on.

"Come this way. We added this wing and the gym downstairs several years ago." Gustavo walks to an adjoining hallway.

"We use this area to accommodate guests like you. There are two bedrooms on each side of this hallway. You may each have one or you may double up as you like." He opens the door of the first room on the right.

"After you have all settled in, come downstairs and join us." Gustavo waves a hand at them as he turns and walks out of sight.

Max stands outside the first bedroom with his friends in silence. He hears the elevator open and Erik brings their luggage to them on a small cart.

"You must be Erik. Thank you." Max says grabbing a bag. The man nods and backs away with his cart. He and Sam take the bags and walk into the first bedroom.

"Check this place out!" Max says. He switches on a light and steps into the bedroom.

Chapter Thirty

A small gold and glass chandelier hangs from the center of the bedroom. There is a king sized bed, a dresser, and a large flat screen TV on the wall. There are dark oak night tables on each side of the bed. The floor is all marble very similar to the blue tint of the floor downstairs. The wallpaper has an intricate pattern of gold shields on a light tan background. Max sees another dark wood door on the left side. After staring at the room for a moment, he walks there and opens the door.

The others follow Max into an oversized bathroom. A huge shower stall and towel rack occupy one side of the room. A toilet and a bidet, a double sink and counter flow across the middle. There is another door next to the sink counter. Max opens the door to an adjoining room.

"Look a Jacuzzi for four!" Max says as he leans over the edge next to a set of towels. Then he hears Sam announce.

"There's a steam room on the other side and another full rack of towels."

"Let's see where that other door goes Sam." Max says opening the door across the room. He sees a mirror image of the first bathroom with another door across from there. He steps across the second bathroom and opens the door to a mirror image of the first bedroom.

"Wow! Separate bathrooms and bedrooms and a big Jacuzzi and a steam room in the middle." Max is impressed.

"If we all stay on this side of the hallway, we sort of have connecting rooms..." Sam says.

"Let's do that!" Ann's voice is slightly shaky.

"I vote for that one." Max points back toward the first bedroom.

"Peggy and I will stay there. Let's all stay on the same side."

"That's fine with me. Ann and I will take the one back here. I think Ann likes that idea."

"Yes we need to stay close to each other tonight." Ann feels worried as Sam gives her a gentle hug.

Max says, "Let's go downstairs in five minutes."

"I hope he has some food for us. I'm hungry! When I'm tense like this I need more food!" Sam's gut is grumbling and slightly knotted.

Ann and Sam move their bags into the adjoining bedroom. After they set out some stuff in the bathroom, Sam teases with her.

"Do you like the right side of the bed?"

"It doesn't matter."

"No, you should try each side; see if you like it."

"You're crazy Sam! Well maybe you should be closest to the bedroom door to protect me." Ann shows a hint of a smile.

"Let's lay down to see if we like the bed."

"Not now, I'm too scared!"

"Well I'm not totally relaxed either. I think maybe we should just cuddle for a while until we go down stairs."

"Just cuddle?" Ann sits on the bed and Sam snuggles up to her.

"Yes." He brushes her hair away and gives her a tender kiss on her neck. He feels her tilt her head back. He embraces her, but a knock on the door followed by

Max's voice interrupts him.

"Is it safe to come in?"

"It's safe." Sam frowns, waiting for Max and Peggy to come in.

"Let's see what Gustavo has to offer. I think he's going to feed us some good old American food!" Max rubs his hands together.

"Some good Italian food I think!" Sam says.

"You must be kidding!"

"Well, I think they'll feed us Italian style."

"I think they'll feed us American food. They are billionaires and they know we are Americans. They can do anything."

Sam recalls the whiff of meat cooking when he first entered the house. *Surely, they will have lasagna or spaghetti to go with it.*

"No, I think we'll get Italian food."

"Bet you a dollar." Max lifts his head up high.

"You're on!"

They walk out of the bedroom and down the hall.

"Let's use the stairs," Sam says.

Max looks indignantly at Sam. "Duh... We came up in the elevator we should go down in it!"

"Amen," Peggy reaches the elevator and pushes the down button. The elevator opens immediately. They smell a hint of tomato sauce as they enter the elevator. The doors close. The elevator whirs, clanks, and stops on the ground floor.

Gustavo is watching the news on a giant projection TV screen when the elevator doors open. He turns off the TV and the screen rises into a cover as he gets up. He looks at Max coming out of the elevator and smiles.

"So you are here. The rooms are adequate?"

"Very nice! Our hotel would not be so nice." Max gives the thumbs up gesture to Gustavo.

"Thank you. You must come dine. I'm sure you are hungry."

"That's a big ten-four!"

"That means yes."

"Definitely!"

Max and his friends follow Gustavo through a partially hidden side hallway. Max did not see the hallway when he first came into the house. He walks into an oversized dining room. A huge glass and gold chandelier lights the room. It hangs over an enormous Teak and marble table. He notices the chandelier has zero dust on it as if someone has just cleaned every glass droplet and polished all the gold. The dining table has wooden bear legs with claws for support. There are twelve high-backed chairs surrounding the table, two on each end and four on each side. Plates, silverware, and napkins in gold rings are set at seven places. The table and chairs all rest on blue tinted marble flooring. The side table is also of Teak wood with the same style legs. Each of seven settings has a tall empty wine glass.

Gustavo Mario and Hera sit on one side. Gustavo motions Max and the others to sit on the other side of the table.

"Wow! This is marvelous." Max says admiring the room. He sees Sam nod in agreement. Sergio dressed in white offers red wine to Max. Max swirls, sniffs, and tastes the rose' wine and asks for more. Sergio fills the wine glasses.

"Thank you Sergio," Gustavo says and sees Sergio make a small bow as he backs out of the room.

"You say Sergio has been with you over thirty years."

"Yes Max, nearly forty."

"That is dedication Gustavo."

"Yes, he does an outstanding job." Gustavo says but he sees Max staring at Hera. "Hera is a unique person, Max. She sees things the ordinary person does not see."

"Pardon me for staring. I'm just tired from the travel. Where is Zeus?"

"Zeus chooses not to dine with us. He will be with us in the meeting room later tonight." Hera interjects.

"If you are interested, after dinner Hera is doing a séance. You are welcome to attend. I am sure it will be interesting. Hera believes she can communicate with our brother Miguel now. We want to tell him we have once again possession of his prized rose diamond."

"Wow! That would be great!" Peggy shouts.

"Peggy! I'm sure they want a private session." Max says, but like when he first saw Hera, a compelling strange feeling rushes over him.

"Not true, Max. We welcome our friends to our séance. Only Sergio is against these. He fears talking to the dead." Gustavo sees Sergio coming back in the room.

"Pardon my words sir, but nothing good can come from these séances. You know how Miguel junior was." Sergio says entering with an open bottle of red wine. He refills Gustavo's glass.

"Hera is psychic. She believes Miggy is still in this house waiting to hear from us. She has tried now many times to reach him. This is special though. We want to tell him about the diamond. We will see what happens."

Max recalls from talking with Gustavo that the staff members were all at the annual celebration away from the estate on that fatal night thirty years ago. He wonders who discovered the bodies. *Did Sergio and the other staff members come back first? I wonder was Sergio the first to discover Miguel Junior?*

"Max, please, we must go!" Peggy whines.

"Yes, I know... We must attend." Max says without knowing why.

Chapter Thirty-One

Max has questions he could ask Sergio, but he knows that will never happen. He sits looking at the brothers seeing their dark blue eyes and jet-black hair except for some gray streaks on Gustavo. As he is taking in all the elegance around him from the furniture to the paintings on the walls, some of which he figures are worth small fortunes, Sergio sets a large bowl of spaghetti on the table in front of them and bows.

Sam nods at Max implying *you owe me a dollar.*

"I hope you like spaghetti." Gustavo says.

"Now we bow our heads."

They bow their heads as Mario Bellasetta prays in Italian. Max silently prays too. *I hope we all get back to America alive and well… and with all that money! Amen.*

After the prayers, Carla starts the dinner.

Ann plays with her meal barely eating. *They're being too nice. Something is wrong. Why are they so nice to us?* She watches Max and Peggy finish their spaghetti and call for a small second helping. While they are eating, Sergio continues to refill the red wine as needed for everyone. *Sergio is so nice to us. It's as if he is apologizing to us for something. Why?* As she finishes her meal, Max breaks her thoughts.

"What work do you do Mario?"

"We are experimenting with a solar project to power one of our warehouses in Port of Gioia Tauro. If it works well here and I am sure it will, we will convert to solar power in all our warehouses."

"It's good for conserving resources. I think the whole world should convert to solar power Max. Think of how much pollution and carbon we would keep from the air. That's why we are so focused on this experiment." Gustavo adds finishing his spaghetti.

"Have either of you been married?"

"I am divorced. Gustavo has a boy and girl. I have three sons."

"I see no children here. Where are they now?"

"The children are in boarding schools until they are older. Then as they are of age, we will bring them here. They are all well behaved, unlike some American children I have seen." Mario continues talking for a while about how much energy the solar panels on the warehouse produce. He explains where the panels come from, how they gradually got off the main electric power, and what precautions they put in place for the installers. Max can tell Mario is deeply committed to solar power. Max finally speaks.

"With all your wealth, I thought you would be spending your time on cruises or basking in the sun on an exotic island."

"Papa raised us to be workaholics. We will always be that way. Our brother Miggy would be too if he were alive."

"I know your brother has passed..." Max is interrupted by Gustavo.

"No, he was murdered! My brother - the thieves murdered him when they came to steal. It was a horrible thing! I would rather not talk about it."

"Please forgive me for mentioning that."

"It is getting close to ten. I will be at the séance,

with Hera and Mario. If you will excuse me, I have to do some planning before then. We will take care of the broken Ford. The Mercedes and the Citroen are stolen vehicles. Mario will take care of it all. In the morning we will discuss what you want to do." He bows before leaving. Mario waits until Gustavo is gone before speaking.

"Gustavo was closer to Miguel than I was." Mario offers waving a hand. "My brother still hurts inside. We were away in America. It was a shock to hear of Miggy's murder. He was deeply hurt. Sergio was the first to come home from the celebration. You can imagine how horrible it was for him to see the guard and Miggy."

"It must have been devastating. Your brother was..."

"Perhaps we talk about it some other time. Oh... Well it is nearly ten o'clock. You will join Hera and us?

"Yes, thank you for your hospitality. You are a most gracious host. If you do not mind I know Peggy wants to go to the séance." Max rises from his chair.

"Very good Max. We will see if we can communicate with Miggy." Mario smiles and nods toward Max.

"Ann and I are sleepier than we should be. Would you mind if we retired for the night?" Sam asks.

"Of course not, Sam. I understand you have all had a long and troublesome journey. Flying across the ocean is very tiring, and then the car incidents. A good night's rest will do wonders for all of you." Mario says standing up.

Max follows Mario and Hera into a small dark

room. There are lighted candles around the room. He sees Hera sit down at the round table; Zeus appears and joins her in her lap. Sergio is sitting on the other end of the table. With her hands face down next to a large candle in front of her, she looks at Mario.

"Hera you may start as soon as we are all seated." Mario says as he sits down at the table.

After everyone sits down, the room goes silent. All Max hears is the purring from Zeus perched on Hera's lap. Hera speaks with a low and eerie monotone chant.

"Miguel G Bellasetta Junior... I call to you. I have a message for you. Miguel G Bellasetta Junior... Talk to me. I have a message for you Miggy. Speak to me! Miggy speak to me!" Hera continues chanting in monotone.

Max listens barely recognizing what she is saying. He daydreams as Hera chants. He feels sad thinking what it would be like to lose a brother. *I consider Sam my adopted brother. In a way, Sam is my brother. If something happened to Sam, I would surely be very sad.* He feels tired and knows Peggy is too. He sees her usual sparkly blue eyes have dark circles under them even though he sees excitement in her face as she stares at Hera. Then Max feels a chill as if an icy wind blew on him. Max starts to speak in a strange voice.

Chapter Thirty-Two

"Oh the pain, the pain! Why?" Max cannot believe what he is saying. He feels he has no control over his voice. His arms feel limp.

"Miggy, is that you?" Hera asks.

"Why? Why?" Max calls.

"Miggy, we want to tell you we have found your diamond. I know you had pain. This should bring you happiness. You are saying why Miggy. Why do you say that?"

"Why?" Max speaks again in the strange voice. His body is rigid as if he were in a trance.

"What is wrong Miggy?"

"My killer is here! Why did you do it?" The voice shouts.

"No, the robbers are not here."

"The truth must come out!"

Sergio rises from his chair as all eyes turn toward him. Henri gently grabs Sergio's shoulder and forces him back down.

"What is wrong Sergio?" Hera asks.

"I was in pain. Great pain!" Max shouts.

"Enough! You torture me even from your grave! I hate you!" Sergio bows his head weeping.

"What are you saying Sergio?" Gustavo asks.

"I did it!"

"At last I have closure! Goodbye my brothers!" Max utters.

"The séance is over!" Gustavo stands and flips on the lights.

"How can this be? You all came back together with

Papa. This has to be wrong." Mario says.

"No, I come back early to prepare for everyone arriving. This guilt has plagued me for thirty years!"

"What did you do Sergio?"

"When I returned, I noticed the gate was open. The alarm was off and the front door unlocked. Inside I saw the dead guard lying in a pool of blood on the floor and a bloody crowbar near him. I grabbed the crowbar and searched around for an intruder in the house. When I go to Miggy's bedroom, he is not dead as I told everyone."

"Miggy was alive?" Gustavo whispers.

"He was alive but covered with blood and badly beaten. I was so shocked I dropped the crowbar. He heard that and opened his eyes. He accused me of working with Tony. How else could Tony get in there to hurt him? You must know he always treats me like dirt! I blacked out and awoke with a pillow over Miggy's face."

"You killed Miggy!" Gustavo shouts and rises to jump at Sergio, but Mario holds him.

"I didn't want to kill him believe me! I just went crazy for a minute. I came to and realized what I had done. I checked Miggy for a pulse. There was none. I wiped my fingerprints off the crowbar and put it back where I found it. Then I called Papa and sat on the floor weeping until Papa and the others arrived. Gustavo, I try for thirty years to make up for what I did."

"You live in our house after killing our brother!"

"I wanted to leave. I stay for your Papa. You and Mario were in America. He was alone. He begged me to stay. He needed solace. What could I do? If I told him what I did, his weakened heart may have failed. Then I would feel even worse."

"Your murder went undiscovered for thirty years!"

"What will you do now?" Sergio is in tears.

"I don't know."

"Gustavo, listen to me. The way you and Mario manage your Papa's business is admirable. Under Miggy, I saw corruption and illegal operations. You know he had thugs and criminals working for him. He treated everyone like dirt including me. I suspect he had his enemies killed. You know Papa's business is much better off without him. He might have had you killed if you tried to interfere."

"Just go away now. I have to think."

"Please consider how things might have been if he lived. Miggy was severely beaten. He might have died anyhow."

"Go!" Gustavo waves his hands and Sergio leaves the room. He sits staring blankly at a wall.

"I think we should go to our room now." Max says. He gets up and helps Peggy from her chair.

"Perhaps we should all retire for the evening. This has been most disturbing." Mario says also getting up from the table.

"We are sorry about what has happened here. I have no idea of what you must be going through now." Max says. He sees Mario nod as he and Peggy exit the room and go to the elevator.

Max enters the elevator with Peggy and waits until the doors close before speaking.

"Wow! Do you know what just happened?" Max whispers.

"A foolish prank disrupted the whole family!"

"No Peggy. I was compelled to speak in there. It's like I felt his presence through me because I brought back his diamond."

"Really?"

"No, I was kidding." Max smiles, not sure what he did.

"Well, you sure upset the family." Peggy shakes her head.

"I exposed a real murderer."

"Let's check on Sam and Ann." Peggy changes the subject as she follows Max out the open elevator doors.

Sam and Ann leave the dining room feeling full and content. They hold hands as they enter the main living room. Ann tries to walk to the elevator but Sam pulls her away.

"Let's go this way." Sam leads her to the stairs.

"Look at all this marble Sam! I think it would be slippery if it's wet."

"But it's not wet."

"It's beautiful but I like a non-slip surface if I had stairs like this to climb." She says catching up to Sam on the stairs.

"Really?"

Sam and Ann jog down the hallway to their room. Ann wraps her arms around him laughing and giggling giving Sam a big bear hug.

Sam stares into her steel gray eyes for a second and then gives her a long passionate kiss on the lips. He brushes her long blonde hair aside and kisses her neck as he starts to caress her. He feels her hands pull out his shirt and wrap her arms around his bare back. Sam reaches back and starts undoing buttons on her blouse.

"Oh golly, not on a full stomach!" Ann says as she pulls away from Sam and takes some deep breaths.

"Oh rats. Okay, let's warm up the Jacuzzi. We can go nude."

"I'll put on my bathing suit. Um... Let's both wear a bathing suit."

"Fine, the suits can come off later."

"We'll see. Let's stay in control and change."

"You're afraid you can't keep your hands off me?"

"Or vice versa!" Ann says and follows Sam to the Jacuzzi after changing.

Sam finds the controls and starts filling the tub with warm water. As the water level nears full, he checks the temperature with his hand.

"I think it's already warm enough. Let's jump in." Before Sam climbs in, he hears a familiar sound.

"Is it safe to come in here?" Max says rapping on the door.

"Come in. How was the séance?"

"You won't believe what happened!"

Chapter Thirty-Three

"It's the weirdest thing I ever experienced! Hey, Jacuzzi! We'll be right back in our suits." Max turns around after seeing the Jacuzzi is uncovered and running. The multicolor indirect lighting in the Jacuzzi looks great.

"What happened?" Sam asks.

"Be right back!" Max says waving.

Minutes later Max is relaxing in the Jacuzzi with his friends. All the room lights are off. Only the dim light from the LEDs in the Jacuzzi cast an eerie glow in the room. As briefly as he can Max tells what happened at the séance.

"So what happens now?"

"We don't know. Gustavo ordered Sergio to leave the room."

"This is hard to believe you had no control over what you said?"

"It's true I felt a presence there. It was weird. I wonder what will happen to Sergio."

"Maybe we shouldn't ask. Let's just relax and forget about that." He sees Max nod at Peggy.

"Absolutely! I'm ready for some R&R. Let's 'Ja-cuzzeee' in It-al-y."

"These warm water jets feel great right now. I'm glad you turned the lights off. It's more relaxing this way." Ann says as she leans against Sam.

"No problem. The Jacuzzi LED lights are enough."

"What I could use now is a good Toscano sigaro." Max says feeling the warm jets gently massage his back.

"Ugh! You'd stink up the whole room!" Ann pinches her nose.

"Yeah, but I heard there's nothing quite like a good Toscano cigar. Toscano cigars are manufactured right here in Italy and have been around for over a century. It must be a good cigar to last that long. You know, when in Rome, do as the Romans do."

"Let's just enjoy the moment. I am sure this is the only time we will ever be here in this house in this Jacuzzi. Especially in light of what happened tonight. Just close your eyes relax and enjoy!"

Sam feels Ann rubbing her leg against his. He stretches out in the Jacuzzi, closes his eyes and smiles. He feels the gurgling of the water jets against his body. He hears Ann humming quietly and knows she is trying to relax. Neither Sam nor anyone else speaks, not wanting to disturb the tranquility. A half hour passes before Sam is overheating.

"I'm going to go pass out on the bed now." Sam says stepping out.

Ann agrees with him and begins stepping out of the Jacuzzi.

"You guys can stay in longer if you want." Sam hands an oversized bath towel to Ann.

"I hope you enjoyed. Whoever wakes up first in the morning, knock. Let's go downstairs together." He bows to Peggy and Max before he walks away. Only a dim nightlight is on as he steps into the bathroom. The shower turns on and he watches Ann step inside it still in her bathing suit.

"You need to rinse off too." Ann says from the shower stall.

"I had that in mind." Sam says and slips in the shower stall with her.

"I want to lather you up but you've got that suit on." Sam says.

"What are you going to do about it?" Ann asks.

Sam embraces her, kissing her and unhooks her Bikini top. Then as if their suits were on fire they both strip and stand naked in the shower.

"I need to lather you up Sam!" Ann smiles as she dispenses body wash in her hands. She begins rubbing Sam's chest. Her passionate hands gently caress their way down the front of his body.

"Oh, let's lather up together!" Sam whispers.

Filling his hands with body wash too, Sam slowly reaches out and gently strokes Ann's shoulders. As his hands work down to her stomach, he wraps his arms around her. He feels the soap ooze between them as he presses her against the shower wall and kisses her willing lips. His hands move up and down her back as they kiss. They twist around and move under the shower spray. Still embracing and kissing he barely feels the warm shower pour over him. Sam forgets about being in this strange house in a strange land and he makes love with his soul mate.

Sam leans against the shower wall still glowing feeling the warmth of Ann nestled at his side. After savoring the moment for a brief time, Sam steps out of the shower. He dries off and trots back to the bedroom and under the covers of the bed. He closes his eyes but feels Ann slide into the bed toward him and stretch her arm across his chest. He opens his eyes to see her face.

"Turn out your light please." She smiles at him capturing him with her steel gray eyes. She stares at him for a few seconds and finally just shakes her head. She rolls away from Sam and turns out her light.

Sam lays in silence for a second, still mesmerized by his love for her and her steel gray eyes. He just turns off his light when he hears Max.

"Is it safe to come in?"

"Come in Max. What's going on?" Sam turns his light on again.

Peggy and Max come in the room now dressed in pajamas. Peggy is carrying the laptop. She plops down on the end of the bed and places the laptop on her crossed legs.

"I've been using Max's computer. He wants me to book a nice one-week Caribbean cruise. This one hits four ports along Central America. We are not into the hurricane season yet so the seas should be calm. It is truly a miracle. I think we should book it now."

"Couldn't this wait? We were um relaxing. What is a big miracle about a cruise?" Sam says realizing he and Ann are still naked under the covers.

"Because whoever booked both of the end suites has cancelled and they are available. We would have the whole end of the seventh deck to ourselves."

"It sounds expensive to me." Sam says.

"Sam, just blow some money. You have more to blow than you know."

"What does that mean?"

"Just do it Sam."

"When does it leave?" Ann smiles and sits up beside Peggy holding the covers up to her chest.

"It's on the Carnival Conquest ship. It leaves next Sunday for the Eastern Caribbean and returns on Sunday. I'll need all your passports and credit cards to book it."

"We'd all need another week off from work. We were going to wait until I had some vacation time built up." Sam objects.

"I think it would be a great way to celebrate our success. Then we can go back to the work scene. What say can I book it for us?"

Max says, "I'm good with it."

"Well I'm not," Sam says.

"Hey, I'm sure Mark will let you take unpaid leave. For God's sake Sam, I gave you a wad of money. You can afford it, even more than you know. Trust me! I'm paying for Peggy and you can pay for Ann. Let's have a party on, uh... what cruise line?

"Carnival."

"On Carnival!"

"What do you mean, more than I know Max?"

"Nothing Sam."

"You know, you're right. I need to spend some of that money."

"Book 'em, Peggy!" Max shouts.

"Let's go back to our room Max. I think they need to get dressed first." Peggy says. She gives a thumbs-up sign as she gets up from the bed and escorts Max out of the bedroom.

"I wonder what Max meant." Sam says.

"Probably some prank he thought of."

Chapter Thirty-Four

After tossing on robes, Sam and Ann retrieve their passports and a credit card. They walk through to the other bedroom and hand the information to Peggy. Twenty minutes later, she makes the announcement.

"We're booked! Thanks to that cancellation, we booked the two huge balcony suites at the rear of the ship! They are incredibly expensive, but so what!" She bounces on the bed displaying a huge grin. She looks at Sam. "Have we hugged yet?"

"No... I don't think so."

Peggy jumps up giving Sam a big hug.

"Me too!" Ann gently pushes Peggy away and grabs Sam.

"A man couldn't ask for a better life."

"Enough! We're going to bed now. You lovebirds can go back to whatever you were doing. Good night." Max waves goodbye to Sam and Ann as he gently nudges Sam toward the door.

"Okay, good night." Sam says and walks Ann back to their room.

"Please lock the doors?" Ann says.

"Right." Sam fumbles around and locks both doors. When he comes back, he sees Ann has rolled away under the covers. He hears her gentle breathing and knows she is already asleep as he gently slides back into bed. Sam feels anxious about the world, wondering what the morning will be like, and what will happen to Sergio.

Carla and Sophia have finished putting away all the

leftover food with help from Erik. The guards and the gardener bring their plates to her from the kitchen table before leaving. She has stacked the dishwasher and put the dirty napkins in the hamper to wash in the morning. As she walks toward her room in the servant's quarters, she hears Sergio weeping through his partly open bedroom door. Struck by compassion, she thinks. *What is wrong with Sergio?* She gently swings his door wide open and sees him hunched over his desk weeping violently. A small travel bag is on top of his bed.

"Sergio, what is wrong? Why is your suitcase out?"

"Go away Carla!" However, Sergio feels her hand rest on his shoulder.

"I have never seen you like this. Tell me, what is wrong?"

"Something terrible has happened. I cannot tell you. I must go away."

"No Sergio! Your whole life is here. Why would you go?"

"Yes, my whole life! Now it is over!"

"Nothing can be that bad Sergio. Tell me what troubles you."

"I killed a man!"

"Impossible! You are a gentle man."

"It is true Carla, and worse it was their brother!"

"No, the thieves killed him. Why do you say such things now?"

"Miggy spoke at the séance. He told everyone what I did."

"Miggy is dead for thirty years."

"Yes, I have lived with this all these years. Go now

Carla. I want to be alone. I must decide what to do."

"May God forgive you Sergio." Carla begins crying as she sees Gustavo enter the room. She rushes out the door and goes to her room.

"Sergio, I have calmed down now. You are right about Miggy but I am not sure I can forgive you for what you did."

"He was a mean man Gustavo." Sergio sobs.

"I know that Sergio, but he was my brother."

"Papa needed me back then. I truly did not mean to kill Miggy. I just went crazy. Can you not understand?"

"I will make arrangements for you with someone else Sergio, some other family can use your excellent talents. I cannot rest easy with you still here. You will be compensated for your years of service."

"I am so sorry Gustavo!"

"I know." As Gustavo turns to walk away, he hears Sergio speak.

"You need not worry about me."

Gustavo pauses for a second but walks out of the room leaving the door open. He slams his hands together still not knowing what to do about Sergio. As he is walking down the exit hallway, he meets Carla carrying a glass of Brandy.

"It's for Sergio. He is not feeling well." Carla offers.

"Yes." Gustavo replies and walks passed her. He is nearly out of the servant's quarters when the silence ends. Gustavo hears a gunshot and a scream from Carla. He hears glass breaking on the hallway floor.

Gustavo turns and races for Sergio's room seeing the Brandy glass in shards and Brandy oozing across the floor.

Carla is standing in front of Sergio's open door staring into the room. As Gustavo nears, Carla backs against the wall and sinks to the floor. Tears are cascading down her cheeks.

He looks in the bedroom and sees what he hoped he would not see. Sergio is face down on his desk with his right arm dangling at his side and a black revolver lying on the floor near his hand. There is blood splattered on the wall and as Gustavo nears, he sees blood start to drip off the edge of the desk.

"No!" Gustavo whispers. He stands over the body seeing part of Sergio's head is missing, replaced by a bloody indentation. Gustavo rushes back to the door closing out the other gathering servants and allowing only Mario to come in the room.

"I heard a gunshot!" Mario shouts at Gustavo.

"Sergio has killed himself. This is all a result of finding that diamond!"

"Gus, we must call the police."

"No! Think of the news reports."

"None the less, it must be done."

"You are right and we must calm the others. This was his doing?"

"Of course Mario, I would not kill him!"

"Carla, are you alright?" Mario helps her to her feet.

"No, sir."

"Carla was bringing him a Brandy."

"Good. She will tell what she saw then."

"Yes. Let us call the police. This will be a long night brother."

Chapter Thirty-Five

Sam wakes from a solid sleep hearing a rapping noise on the hall door. He is surprised he has not had any wild dreams that he remembers. Sam sits up on the edge of the bed still groggy. He pats Ann as she gets up and trots to the bathroom.

"Hey sleepy, it's us. Are you decent?" Max says.

"I've been called worse."

"Hey Sam, something happened last night. I think I heard sirens and strange voices. I did not venture out though. Maybe that's normal for the Bellasettas. Then considering what happened at the séance, I wonder..."

"Give us ten minutes." Sam says.

"Okay, come to our room when you're ready."

Sam flops back on the bed but a beep and voice from the intercom over the headboard startles Sam. *Funny I didn't notice that intercom last night.*

"Hello! This is Gustavo. Will you join us for breakfast?" There are red buttons on the intercom numbered one to eight. Sam guesses the flashing number eight button is a talk button and presses it.

"We'll be down in ten minutes."

"Bene, come to dining room when you are ready."

"Okay." Sam does his calisthenics. As he finishes his exercises, Ann comes out of the bathroom wearing a light tan blouse and tan slacks. She waves at him and goes through the center room to see Max and Peggy. Sam eventually joins the others and they all migrate to the dining room. After saying good morning to Gustavo, Sam sits with his friends in their same places. He can tell something is wrong and is about to speak when

Gustavo talks.

"I suppose you are all wondering what happened last night."

"Yes and where is everyone?" Max asks feeling tension in his voice.

"Hera is meditating in her room. Mario went to the police station this morning. As you know both the Citroen and the Mercedes are stolen vehicles. Mario will explain what happened with them. Your Focus is another problem. The rental company may charge you for all the damages. I suspect Mario will not be back before lunchtime."

"I hope all will go well there."

"There is no unsolvable problem. Now enjoy the breakfast."

"Mario is answering questions about the men in the Citroen and the Mercedes and about the Ford Focus too?" Max asks.

"Mario will do fine. You may have heard a commotion last night."

"We heard sirens." Max says.

"Yes." Gustavo says. Before he can explain, Erik enters with a platter of roasted birds.

"I hope you like Quail for breakfast. They are fresh. I shot them only last week. Erik is an excellent preparer of Quail"

"I love quail." Max sees Peggy making an ugh-face at him.

"After breakfast we go to church." Gustavo sees Max studying the back of his newspaper.

"You said Mario is with the police."

"Yes. Henri and I will go. Do you want to go with

us?”

"We do not speak Italian. I am curious. Where is Sergio now?”

"Sergio had an accident last night. He is in hospital. That is why you heard the sirens last night.”

"Is it serious? He seemed distraught at the séance.”

"Yes it is serious. We are all upset about what happened. Sergio shot himself in the head. However, unlike killing Miggy, he botched the job. The bullet glanced off his skull barely penetrating his brain and knocking him unconscious. I heard the shot and if I had left him alone, he would have bled to death. I could not do that. I got medical attention for him. He may very well survive the wound.” Gustavo's face strains to remain calm.

"We are all in shock about last night. What will happen to Sergio?”

"Thirty years. There is no proof of what Sergio did except for his own confession. A smart lawyer will advise him to never admit to the crime now.”

"So he is off the hook so to speak.”

"Yes.”

"What will you do? I think I would do something.”

"Sergio has been a loyal servant for the past thirty years. Even though he killed my brother, I cannot do something I would feel guilty about now. I have found work for Sergio with someone else. I could not have him living in this home knowing what he did.”

"What if he decides to tell his story to the news and hopes for a light sentence?”

"That would be unacceptable Max.” Gustavo pauses for a few seconds as if thinking intently.

"Henri and I will be back for lunch. You can enjoy relaxing or using the gym. Erik can show you whatever you want."

"I see an article on your paper shows a diamond like yours."

"Indeed it is. The Sunday paper is running an article about us donating the diamond to the museum tomorrow. We want to see a crowd there when we place it in the enclosure. I am sure the diamond will attract more visitors to the museum."

"How will you get the diamond there?"

"It is already there in their safe. We will take the Limo there. We will in person place the diamond in its new display in the museum. Reggio Calabria is only about fifty kilometers away. You will ride there with us."

"Why would you announce such a thing?"

"Perhaps a mistake, but we wanted to let the public and the news people know so they can all be there for the ceremony. At the museum, robbers would not attack in a crowd of people. My guards will be on alert along the way and at the museum."

"These are the same guards who dealt with the Cresto guys?"

"Yes, trust me we will be safe. The streets are usually safe Max. Now we go to church."

"There are unsafe times?" Sam asks.

"No more than in America."

"You are welcome to drive around in the Qubo if you want to explore the country." Gustavo says as he prepares to leave.

"I think I would prefer staying here today. Don

Cresto is still around somewhere." Sam says.

"Bene! We have a game room and a gym. You can play games or work out, or watch a movie."

"That sounds great to me." Max says. Gustavo briefly shows Max how to work the remote for the projection TV before he says goodbye.

"I wonder where the game room is." Max says, but he sees Erik approaching from the kitchen.

"It is to your left Mister Max." Erik says as he joins the group.

"I'd like to go to the gym." Sam says.

"It is to your left Mister Sam."

"Is everything to the left?"

"Yes sir."

Max stays behind as the others head for the gym and game room. He taps Erik on the shoulder to stop him.

"Erik, really where is Sergio?"

"I do not know sir."

"Where you here 30 years ago, did you see the murders?"

"Yes, my first year here. The killer left a bloody crowbar in the living room. Miguel Junior and the guard were drugged. The thief could have robbed the home without killing them. It was a brutal scene. The guard was killed with one blow, but Miguel was severely beaten and then suffocated."

"Did you like Miguel very much?"

"Miguel Junior was not an easy person to like. I think the two remaining brothers run the businesses much better."

"I take it Miguel Junior was not liked by many people."

"Miguel senior loved him very much. I will leave you now. Enjoy the game room sir."

The rest of the day and evening they spend between the game room and afternoon naps. They retire early Sunday evening after another superb dinner but no word about Sergio.

Chapter Thirty-Six

Max is famished as he and his friends meet in the dining room for breakfast Monday morning. He sees Erik bring out Spanish omelets with extra sausage and fried potatoes garnished with parsley and sliced tomato. He enjoys the meal along with the others. Finishing his breakfast, he questions Gustavo.

"So how is Sergio?"

"Unexpectedly he died last night Max." Gustavo frowns.

"You said he would be okay. What happened?"

"We must forget about Sergio. The tragedy is over. We must think about positive things. Now today we put the diamond in its final home. The National press will be there to take pictures of all of you and me and of the display for the donation. Extra guards will be at the museum as a precaution. It is time to go. You are going?"

"We all came here to see the ceremony. Yes."

Max follows Gustavo and Mario outside to the Bellasetta's large navy blue Limo. He sits in a circle with his friends in the back of the Limo. As the driver starts out, Max sees a van follow the Limo. The small caravan streaks along the roads headed for Reggio Calabria.

Since leaving the estate, Sam is nervous about this journey. However, with a mass of firepower behind the Limo, it seems foolish for anyone to ambush them. He leans back in the cushion seat to relax as the Limo turns onto the main highway heading for the museum. *No worries.* He thinks stretching his arm around Ann, yet his face is worried.

"Relax Sam. It's only about forty kilometers to the museum. We should be there by eleven." Gustavo says sitting across from him.

"I am relaxing. I am hoping the journey is uneventful."

"Enjoy the journey." Max says.

Other than Gustavo expounding on his beautiful country, nothing exciting happens along the way and the Limo approaches the museum on Via Lia within the hour. Crowds of reporters aim cameras at the Limo as it stops in front of the main entrance. Gustavo and the others exit the Limo and start toward the entrance. People separate to make a path for Gustavo and company to enter the front doors. Inside more cameras flash. The head of the museum greets Gustavo with a warm handshake.

"Welcome Mister Bellasetta. We were worried you'd arrive late." The curator Mister Diego says.

"Yes, there was a small traffic delay but we are here now. Show us where the diamond will be housed."

They walk to the new display and Gustavo asks for the diamond. Mister Diego goes to a storage room and opens a safe. He retrieves the black pouch with the diamond. Opening the pouch, he rests the diamond on a small yellow cloth before handing the Bellasetta Rose diamond to Gustavo.

"Thank you Diego. Henri, check the marks." Gustavo hands the diamond to Henri who examines the stone with his eye loop.

"The serial number is correct and the mark." Henri says.

"Just a minute! We have an expert gemologist here to check the diamond." A reporter from The Local newspaper shouts.

"You doubt the authenticity of the diamond?" Gustavo asks.

"Please, let us check it to remove all doubts!"

Gustavo pauses for a few seconds before agreeing. He hands the diamond to their gemologist who is sitting at a small table near the display. The man carefully wipes the stone, weighs it and examines it with his eye loop. He nods indicating the diamond is indeed the real thing and hears a small cheer from the crowd of reporters and visitors. Gustavo raises his hand to silence them.

"This diamond is most beautiful and is indeed the largest red diamond known to exist. You all have the privilege of seeing it whenever you like here. I hope we have removed all doubts about the diamond now. Let me put this in its new home so everyone can enjoy it." Gustavo says taking the diamond back. He follows Mister Diego to the new display.

"We have the very best security for the diamond Mister Bellasetta. Between the laser beams, the vibration sensors, and of course the unbreakable glass and lock, no one will steal this precious diamond. The alarms are off for you to place the diamond inside."

"Let me place it there and let it shine." Gustavo says. He sets the diamond on its perch and the pouch next to it with the initials showing. When the display closes, two spotlights come on causing a plethora of red tones to emit from the diamond.

Sam marvels at the beauty of the diamond but he is still worried about Cresto showing up since the event is on television. He searches the crowd as he walks around in the museum looking for any sign of trouble. There is none.

Max takes pictures of the people, the diamond in its display, and some of the artifacts in the museum. Impressed by the sheer beauty of some intricate wood-carvings, he is lost in his picture taking until Gustavo taps his shoulder.

"It is time to go Max." Gustavo motions toward the front exit and follows his new friends out the front door. The Limo takes them back to the estate without incident. Gustavo stops everyone in the living room to speak.

"We thank you for doing this. There were skeptics among the reporters who did not believe we have indeed recovered the real rose diamond."

"Why would they doubt?"

"It is nicknamed the 'Deadly Diamond' for years until now. Everyone assumed the main reason for the robbery was lost in New York somewhere as Salvatore Cresto professed. The diamond is a legend in its own time. Some reporters thought it was lying in a New York sewer. Now they know the truth."

"Yes, I remember reading about Cresto claiming he dropped it from his pocket in the airport between plane flights."

"We doubted that happened and now we have proof he lied."

"So many people searched in the wrong place."

"Yes. This concludes our business. I apologize for the incident with Sergio and for his ultimate demise. Now you are free to do whatever you want. Mario and I appreciate your coming here. We enjoyed learning some things about you and your friends. Have you made any plans?"

"I think we already know what we want to do."

"You have discussed plans for today?"

"Yes. If we are finished here..." Max shrugs.

"You want to go back to the USA?"

"Your hospitality has been most kind and unexpected. I believe we would have had much less luxury at our hotel. We do not want to impose on you anymore. I am very sorry about Sergio."

"It all makes sense now Max." Gustavo says.

Chapter Thirty-Seven

"When Mario and I came home from America we thought Sergio was overly depressed about the murder. We always thought he became too subservient. However, over the years, we got used to the way he was. How he was able to live in guilt all this time is hard to imagine." Gustavo explains.

"Maybe he is in peace now." Max says, but Gustavo just shrugs and changes the subject.

"Do be careful. We still do not know where Cresto is. I suggest you change your flights to leave from Reggio Calabria instead of Rome. It is much closer as you know and Henri can transport you there."

"Yes, perhaps that would be better. Maybe we will explore Rome another time." Max smiles at Gustavo.

"I understand. When you are ready, Henri will drive you. Ring me on number one." Gustavo pats Max's back. Max and the others shake hands again with Gustavo and go to the elevator.

Back in his room, Max makes phone calls to Reggio Calabria while Peggy finishes packing. He books two rooms at the Apan Hotel for the evening. After some more calls cancelling the Rome flights, he books the four on American Airlines from Reggio Calabria to Fort Lauderdale leaving tomorrow at noon.

"I got it done. We just get Henri to take us to Hotel Apan in Reggio Calabria and we are good to go from there." Max announces as Sam and Ann join Max and Peggy with their bags. Max presses the number one red button. "Hello Gustavo we are ready."

"Bene! Come back to the walkway area. I will meet

you there. Leave your bags. Eric will take them to the Limo."

"Okay!" Max pauses before he leaves the bedroom. He looks around at the wonderful surroundings and amenities. Then with a sigh, he joins the others to leave.

"Come this way." Gustavo motions Max to follow him along the walkway.

Max and the gang follow him to Papa's old bedroom. As Max walks into the room, he sees it is a bragging room - a history of the Bellasetta family. There are display cases with medals and family pictures of several generations inside. The walls have pictures of various ships and company buildings including Banc Bella. One wall has rows of children's pictures. All of the trophies and good things that the Bellasettas have done in their lives are on display in the room. A new picture of Miguel G Bellasetta Senior adorns the wall directly across from the entrance door.

"We wanted you to see this room and what Papa kept here. Papa was a great man. He created an empire worth several billion Euros starting with nearly nothing. I wanted you to see all the good things we have done." Gustavo tells them as they enter.

Max nods gracefully at Gustavo. He touches the photo of Papa Bellasetta.

"Did your Papa get to see the diamond?"

"No Max, only a picture of it."

"Your Papa waited all these years then failed to see it."

"Perhaps he is looking at it from above now."

"The Bellasetta Rose is home in the museum where

it belongs."

"Yes, and we have replaced Miggy's picture with one of Papa."

Max looks at the picture for a moment and has to ask.

"Would you mind if we take pictures of this room? It's like a whole history of the Bellasetta family." Max watches Gustavo hesitate and then nod to Max.

Max takes his smart phone out, and snaps a few shots around the room and snaps shots of Gustavo. Sam and the girls do the same. When Henri comes in the room, Max has him take a picture of him and his friends standing next to Gustavo. The pictures are ones he hopes to show his parents and maybe his kids someday. After the picture taking, he shakes hands again with Gustavo before leaving. It is time to go and Max follows Gustavo out of the room.

Gustavo escorts them down in the elevator and out of the house. Max holds Gustavo back from the others. "I really appreciate what you have done for us. I am still not sure why you have been so nice to us." Max sees Gustavo's face wince.

"Max we try to make up for the bad things our brother did. As you know now, he was not killed because of a robbery. He was beaten and killed out of hatred. The secret Papa never knew and we thank you for not talking about that to anyone. As soon as you are home, you can tell the others what I told to you, or not. It is up to you then." Gustavo pats Max on the back and watches him catch up with the others.

Outside the sky is thick with black clouds. Max can

feel the tension in the atmosphere as if rain and lightning are soon to come. He sees raindrops hitting the pavement outside of the overhang. He sees a few raindrops on the Limo and Henri is waiting next to the open trunk.

"Please examine to be sure we have all of your belongings. The rain will be starting soon. We must move along." Henri watches them check the bags.

"Thank you Henri. It all looks fine." Max says. He snaps a few more pictures of the Bellasetta house and Henri and the Limo as Henri closes the trunk. With a saddened heart, Max blows a kiss toward the main house. Standing by the trunk, he feels the dense air before a rain starts.

"Please go inside now, Max." Henri points to the Limo.

The sky grows darker as Max reaches the Limo door. He enters the Limo as a loud bolt of thunder strikes nearby. Max closes the Limo door hearing another clap of thunder. He feels the Limo start to roll away from Gustavo and the Bellasetta estate.

Max lowers the window and waves goodbye to Gustavo.

"Goodbye, safe journey!" Gustavo waves watching the Limo roll toward the iron gates.

Max waves to him again as Henri drives them away. The large wrought iron gates open as the Limo approaches. Max takes a last look at the estate as the Limo passes through the gates. *Goodbye magnificent estate!* It is a moment he locks in his memory knowing he will never see the estate or Gustavo or Mario again. *Goodbye!*

Chapter Thirty-Eight

Henri drives down the winding path and eventually onto a main road. He has made the journey to Reggio Calabria many times taking company executives there after staying with the Bellasettas. This is a more casual trip since he genuinely likes Max and the others. Sometimes the company men have been abusive. He remembers being close to throttling men several times.

A light sprinkle pats down on the Limo as Henri accelerates to cruising speed. His thoughts switch to Sergio. *I wonder how Sergio managed to be silent for thirty years. Maybe he was afraid of what Gustavo or Mario might do. I have never seen Gustavo so upset. However, from the rumors I have heard, Miguel Junior was a rat. Perhaps Gustavo will forgive Sergio. We all do wrong things. I hope Sergio rests in peace.* Henri thinks as he slows and eases onto the main highway to Reggio Calabria. Max interrupts his thoughts.

"Henri, how long have you worked for the Bellasettas?"

"Many years, I protect Gustavo."

"Is he as nice as he seems?"

"He is a most generous and honest man. You have seen only the slightest amount of his kindness to others. I would give my own life to save his!"

"Wow! That's dedication!"

"I am very good at what I do so no worries. I love what I do Max."

"That's great. I always say, enjoy the journey."

The rest of the trip consisted of idle chitchat until Henri stopped the Limo at the entrance of the Hotel Apan in Reggio Calabria.

"Let me help you with these." Henri retrieves the luggage from the trunk and Helps Max and Sam set them on the curb.

"Well, goodbye." Max says shaking Henri's massive hand and passing a one hundred Euro bill to Henri.

"Arrivederci to all of you. Oh no..." Henri says. He smiles grabbing Max by the shoulder. He stuffs the bill back in Max's shirt pocket before he leaves.

"How about that." Max whispers as he watches Henri get in the Limo and drive away.

"Why are you smiling Max?" Peggy asks.

"I feel free again. Maybe it is too much opulence. Maybe it is my lack of control over anything. Whatever it is, I'm glad to be away from the estate and away from the diamond and the Bellasettas!"

They follow the bellhop taking their bags to the lobby.

"See if you can get rooms on the third floor. I like the third floor." Sam says following Max to the front counter.

"You would! Let's hope we don't have to run down the stairs!" Max looks at the girl at the counter, a thirtyish red headed beauty wearing a blue and gold uniform. He would be flirting and trying to get her phone number and a date less than a year ago. Today he barely looks at her.

Max fills in some paperwork and smiles at the woman. As he stands at the counter, he reflects on his life. He always felt like something was missing in his soul. He chased women all his adult life trying to fix whatever it was, and then recently all seems okay with his inner self. His relationship with Peggy seems to have changed. He realizes he wants to be with her all the time. Max finishes the paperwork with the clerk and gives Peggy a gentle hug.

"I got your wish for the third floor Sam. It must be the off-season. The hotel is obviously not booked solid." He says and leads the others to the elevators.

On the third floor, Max comes to his room first along the hallway and waves goodbye as he opens the door. Max starts to go in but Sam pulls him aside.

"Max, I am glad you agreed to not roaming around Rome."

"I am glad too." Ann says hearing Sam.

"I'm happy!" Peggy agrees.

"We can tour Rome another time. I'm concerned about the guys who got away, especially Don Cresto. Who knows what he is planning. I'm surprised we didn't have trouble with him at the museum." Sam adds.

"Gustavo said they were wounded so maybe they are recuperating somewhere. However, I have doubts about staying in Italy too. Something is still bothering me. I am having trouble handling everything." Max says.

"I'm starving. Let's check out a restaurant as soon as we dump our stuff. I could eat a cow right now!" Sam pats his stomach. He rushes to his room and sets the suitcases inside. A moment later, he and Ann are back at Max's room.

"It's time for some food!" Max says. He gets up with

Peggy and locks the door behind him.

"Not another McDonalds." Peggy gripes.

"Okay, let's see what we can find."

"Is there a cozy little restaurant nearby?" Max asks the clerk as they walk into the main lobby.

"I like a place called Mama's on Viale Calabria." The clerk says.

"Good food and cocktails?"

"Yes, and it is open at eleven."

"Very good, call a taxi for us."

"There should be one out front sir."

A taxi delivers Max and the others to Mama's within minutes after eleven. They walk inside the small restaurant and a waiter seats them.

"May I take your drink orders?" A waiter says.

"Sure. What is your name?" Max asks.

"Lenny, sir."

"Bring me hot tea with lemon Lenny. This is fine. Today we celebrate! Let's get some lunch!" Max says.

Sam is skeptical. "We're not home yet."

"Yes, but no one is following us. No one knows where we are. Relax Sam. It's over! We are as good as home now." Max smiles confidently although something is bothering him. *I just do not understand so many coincidences.* Max thinks but shrugs it off.

"When I'm sitting on my balcony at home and enjoying the Florida sun. Then I'll relax!" Sam replies.

"That will be real soon. Someday I still would like to tour Italy. The people here have been great, except for the bad guys."

"Someday later but let's go on that cruise first. That's why we got the passports."

"Yes, Peggy already booked that cruise for us. Let us feast now."

"If you guys have this big wad of money maybe you could take all our parents on the cruise with us. The suites are certainly big enough." Ann says and sees Max's jaw drop. Peggy is silent too.

"Much better if we just buy them a separate cruise." Sam says.

"Yes. I'd feel kinda funny with my parents along. It might cramp my style." Max says.

"Ten-four on that!" Sam agrees.

"I was kidding." Ann giggles.

Sam originally planned on a cheap inside cabin for his first cruise. Now Peggy registered him for an expensive balcony suite. He thought about his new friend Chet Hatter the lead guitarist for the Danglebatts band. Chet told him '*It's peaceful and very relaxing to sit out on the balcony and listen to waves splashing against the ship at night as it sails from port to port.*' *Since Max gave me a half million dollars, the balcony suite is no problem.* Sam smiles.

"Here is the lunch menu sir." The waiter says handing a menu to Max.

"What do you recommend Lenny?"

"We have a delicious Salmon fillet."

"Sound good?" Max asks and sees everyone nod.

"Bring us four of your best fillets Lenny."

Lenny nods, announces what the side dishes are and takes their orders before leaving.

Max tunes out the chatter from the rest as he remembers the enormity of his new bank balance. *My God! Four more million! It's like winning the lotto! Let me think of what I can do now. I wonder if mom and dad have a mortgage. I can pay off my own mortgage on the house and the boat. I have to give two million to Sam of course. Maybe I should include the girls in this fortune. The girls risked their lives too. Should I do some charity work?* Max is still daydreaming in his own world when the waiter places the Salmon and mixed vegetables in front of him. He eats and drinks almost in a stupor feeling unusually tired after the meal.

"This was excellent! Kudos to the cook and Lenny! I'm ready to go back and take a nap."

"That's a good idea Max. I'd like to rest up so I can party tonight! Let's meet up about six." Sam feels good about the day. The knot in his stomach is not so bad now. They take the quick taxi ride back to the hotel. He and Ann go to their room. He unpacks a few things before stretching out on the bed and falling asleep. At six in the evening, he rings Max.

"Wow we slept well! Let's meet outside in five."

Chapter Thirty-Nine

A new Italian band is rocking in the lounge with a strong bass beat. A waitress seats them near the dance floor and takes their drink order. As she leaves, Sam coaxes Ann onto the dance floor just as the music slows to a waltz.

"Fine by me," Sam says snuggling against Ann. He feels her hand on the back of his neck and her body pressing against his. Sam shuffles around the floor deliberately as slow as he can, enjoying the moment.

The foursome drink and dance to the music and the night passes quickly. By nine, they are ready to go back to the rooms, still feeling the effects of the time difference. They are having fun but decide on a good night's sleep before the flight home tomorrow. They say goodnight and go to their rooms.

Back in his room, Sam turns on the TV as Ann goes into the bathroom. A reporter named Dom Figuero is telling the news in Italian. Sam switches to several different stations before finding one speaking English.

Sam is about to change channels again when Ann comes out of the bathroom.

Wearing a shear negligee, she looks sheepishly at Sam as she slides under the bed sheets. "Why are you watching TV?"

Sam wakes at eight o'clock fully refreshed from a pleasant romp and a quiet night of sleep. He smiles as he thinks. *It's morning and I haven't had any weird dreams.* He remembers the flight from Reggio Calabria leaves at noon so he has plenty of time to get to the airport. He and Ann pack their stuff and meet Max and Peggy in the lobby. After checking out Sam dons his coat walking outside to board the hotel shuttle to the airport with the others.

At the terminal, Max tips the driver. He grabs bags and walks inside with the rest. They go to the American Airlines counter. After checking the bags, they wander around the terminal but find nothing interesting to do. They have lunch in a small café and relax at the gate waiting to board. Max is strangely content just to sit quietly. He still has a feeling that something is not right. Finally Sam speaks.

"You must be out of pranks Max." Sam remembers the rubber spider and wonders if Max still has it in his carryon bag.

Max just shrugs and smiles still thinking about the extra four million dollars. *I promised not to say anything until we are back in the USA. I wish he had said until we are out of Italy. Then I could tell everyone about the money on the flight.*

Max boards the plane for Philadelphia with the others just before noon. The plane taxis to the runway and immediately catapults into the cool air. When the plane reaches altitude, Max walks the aisle scanning the passengers all the way to the rear restroom. He sees no one suspicious. Content not to worry about Cresto, he settles in his seat and sleeps for most of the flight. Gaining six hours, it is only four o'clock in the afternoon when the plane lands in Philadelphia.

They switch planes to fly to Fort Lauderdale. Before the plane can take off it develops a mechanical problem and the flight is cancelled. They reschedule on the only thing available leaving Philly at eight in the evening.

"Let's find a bar." Max says and he thinks. *Maybe this is all there is to that bad omen that is nagging me.*

Peggy clings to Max keeping him from attempting any more pranks, but Max stays calm content to sip on several Jack Daniels drinks. They finally board the plane to Fort Lauderdale at nearly eight at night.

"Hurray! We're going home!" Max slurs his words.

"Shush!" Peggy covers his mouth.

"I'm just happy sweetie. Aren't you happy?"

"Yes Max. Please be quite."

"Hey guys, we forgot to eat." Sam says.

"We had our dinner. We ate a pound of pretzels and peanuts. Maybe I'll just get another drinky-poo. Nurse!" Max pats the flight attendant's arm as she starts to go aft.

"I will take care of you as soon as we are airborne." She says.

"I just want a drink ma'am." Max laughs.

"That's what I meant sir!"

Max laughs again as he watches the woman walk to her seat.

The plane is far away from Philadelphia as it levels off at thirty thousand feet aimed toward Fort Lauderdale. After a few more drinks, Max feels the plane touchdown and roll to the terminal.

"Now I'm totally inebriated!" Max blurts after the plane halts at the terminal. "I want to go home and check my house and see if Cresto took anything. We need to get some beer to sober up with."

After they retrieve their luggage, Max hails a taxi

and has the cabbie stop at a local seven-eleven store. He picks up two six-packs of Michelob. He yells to the driver. "Take us to 812 Clifton Street! Sam, order some pizzas!"

Sam dials his favorite pizza place and orders two large pizzas. "Let's hope we get there before the pizzas do!"

Max taps the driver. "Big tip if you beat the pizza man!"

After some seemingly dangerous speeding and maneuvering, the driver squeaks to a stop at 812 Clifton Street.

"I think you beat the pizza man, so here." Max gives the driver a generous tip. He staggers up his front steps opens the front door and pours into the living room with his friends. Peggy rushes to her bedroom to check her things before she breaks the silence.

"I hate to wish harm for people, but I do hope Gustavo puts an end to Don Cresto and his friends."

As Max opens a beer, he hears the doorbell ring. Max peeks through the lens on the door before opening it for the pizza man.

"You got the last order man. We were closing." Pizza man says.

"Well, thank you pizza man." Max says. He pays the tab along with an extra big tip. He carries in the pizzas to the dining room table and starts eating as his friends join him.

Max finishes one slice, and retrieves his laptop. As he munches on a new slice of pizza, he begins typing.

He mumbles a bit from his full mouth. "You know I still can't figure out how Don Cresto knew we were going to Rome and what flight we would be on. That is what still bothers me. Was that just a coincidence?"

"Another good question, how did he know you split the reward? I have no answers Max. Maybe we can work on that in the morning." Sam sees Ann finish her second slice of pizza and look at him.

"Yeah Sam, let's go fishing in the morning. I bet we can catch a ton of Snappers or something. I feel lucky!"

"On a Wednesday? Sure, why not. Eleven o'clock, no need to rush."

"I'm tired. Let's go home." Ann leans back on the couch closing her eyes.

"You guys are welcome to stay here." Max says.

"No, if it's alright with Sam I'd like to go to the apartment."

"No problem love. We can get a taxi and be on our way."

"Oh, there is one more thing I forgot to tell you Sam!" Max slurs a bit. "We are back in the USA now so it's okay. Gustavo wired four million dollars to my account."

Chapter Forty

"It was only one million Max. I saw the printout."

"No Sam, four million more."

"That must be the booze talking. Why would they do that?"

"Gustavo said their brother was a bad seed. Miggy bought the diamond with drug money. Because they are very proper people, they wanted to pay for the diamond with honest money. The money is there Sam, I checked."

"Then you can pay for my cruise with your extra money."

"The deal was fifty-fifty Sam. I owe you two million dollars! Better still, I can give you and the girls each a million. After all, they were at risk too."

"Yeah, why not... Hey let's talk about this in the morning." Sam does not quite believe Max, being rather schnockered himself.

The cab arrives ten minutes later. Ann grabs two of the remaining beers. Sam grabs their luggage, and they wave goodbye to Peggy and Max.

"See you all in the morning! We'll go fishing!" Max waves back.

As he rides back to the apartment, all the excitement winds up Sam's brain. He feels good having Ann pressing on him. They lean against each other until they get to the apartment complex. Sam pays the cabbie and they go inside the building and into his apartment. He switches on the TV and watches a mindless show with Ann until the beer is gone.

"It's nearly three in the morning Ann." Sam has finally unwound from all the excitement and too sleepy and drunk to do anything else but flop back on the couch.

"I'm going to bed." Ann stands up quite wobbly as she weaves her way to the bedroom.

It takes Sam a moment to realize she has left him. *Good idea*, he finally thinks. He turns out the lights and heads for the bedroom. Ann is undressing when Sam staggers into the bedroom. The only lights still shining are from the nightlights in the living room and bedroom. He sees her waving her bra around in the air at him.

"You like what you see?" she says leaning against the side of the bed for support as she sways back and forth.

"Yes I do!" Her beauty still shocks Sam even more in the shadows of the darkened bedroom.

"Then come to mama!" She throws her bra up and into the paddle fan and extends her arms toward him. Her bra slowly spins around and flies onto the floor. She giggles seeing Sam stagger toward her with arms outstretched. She feels his warm embrace and falls onto the bed wrapping her arms around him. She enjoys a passionate kiss and then goes limp, passing out in his arms.

Sam looks at her closed eyes and thinks. *We got a little too drunk! She is so exciting, vulnerable, and beautiful! The entire world seems right!*

"Well... Even so..." Sam mumbles as he rolls off Ann and closes his eyes next to her. He smiles, forgetting about Don Cresto for the moment.

Three days after the gunfight, Don Cresto is still feverous and spends an hour listening to the recordings from Arturo's laptop. He scowls learning of their return to America and of the cruise. *Maybe I can get Arturo's friend Bruno to stop them.* Don thinks before speaking.

"They go on a cruise with our money! I must get well. I must stop this pain! I must stop them!"

"We go to hospital Don. You must get help!" Angelino says.

"Let me call Bruno first. If he can force the money from them, I can stay here and fight the Bellasettas! Arturo says Bruno is a loyal man."

"Okay Don, call but then we go."

"No. I am feeling better. I want to hear from Bruno in Fort Lauderdale. If he succeeds, I can stay here and recover. If not, I have to go to America."

"Hello Bruno!" Don says when he answers.

"Hello Don. Why did you go to Italy?"

"It seemed like the right thing to do. I need some help now."

"Carl told me of your plan before he left with you. How is he doing?"

"I think Carl is dead."

"Dead, what happened? I know the plan seemed risky to me when he told me Don."

"It would have worked but we had some misfortune. Carl started a gunfight. Angelino and I barely escaped but we are each wounded."

"This is bad news Don. Carl is dead and you and Angelino are hurt. The plan was for no one to be hurt.

You say you need help. What do you need?"

"Let me explain what happened and what I want you to do."

Don tells Bruno all the rest of the details. He feels better being reassured that Bruno will get the money for him. Don settles stays in the house in spite of Angelino's pleading to take him to a hospital.

The next day however Bruno does not call. Don checks the laptop and hears what happened to Bruno.

"This is outrageous! I must go to America!"

"You look worse today Don. I will take you to hospital now." Then against Don's protests, he loads Don into his old truck. He hears Don complain the whole way to Paidos Medical Center in Gioia Tauro. Finally parking the truck, Angelino helps Don into the hospital.

Don's side and shoulder still are throbbing as he attempts to fill out the medical forms the nurse gives him. He watches a nurse administer a shot of antibiotics and she gives him a pain pill to swallow. Don winces as she cleans his wounds and tapes large gauze pads on them.

"I will be back in a moment. Please complete the forms." The nurse says. She leaves the room as Angelino returns from the restroom. Don's side is still oozing a little blood onto the bandage the nurse just put on him and he grunts as he listens to Angelino.

"I am glad we came here. They can fix whatever keeps this fever in you. You are better to chance being caught here than dying."

"It is time to go!" Don staggers as he walks tossing the forms on the bed.

"You still need attention." Angelino argues.

"No, we must go now. She will call policia! She gave me an antibiotics shot. I will be fine. We must go!"

Chapter Forty-One

"I hope the shot is enough. We go as you wish." Angelino follows Don into the hallway. He looks in all directions and sees no one. He follows Don out the hospital exit unnoticed. After he helps Don into his truck and starts the engine he speaks.

"So what are your plans Donny?"

"Well, our best plan did not work."

"It would have worked if Carl had not been so careless with his gun!"

"Yes, and why he shot at the policia..."

"We all crammed in that Citroen when they got away from us."

"Maybe we should have thought of another plan at that time."

"For sure we should not have waited near the Bank for them." Angelino sees Don grab his side when the truck hits a pothole in the road.

"We screwed up! We had them on that side road. Now they are safe in America. I will need to avenge the deaths." Don says.

"I am afraid of doing anything else Donny."

"Are you afraid of avenging the death of your friends?"

"Yes I am. I have family here and children. Albert and Carl too, they were the shady ones. I go along because of you Donny. I see now so much death and trouble. Can you forgive me?" Angelino tilts his head down as he drives.

"I was wrong to come to Italy Angelino. I could deal better with these rats in America. I must go back to the

USA. Can you help me?”

“Are you out of money?”

“Well almost...” Don thinks for a moment. “No, I have money in a 401k, but it will take a week or more to get it.”

“What is a 401k?”

“It is like a retirement fund. I never touch it or tell Arturo about it. I know I have a lot of money in there, and all I need is a few thousand.”

“Maybe we can get help Donny. I do know a dangerous man who will loan money. Kyle charges a lot, but he can get cash for us today. I also know Albert’s friend Gino makes fake passports and ID’s, but he charges a lot too. I am thinking, perhaps you should wait until your wounds heal. It gives you time to get your own money Donny.”

“No, Angie this must not wait. Max made a deal with the despicable Bellasettas. Because of Max and Sam, Arturo is dead and my friends are dead! I need money and a different passport. I am sure authorities are looking for you and me. Let me do this now Angie! Make the calls!”

Angelino shakes his head but he calls Kyle as he drives away from the hospital. He talks for a moment before hanging up.

“Because you are not living here, I will have to guarantee the loan personally Donny. This man will be ruthless if I do not repay with interest... Are you sure you will pay this within the thirty days?”

“Would he kill you?”

“Maybe worse, he may hurt Camilla or our children.”

"I promise you Angie, I will pay you with my retirement money if I cannot get the money from Max. God forgive me. The Bellasettas will have to wait. I will get the money back to you, but then Max, Sam, and their women must die! I will kill them – every one of them!"

At nine o'clock in the morning, Max rolls out of bed leaving Peggy still asleep. He eases out of the house and drives to his bank to talk to John Thurman. Knowing Peggy and his friends Sam and Ann all have accounts at his bank, he signs orders for John to transfer a total of three million dollars, one million dollars each to Peggy's, Sam's, and Ann's accounts.

"Are you sure you want to do this?" Mister Thurman asks.

"Absolutely, they all shared in the risks."

"Okay Max, I'm sure you've thought this through." John makes the transfers. A moment later, John sees the computer updates on his screen as the orders complete.

"I see your expression changed. Does that mean the transfers are done?"

"Yes Max, you're three million dollars poorer." John shakes hands with Max and says goodbye and watches Max walk away.

Max slips into his Corvette, lets the top down, and drives back to his house on Clifton Street. As he speeds along with the cool breeze blowing his dark hair around, he smiles thinking about telling the others what he has done with the money. By ten Max is back home. He parks and quietly opens his front door but Peggy is already out of bed.

"Hello love. Where did you go so early?" Peggy asks from the kitchen seeing Max come in.

"I went to the bank. You and our friends are all millionaires now."

"What?"

"I split the money almost evenly now. I transferred a million each to you and Ann and Sam."

Peggy is speechless nearly dropping her plate of pancakes she is carrying to the table. All sorts of thoughts run through her brain. *Why did he do that? He hinted he would do that. What am I going to do with a million? Oh, I'll think of some things!* Her thoughts were broken as she found herself sitting in a chair with Max rubbing her shoulders.

"This is a good thing Peg. I did it for two reasons. First, we all shared in the dangers, and I want to be sure you marry me for love and not money. You have enough to do well without me now if you care to do that."

"Max, it never has been the money. I love you. I love everything about you, even the pranks." She turns to kiss Max but hears the doorbell ring.

"I'll get it. We eat and we get ready to go fishing." Max says. Giving Peggy a quick kiss, he walks to answer the door.

Chapter Forty-Two

Sam awakes at nine o'clock in the morning. He thinks about Don Cresto as he sits up. He remembers Gustavo saying not to ask what he would do to Cresto if he found him. *Maybe Gustavo will seek revenge for his brother. He would see that his men act in self-defense, or maybe his men would save Don for him to take personal revenge. Maybe he will do nothing to Cresto.* His mind rambles through what may happen to Don Cresto. In any case, he believes Don Cresto will stay in Italy and try to harm the Bellasettas. He feels safe from Don Cresto and company at least for the moment.

Even so, he still has a question nagging at his brain. *How in the world, out of all the flights to Rome and all the different airlines, how did Don Cresto book the same flight to Rome as we did? It seems like far too much of a coincidence.* He knows the thought has occurred to the others too. Now that the threat is maybe over, he tries to brush that question aside, but to no avail.

Sam does his calisthenics, showers and dresses. He goes into the living room. Ann is in the kitchen cooking some leftover ham from the refrigerator and the last of the eggs. She already has the table set for two. He knows they have an hour to get to Max. Ann walks out of the kitchen and smiles at him.

"Have we hugged yet?" She asks as she looks into his eyes putting her arms around him.

"No... I don't think we have." He smiles at her and hugs her, elated to see the sparkle is back in her bright gray eyes.

"I'm stealing that line from Peggy you know." She tightens her arms around Sam and holds him close to her.

"It's a very good line. I'm hungry woman!" Sam gives her a healthy squeeze too.

"I'm just finishing the eggs." She dances away from him.

Sam likes the way Ann uses just the right seasoning on the eggs. It is not a lot of salt and pepper but something else that makes the eggs taste great. *It's Ann*, he concludes, *just Ann*.

She divides the eggs and he eats a slice of toast with the eggs and ham. He has some orange juice and coffee.

"No time to rest after breakfast. We better get going. We told Max 11. It's almost ten thirty now. We have to take your car. The van is still over there."

He hustles Ann along to the car and heads to Max's house. He wants to see how Max and Peggy are doing after consuming so much alcohol. Half way there, he rings Max's cell phone.

"Hello... We are on the way. Are you up yet?" Sam jests.

"Oh yes, we are. You're supposed to be here by ten, you dumb ass!" Max says sounding depressed.

Sam's gut wrenches. He remembers the code words and hopes Max has merely used the code accidentally, but Max continues.

"I hate to call you a dumb ass but you must have overslept. Come here right away and bring Ann. Someone here wants all the money to invest. I need both you and Ann here to do that."

"I really do feel like a dumb ass Max. We'll be over

as soon as we can." Sam tries to sound calm. He rings off closes his eyes for a second tilting his head back.

Ann begins stretching and smiles at Sam before noticing how pale he is.

"Why did you say you're a dumb ass? Is everything okay?"

"Not exactly, Max wants us to come to his house but I think I should just drop you off somewhere." Sam tries to sound normal.

"Why do that?" Ann says as she brushes her hair back in place.

Sam is lost for words. *Should I tell her Max is in trouble and I don't want her in trouble too? Maybe I should take her back to the apartment, but what can I tell her?*

"Well?" Ann questions after an awkward pause.

"Okay, the thing is... Max called me a dumb ass first."

"What! Of all the nerve! After what you did to save our lives and he has the nerve to call you a dumb ass! What possible reason..."

"He says because we're a little late." Sam interrupts her.

"Late for what? Oh, let me give him a piece of my mind... Oh no!" She takes out her phone to call him, but promptly puts it away.

"You remembered the code word."

"The code word, yes." Ann nearly faints. She feels Sam pat her leg.

"Yes, Max said he needs to take back the money. He said to get my dumb ass over there and bring you. Why would he want you there if he were in trouble? He mentioned dumb ass twice. Maybe someone is holding him and Peggy at gunpoint and wants the reward money."

"How could this be? Didn't Gustavo say Don Cresto would be history? Didn't he say we have no worries?" Ann begins sobbing.

"Yes to both. I don't see how Cresto could get out of Italy, but the news of the reward is out. Maybe it's someone else. All I know is Max can't tell me what it is."

"He's joking with you. This is another one of his pranks!"

"Ann, Max and I have a pact. We never prank each other. He would not call me dumb ass unless he is really in trouble."

"So what do we do now?" Ann's face is ashen. She grabs his arm with both hands.

"Let me think for a minute. We do have an element of surprise on our side..." Sam continues driving toward Max's house only a few minutes away.

"I need to call Mark." Sam's brain begins working on a solution.

"You mean Mark Goodman? Why call our boss?"

"Well, even though I haven't known him long, he is like a mentor to me. He can help us." Sam calls Mark at Silvan Enterprises.

"Hello Sam, you're back in the USA already!"

"Yes Mark but we have a problem. Max is in trouble. I suspect someone has Max captive in his house probably at gunpoint."

"What? Who would do that?"

"I don't know. It could be anyone. All I know is Max

is in trouble."

"How would you know Max is in trouble?"

"You know Max never pulls a prank on me right?"

"Yeah and me too if he knows what's good..."

"So remember the code - the dumb ass code? He used it."

"I remember you saying that. So you think someone is with Max now?"

"Yes, it's the only thing that makes sense. Max called me a dumb ass and he wants to take all the money back. He used dumb ass twice. It can't be a mistake. I think it has to be someone after the money. Max wants me to come there and bring Ann. We need help Mark!"

"Okay Sam. I will call my friend Police Captain Fred Holland. He can help. You'd better be right about this Sam! If it's a prank, you and Max can kiss your butts goodbye! You'll have to pay for everything and possibly get some jail time."

"There is no doubt in my mind Mark. I'm not sure what it is but I bet it's someone wanting the money from Max."

"Okay, Sam. Go there but do not go in. Wait for the police to arrive."

"I'm almost there Mark. I think I have to go in."

"No Sam! Stay away. This could be very dangerous!"

"What would you do if he were your best friend?" Sam waits but hears no answer.

"Wish me luck Mark!" He says goodbye and hangs up as he stops the car and shuts off the engine. He sits silently a moment before speaking.

"I have to go in Max's house. You should stay in the

car love. Mark will get the police to come here."

"I'm going with you!" She wraps her arms around him as best she can.

"No love. Look at you... You're shaking. This will be dangerous. Someone may be shot or killed. I don't want anything to happen to you."

"If you die I want to die too!" She says and hugs him tighter.

She has a way of choking up Sam and this is one of those times. He strokes her hair and kisses her. He takes a few seconds to regain his composure before he can talk.

"Okay my love. Let's go say hello!"

Chapter Forty-Three

Mark Goodman hangs up the call from Sam and sits thinking for a moment. He wonders what trouble Max is in now, and then he shrugs and dials the police station. After one transfer, he connects to Fred Holland.

"Hello Fred. This is Mark."

"Hey Mark. How are things at Silvan? I'm asking because it's a boring day here. We got nothing going on."

"No axe murders to solve today?"

"I have nothing exciting to tell you about, just some minor crap."

"Perfect Fred. I have something I need you to check out. It may put some excitement in your day." Mark explains the situation to Fred and asks for help.

Sam and Ann hold hands as they leave the car. Sam sees an older black Chevy parked on the street next to Max's house as he walks.

Sam stops, takes a deep breath and exhales noisily before continuing. He staggers a little holding on to Ann for support as he walks to the front door. Sam rings the doorbell. The knot in his stomach is back.

He sees Max stare at him with sad eyes when the door opens. His eyes seem dark and sunken. Behind Max, a dark man is standing with a large black revolver pointed at Peggy's head.

"Come in Sam and Ann," an unfamiliar voice beckons them from behind Max. They hesitate but Max motions them inside. Sam steps inside and then he cautiously steps to the window next to the door. He moves the curtain aside to look out at the street.

"Get away from the window!" the man shouts.

"Is that your car out front?" Sam asks, leaving the curtain askew.

"Yes. I will soon replace it with a new one." The man lets Peggy sit down in a chair and sees her begin weeping. He waves Sam toward the dining room table.

Sam moves through the living room with Ann behind him. He watches her barely make it to a chair and collapse there.

The man looks strangely familiar to Sam but he cannot determine who he is. *This is not Arturo.* Sam thinks seeing the man's dark complexion and nearly black hair. His dark gray suit looks rumpled and his shirt is open three buttons down revealing a hairy chest. The man continues talking.

"You wonder who I am Sam."

"You look a little familiar." Sam says. He turns to Max for a second and mimes "STALL!" to Max before looking back at the man.

"I am Bruno. My friends Arturo and Carl are dead because of you. I feel you are responsible for that!"

Sam sits across from Bruno. Max plops down next to Peggy.

"Why are we responsible? How did you know we were back in the USA? We just flew in last night."

"Ah, I've been watching and waiting for your return. Of course, Don called me too. He wants you and Sam to transfer the five million to his account in Italy. He will stay in Gioia Tauro to see what he can do to the Bellasettas. The money will help a lot."

"Not five million. The reward was only one million." Sam says.

"Don't lie! I know it is five. I know why too! The Bellasettas want to clear their conscience but they never can. Arturo told me everything about them! You gave money to Sam, Ann, and Peggy this morning too. We need to transfer it all to Don Cresto. I will watch with my gun on your lovebirds.

Max says, "You are not entitled to that money. I won't do that!"

"I will kill your women one at a time if you don't, Max. I will start with Peggy now!"

"Okay, okay. We can do that... but I think we each have to sign a form at the bank for such a large transfer. Since you have control... please tell Sam how Don Cresto knew what we were doing every step of the way. Tell him how that was all possible. Sam is curious to a fault!"

"I already told you. Why should I tell him?"

"Not for me, for my friends Sam and Ann. This has been a mystery for some time now for them. They want to know."

Sam edges closer to Bruno hoping to kick his gun away. He casually slides forward in his chair but Bruno instinctively leans back, moving too far away for Sam to reach the gun. He sees Bruno pause for a few seconds and then face Max.

"I will tell your friend only because it is fun to see how you react and it does not matter to keep it secret anymore." Bruno says looking smug. "I am a private eye by trade as well as Arturo... was. We both specialize in surveillance. Don's Papa Sal told him about the diamond in your attic. Their Papa was very sick. In fact, he is now dead. Cancer you know. He still was smoking cigarettes even though it was killing him. Why do people do that?" Bruno waves off any answer and continues his tale.

"No matter, Papa told Don and Arturo about the diamond in the attic. Don tried to buy this house several times. He offered Max far more than the house is worth. What is wrong with you Max! Why you not sell? That would have been the clean way for everyone. You refused. You said you would think about selling."

"That was not good enough. He wanted to get the diamond and sell it so his Papa would know they did that before he died. His Papa wanted to give half the money to his friend's family in Italy if Don could find some relatives and then split the rest with Arturo."

"What friend - you mean Tony Albero!" Sam asks.

"Yes of course!"

"Sal killed Tony."

"It was love only. Tony was his friend!"

"I don't understand. Well please first tell me how did Don book on our flight? How did he know we flew back yesterday?"

"Arturo was brilliant. Let me tell you why!"

Chapter Forty-Four

"Arturo first put a bug in the living room so maybe he could hear something and blackmail Max into selling."

"A bug in the living room doesn't answer the question. Max booked our flight home in Italy. A house bug would not have heard that." Sam cautiously raises an open hand toward Bruno.

"You are correct Sam." Bruno gestures back at him.

"Arturo did originally plant a bug in the living room for Don. It transmits to a unit outside that he could access from the internet."

"It was when Arturo and Don came here while you were at a concert. Arturo put malware on Max's laptop while Don was in the attic. Don could not get to the diamond because Arturo became sick just after installing the bug on the computer. The bug works very well. Max's computer sends what is said to Arturo's laptop through the internet."

"Good God! You can do that?" Sam is appalled.

"Yes and Arturo was shocked when he heard you talking about the diamond you accidentally found in the attic. He was outraged. Arturo wanted to storm the house and take the diamond then but that would start a huge investigation. He heard Max wanted to return the diamond to the Bellasetta thieves in Italy!"

"Then the Bellasettas took possession here and gave you the money. Arturo planned to take the money from you here, but then he died. Something happened to Don when that happened. He heard you were flying to Italy for that celebration. He and Carl got on the same flights and called his friends in Italy for help. The rest is history."

"So then he was going to force us to give up the money or kill us but it's easier to do that in Italy..."

"Yes, the plan was to kidnap the girls. Don took Arturo's laptop with him to Italy since as you know, Arturo passed."

"I just found out."

"Then the unfortunate incident with the shootout left Don unable to do much for days. The laptop still recorded any time you talked about anything. Did you know he could also tell where you are from the GPS program built into your laptop? Don stayed informed of where you were. He knew what flights you booked to Rome and when you came back here."

"That's crazy! I thought Max was safe using the internet to book. I know his laptop has the latest antivirus software, the most expensive one!" Sam says still in awe.

"Arturo's malware bypasses antivirus programs. Don is still tracking you today. I am very sad that my friend Carl died too but at least I can give Don some comfort when I get the money for him. Why you had to return the diamond to the Bellasettas is a mystery. Arturo had a buyer in Miami willing to pay ten million dollars!"

"Ten million!" Sam gulps.

"Yes! With some haggling, I am sure someone would pay even more. That diamond is priceless!" Bruno gets visibly angry.

"Five million is a pretty hefty sum to give to Don don't you think? What is your cut?" Sam asks.

"I get half a million, ten percent."

"We did the right thing returning the diamond to its real owner!"

"You're crazy!" Bruno rants louder.

"You did not return it to a rightful owner. The Bellasettas are crooks and murderers! Miguel junior bought that diamond with drug money - the blood of others! The Albero family should be the rightful owner of the diamond and the money now! Did you ever wonder why their Papa Sal robbed the Bellasetta house? Did you know why Tony killed Miguel Junior? Do you wonder why we would not deal with those crooks?"

"Not for sure but maybe you're a crook too!" Sam pushes his luck trying to keep Bruno talking.

"I may be a crook but the Bellasettas are worse, much worse! Miguel ruined many lives including that of Sal's friend Tony. They murder people to get what they want! I am surprised they did not have you all killed here and just take the diamond from your dead bodies!"

"Gustavo seems like a nice man... The whole family seems nice. They were extremely generous and accommodating toward us. Miguel Junior was the only bad person. You base all your accusations upon the works of one man." Sam says hoping Bruno would lean just a little closer to him.

"Maybe the others are but Miguel Junior was a rotten apple! Let me tell you what happened." Bruno pauses a moment to calm down. His gun hand begins to shake a little as he prepares to explain what happened.

Outside the house at 812 Clifton Street, a black van silently rolls to a stop. The lead man Matt Garner stretches his tall body outside the van. He feels the excitement of a possible confrontation as he checks the tightness of his Alpha Elite vest wrapped around his chest. He stands outside the van and watches his four men in black suits surround the house. Matt hears his ear bud click and the man on the front porch talks.

"There is only the one gap in the curtain by the front door. All the other windows are covered." The man in black tells Matt.

"Get a scope there. See if you can pick up sound and video from inside." Within a minute, a man with a small periscope peeks through the window. He reports again to Matt through his headset.

"There is only the one man holding a gun on the others. They have him talking Sargent. He was calm but now he is getting excited. He's saying something about worst criminals."

"Not good... Get two men at the door in case we have to rush in." Matt says and hears another man cut in.

"The perimeter is clear. Nothing else going on we can see."

"If he looks like he's going to shoot, or relaxes his aim we need to break in. We may not have a choice."

"Yes sir, we need him to relax that gun just a little."

"Give me a signal if you see an opportunity. The chance he will shoot someone is lower if he is not pointing at someone."

"It looks like he is relaxing now Sargent."

Chapter Forty-Five

Bruno keeps talking. He feels compelled now to let Sam know everything. "Miggy was the worst of all criminals! Their Papa Sal worked for the Bellasettas but more specifically as a house guard. Don and Arturo were young children just starting in school there. Papa Sal knew of several dirty deals Miguel junior did. He thought the old man Miguel senior was in on it. Then his friend Tony Albero told Sal about the drug dealing and the murder of his father."

"Yes, but Sal killed Tony Albero!" Sam shouts at Bruno.

"Let me explain that... but why I should bother I don't know."

"You want to clear the conscience of Arturo and Don and their father as well." Sam offers.

"Yes, maybe it is time everyone knows what happened back then. Tony's Papa would have lived comfortably if he had accepted Miggy's bribe. Miggy offered Franco huge money for each shipment brought in, if he would stay quiet about the drugs. Franco said no. What else could he do? He was an honest man."

"Did Franco turn up dead?"

"Yes, but how do you know that? You've stalled me enough."

"So now you think you should get the money?"

"Yes Sam, I think it is time to transfer the money. You all have online access. Let's try to transfer money from the laptop."

"Answer this please. Why did Sal choose to come here?"

"One last answer Sam is all I give. Sal and Tony wanted to live in America. Now, get the laptop Max!"

"Please one more thing. Why did Sal kill Tony? I read that he caught Tony with his girlfriend. How did he feel so strongly about a woman to cause him to kill his lifetime friend?"

"It was a jealous rage. Sal was going to marry Pia! I need to get the money!" Bruno waves the gun at the laptop in Max's hands.

"Some friends! Where were Don and Arturo?"

"Donny and Arturo came home after school that day and found the bodies. Several foster parents raised them. Now shut up!" Bruno shakes the gun at Sam upset recalling what Arturo told him. Bruno raises his gun to scratch the side of his face about to speak when the front door bursts open and two men in black storm in.

"Police! Drop the gun!" One man shouts. Ann screams. Sam kicks at Bruno's gun but misses. Bruno fires a shot blindly missing everyone. The men return fire. Four loud pops ring out and the gunfight is over. Bruno slumps to the floor.

Sam looks at Bruno's unseeing eyes staring at him. Blood is gushing from several parts of Bruno's body. He knows the man he just talked to is already dead.
"Is everyone okay?" Matt Garner shouts entering the room with another man. Ann buries her head in Sam's chest and squeezes his sides. Peggy and Max huddle together. Everyone nods for Matt. Then Matt sees Fred Holland walk into the dining room.

"Hello Max, Sam, Ann... Matt told me what was going on. I decided to come here. We will need statements from all of you." Fred watches one of the men pick up Bruno's gun.

"You're lucky to have Mark trust you so much. I would have trouble believing your story from anyone else. Who holds people for ransom in their own house?" Fred reaches down to check Bruno's pulse.

"Yeah, he's gone. I just wanted to check that myself." He explains to a man in black and looks at Max.

"They were able to look inside from the one curtain pulled aside. Matt's man Tom found a small gap in that front window curtain. He used a special periscope to look into the dining room. He really had no choice when he saw and heard what was going on. I am sorry this guy is dead. I would've loved to interview him."

"We are lucky he was in a talky mood. He chatted right up until the men stormed in." Max says.

Max sits in the living room with Fred and his assistant as a man begins taking pictures of the body and surrounding area. Fred takes statements from everyone. Max is the last to talk. The coroner takes several pictures of the scene. Eventually some men remove the body. Flashing red and blue lights are still everywhere outside.

"It's thirteen hundred hours. I think that's a wrap on the statements. We'll be going." Fred tells Max.

"Thank you Captain Holland. You saved our lives."

"It's our job Max." Fred Holland waves a hand at Max.

"Are we all free to go now?"

"I see no reason to hold any of you." Fred nods an okay as he walks out the front door.

"Thanks Captain." Max turns to look at Peggy and

the others. "How are you guys doing?"

Sam shook his head. "My nerves are shot but I feel relieved."

"Me too," Peggy says. Ann nods her head.

"Okay, then I'm starved! Let's go somewhere." Max says.

"Wait a minute, what about your front door? We can't just leave it like this!" Sam shouts.

"Right, Sam. I think I can just push the frame back together and pound some nails in it or something. This poor house has had too many break-ins!" Max trots off and comes back with a drill and a bag of drywall screws. He pushes the doorframe together and secures it with several screws. It looks bazaar to Sam but it is a good temporary fix.

"I bought these screws to put up some privacy fence in the back. They sure came in handy again."

"Very creative, you should maybe paint the screw heads and just leave it that way." Sam says.

"Maybe I will. That should hold it." Max says admiring his work.

"Where should we go now?" Sam heads for the door.

"Okay, there's a good Chinese place two streets over."

"No problem, we can go in the van. I'll drive."

"Of course! I need to get out of this house. It's giving me the creeps now." Ann grabs Sam's arm as she walks out the door with the others.

Chapter Forty-Six

Sam goes out the front door with Ann and walks around to the minivan with Max and Peggy. Before Sam starts the engine, all the danger catches up with him. He leans into the steering wheel and takes a deep breath.

"Are you okay? You look pale." Ann says.

"I'll be okay. It's all these things that have happened. I just need to regroup. You could have been killed if Bruno had been a better shot!"

"But he wasn't and I'm not shot. Bruno did not shoot anyone. You are supposed to be my tower of strength. I couldn't get along anymore without you." She stretches her arm behind his back and snuggles against him.

"I'm alright now. Let's hope Don Cresto stays in Italy."

"I thought he was dead until we met Bruno."

"If luck is with us, he will die in Italy. I'm ready for some food. I'm really starving!" Sam smiles, but his stomach is in knots.

"Yes." Max says as Sam drives to the restaurant.

After ordering food, Max makes a statement. "At least three people have died in my house. I'm sure I need to sell it now. It has bad Karma!"

"The bad Karma is dead now." Peggy says.

"Yeah but I'll always remember. I can't erase my memory. I don't think I can stay there anymore."

"You and Peggy are welcome to shack up in our place until you feel better. Is that alright with you Ann?" Sam asks.

"Yes. I understand how you feel Max."

Peggy leans against a nodding Max. "Well I'm relieved Max. I was hoping you didn't want to sleep there tonight."

"At least we know Arturo and Bruno are dead and Don is stuck in Italy so we have little to worry about. I'll still have trouble living there with all the memories of what has happened." Max says.

While he eats, Max calls Mark thanking him from everyone. He talks a long time between munching on his food that is cooling down explaining what happened. He tells Mark about the diamond, the pursuers, and the flight to Rome, the remarkable Bellasettas estate, and Bruno holding them at gunpoint. Mark is impressed that they are still alive. Max says they need the rest of the week off, and next week for the cruise, to recuperate from all the strain and stress. Mark reluctantly agrees before he says goodbye.

"Thank God, we're through with that diamond at last! Now we have to figure out what to do with all this money."

Since the house is somewhat secure, they spend the rest of the afternoon grocery shopping to stock the refrigerator at Sam's apartment.

Peaks and valleys Sam thinks to himself remembering his dangerous trip to Jamaica with Max. *The end of another near death experience but this time I have a wad of money to show for it.*

"I know we got all this food, but I'd like to head for

the beach. I know a neat little Bistro there. It's five now, we can have an early dinner." Max says nudging Sam.

"Sounds good to me. Let's go."

"I think I know the place." Sam says walking out of the apartment. He drives to the beach and finds a parking spot near Topy's Café.

As Sam approaches the café, it looks as beach-worn as ever to him with the same old faded red and yellow sign outside. He finds a table on the back patio jutting over the beach. Sam dines with the others enjoying a gentle breeze that sweeps across the patio.

After dinner, Sam strolls along the shoreline with Ann and the others, his shoes and socks and shirt in hand, enjoying the ocean and the late afternoon sun warming his bare back.

"Well we made it, my love." Sam says. He digs his feet in the sand and feels a cool wave roll over his ankles.

"I love to hear the waves pound the shore and feel the sand between my toes." Ann says holding on to Sam's arm as she walks.

"The knot in my stomach is finally going away. Gustavo's man said Don has bad wounds. He could die, even though he was able to call Bruno. He has to be broke. I think the last of our worries is stuck in Italy."

"We have each other too. I'm excited about the cruise Sam. Thanks to all that money we have our own luxury cabin to relax in." Ann smiles at Sam and tilts up, kissing him on the cheek.

"This has been another thrilling adventure with Max.

But this time I came away with some money!"

"Yes. I think we are all ready for a relaxing cruise."

"I never spent so much on a vacation. Let's hope it's not blah!"

The night passes into morning in the Fort Lauderdale apartment and all is quiet. Ann and Sam are reading the morning paper in the kitchen as Max cooks ham and cheese omelets in the kitchen. Peggy cheerfully bounces into the kitchen from the living room.

"Good morning!" She shouts carrying Max's laptop. "Hey, I just looked at our suites for our cruise! I think we'll love them. They are huge!" Peggy is still bouncing up and down a little as she talks. Then she looks at Sam. The dark circles under her bright blue eyes are gone.

"Have we hugged yet?"

"No... I don't think so." Sam stands up just to give her a big hug.

"I need a hug too," Ann says. She stands up and gently pushes Peggy aside so she can grab on to Sam.

"What a great way to start the day."

"We have the whole day to ourselves Peggy. Sam wants us to go to Marcy's Café for lunch. He wants us to do something 'normal' if that is possible." Ann says.

"Sounds like something to do after we shop. Let's go shopping!"

"I'm a happy man!" Sam says. He feels at home again. The knot in his stomach is nearly gone. He can smell the omelets cooking and the coffee brewing. He smiles and sits down again.

Max begins whistling flipping the last omelet in the frying pan.

"Wow Max, you're whistling a Danglebatts tune!" Peggy says.

"Yeah, they're not so bad. I kind of enjoyed the concert after all." He stands next to the stove looking at the frying pan. He stops whistling to answer his phone ringing.

"Hello… Gustavo. Hey we all thank you for…" Max pauses listening in silence. He stops flipping the omelet.

"Thank you Gustavo." Max rings off and stares at the phone.

"What did he want? He isn't taking back the money is he?" Sam asks.

Max pauses for a moment and says, "No… The money is fine. It's worse than that." Max pauses to take a deep breath.

"He told me the Paidos Medical Center in Gioia Tauro treated Don Cresto for bullet wounds but he left unexpectedly. However, the nurse recognized Cresto's friend. Gustavo's men found Don's friend Angelino Petroni. He has a bullet wound in his shoulder. Petroni talked after interrogation saying Don Cresto now has a false passport and a lot of money. Angelino said Don is in route to America. Angelino took Don to the airport, but has no idea of when he will arrive in the USA."

"Oh my God, then he's still alive!" Ann cries.

Chapter Forty-Seven

"Cresto can't do anything Ann! They probably gave him a temporary patch job. He may not survive if he makes it here." Sam says.

"Gustavo requested the hospital call him instead of the police. He wanted to deal with Cresto without the police involved. The hospital called Gustavo but he could not get anyone there in time. Cresto vanished again!"

"Cripes!"

"Don Cresto is in critical condition. The nurse at the hospital said and they were going to admit him as a patient and expected him to be there for a few days but he left. The good thing is she recognized Don's friend Angelino."

"The nurse should have called the police! Cresto should go after the Bellasettas instead of us. He knows it is Miguel junior who ruined his dad's life and not us!" Ann says feeling Sam hug her.

"Yeah but we are a much easier target than the Bellasettas! We have the money from the diamond too. That's why he is after us." Max's sees his last omelet is smoking and black in the pan.

"Damn!" He dumps the omelet in the trash.

"I'm not hungry." Ann says. She sinks into her chair.

"We'll split them." Max says setting the omelets on the table.

"No I'll just have some fruit." Ann bends her head to say prayers as usual.

"Well I hope he tries to attack the Bellasettas before he comes here and I hope the Bellasettas finish the job this time!" Sam feels the knot in his stomach tighten up again.

"I think we have to go on with life as if he doesn't exist anymore. We should notify the police to be on the lookout for Cresto. Maybe he can't get plane fare back to the US anyway." Max tries to sound confident but his voice lacks its usual confidence.

"He wouldn't get a fake passport if he didn't have a way to fly back here." Sam says and eats his breakfast in silence after that. Suddenly the nightmare is in his mind again. He feels the money is siphoning the life from him and Ann.

"I still vote for shopping." Peggy says. "What the heck, we might as well enjoy shopping while we are still alive!"

Ann sinks back down in the chair after just getting up.

"Joking Ann, I was joking!" Peggy says with a nervous laugh.

"Shopping, you want to shop with this hanging over our heads?"

"Yes it'll take our minds off of this creep."

"Go Ann. Try not to think of Cresto." Sam urges.

"Well, okay. Let me get my hat. You know my car is at Max and Peggy's house." Ann realizes.

"I'll take us back there." Sam says. Sam and his friends head for Max's house to see what they can do. Sam drives mostly in silence until he parks in the carport again at Max's house.

"Go ahead and take your car Ann." He sees Ann and

Peggy switch to Ann's car as he and Max walk to the house. Peggy and Ann leave to go shopping.

Max suddenly turns to Sam as they walk. "You know we've been through a lot Sam. I think of you as more than a friend. You're like a real brother to me... the brother I never had!" Max is nearly in tears as he grips Sam's shoulder. After an awkward pause, Sam clears his throat to speak.

"Yes we're still standing Max and we are adopted brothers, you and me!" Sam grips Max on the shoulder too. Then he releases his grip and smiles realizing how close the two of them really are for each other as he walks silently to the front door.

Inside they see the yellow police tape still in the dining room. The paddle fan is still on the floor in the spare bedroom, but their heart is not in to working on the fan. They stare at it for a moment.

"Maybe I can get someone to install the fan for me." Max says.

"That might be a better idea Max. Let's swing down the ladder. I want to get the tools I left up there."

Sam climbs up the ladder again and lifts himself into the attic. He sees the extra tarps Cresto left behind as he crawls out on the beams and retrieves the wire and tools. Sam looks again at the lifted up insulation where he found the diamond. He carefully covers the bare spot with insulation again before coming back out of the attic. He folds the ladder and pushes it back up to the ceiling.

"I guess we just relax now until we go to Marcy's" Sam says.

"I have what we need right now. I bought some in

the Bahamas."

Max retrieves two Cuban cigars from a humidor in the living room. He motions Sam to go outside to the front porch. Max settles into a rocking chair next to Sam and lights up the two cigars handing one to Sam. Max leans back in his chair before taking a quick puff.

"Peggy won't let you smoke in the house?"

"True, Sam. Now as Jack Nicholson would say, 'There's nothing quite like a good Cuban cigar'" Max draws in and puffs another small cloud of smoke. He sees Sam do the same.

"Good cigar Max."

"You know I don't think I can live here anymore Sam."

"Of course you can stay as long as you want at our apartment. We have the spare bedroom. Peggy and Ann get along just fine and..."

"I know that Sam. I'll put the house on the market tomorrow. Peggy and I can store our stuff in a pod until we can find a new home."

"You're serious. You want to leave this house?" Sam puffs again.

"I'm selling as soon as the tape comes down." Max sends out another puff of smoke. "You know I should have bought a box of Toscano cigars in Italy."

"What does Peggy think, about the house I mean?"

"All that sentimental crap is gone now. She says this house gives her the creeps now. She'll move back in with her mother if I stay here." Max puffs on his cigar blowing a perfect circle of smoke.

"If I were you I would not let that happen."

"I won't. As much as I like this old place, I really

think it has bad Karma Sam. I hope I can find a block house with extra tall ceilings like this place."

"Good luck on that." Sam remarks. Sam stays silent with Max enjoying the fine cigar and the company of his best friend until it is time to go to Marcy's.

Chapter Forty-Eight

At noon Max and Sam, meet the girls in Marcy's parking lot. Sam admires Ann in her yellow dress with a yellow wide-brimmed hat blocking the sun from her smiling face. The bright sun makes Ann's dress seem to be alive with color. Peggy is clad in a hot pink dress. They group together and enter the restaurant.

"¡Hola!" Max shouts as he walks inside and sees Marcy.

"¡Hola! Max!" Marcy answers Max and races toward him surprisingly fast for an older heavy-set Cuban woman.

"Wow! What hot ladies you have with you!" Marcy flaps her hands at them and smiles.

"Marcy this is Peggy and Ann, and you know Sam. I want you to meet them." Max says pointing to the girls. He watches the girls chat with Marcy and shake hands.

Sam interrupts Max. "We are trying to get back to normal Marcy. Do you still have that great clam chowder? It's the best clam chowder in the world!"

"Of course! I always keep that for you." She laughs a little.

"Well I'm glad you have some. My mouth is watering already."

"Yes we have, you get whatever you want. You stay and eat! I like your new girlfriend Sam. She is not like your old one. She's a happy person."

"I'm happy and lucky." Ann says.

"Hey Sam!" Chet Hatter shouts from across the dining room.

"Chet?" Sam says walking to his friend from the Danglebatts.

"It's a small world Sam. This is one of our favorite hangouts."

"Hello Katie. What's the baby's name?" Sam barely remembers Chet's wife and sees she has their new baby with them.

"Hello Sam. This is Chester named after Chet's father."

"So what's new Chet? Are you still with the band?"

"Yeah, they can't live without me. Katie is okay with it, but her favorite neighbor is moving out. Casey and Katie used to do stuff together. Now she is moving out with Brad and selling the house."

"So the house next to you is on sale?"

"Yes. You know someone who wants to buy their house?"

"If not me, maybe Max would. He's had some trouble with his house. Does the house have tall ceilings?"

"Yes, ten foot ceilings. Tell me what happened."

Sam updates Chet on all the events including the five million paid by the Bellasettas and the trouble with the Crestos. The last problem Sam finally talks about is why Max wants to sell his house.

"He's looking for a house with tall ceilings." Sam concludes.

"Wow. I had no idea you guys were having all this trouble. I know Brad and Casey would be happy to show the place to you and or Max. It is a lot smaller than our place but a lot less money too. I think it's around a half mil."

"Not bad. Well, let me get back to my group. I'll be

in touch." Sam returns to his cooling clam chowder and his friends.

"Max, we need to go to Lux Lane." Sam says smiling.

After lunch the girls decide to go back to the mall and shop some more. Sam follows Chet back to Lux Lane to show Max the neighbor's house. Then he drives back to 812 Clifton Street.

"I have to pack a few more things."

"That house on Lux Lane is almost as big as this place. It has the tall ceilings you want and it's a concrete-block house. What say Max?"

"I have to think about that Sam. Thanks for everything. See you later."

Sam heads back to his apartment. At four o'clock Ann comes in carrying two bags full of stuff she bought. A big Macy's bag has smaller bags inside it. The other bag has more groceries.

"You look like you had a good time." Sam says eyeing the bags.

"Oh yes. The last thing we did is more grocery shopping and then I dropped Peggy off at her place. She and Max are packing up some stuff. I hope she'll be alright in that house." Ann sets the bags down and plops on the couch.

"You look worried." He says turning the volume down on the TV.

"I can't get Don Cresto out of my mind."

"I have the same thoughts. The Bellasettas failed to wipe out Don the first time. I know if they got another chance they would succeed!"

"You want them to kill him? I hate to wish that on

anyone!"

"Sometimes it's better if things happen you know."

"I guess so... Now, what have you planned to do with all your money? You're not going to leave me now that you're a rich man are you?"

"I have very few plans for the money. I say I am stuck on you!"

"I'd say I'm stuck on you too!" She leans against Sam. He turns her head toward him and gives her a passionate kiss.

"I like that! There is not much to do until seven or so. Let's forget about Cresto and the Bellasettas for now." Sam says smiling.

"I can stash away the stuff later." Ann scoots over to Sam on the couch and snuggles up to him.

"Now you're talking!" Sam says. He wraps his arms around her as an ad from Carnival Cruise Lines comes on expressing the virtues of going on a relaxing cruise.

"We will be there soon." Ann smiles as Sam turns off the TV. She kicks off her shoes to relax.

"I'm ready for that cruise." Sam squeezes Ann and smiles but his eyes are tired. Outside a sudden storm pelts the balcony with rain and he hears a low rumble of thunder. Sam always likes to nap during the rain. He slouches over and dozes off into dreamland.

In his dreams the old expression time flies when you are having fun seems to come true for Sam. He finds himself sailing out of Fort Lauderdale on the ocean liner Carnival Freedom. Ann and he are settling in their room when someone knocks on the door. Sam opens up and sees Don Cresto pointing a gun at him.

Don is wearing bloodstained clothes he wore in Italy. His face distorts with pain. His hand is shaking as he waves the gun motioning Sam to back up.

"Get inside! Call Max. Have him come here."

Ann shrieks. Sam is dumbfounded. *Don knows we are on a cruise! How did he get to America?* Sam backs up inside the cabin. Don follows him inside and closes the door.

"Call Max!" he shouts again.

Sam dials Max's room. Max answers after a few rings.

"What do you want? Peggy and I are about to go up on deck to watch the shoreline go away."

"You dumb ass, you are supposed to come here first so we could all go up there together."

"Oh yeah, we'll be right there." Max responds after a moment.

"Let's get there before the view is gone you dumb ass."

"I got it, I got it. See you in five you dumb ass." Max replies.

Max remembered the code words. Sam silently mumbles.

"I want that money! You must give me the money." Don shouts.

"How are we going to do that on the ship?" Sam asks.

"Never mind how, just get Max here so I can get the money."

"He said he will be here in a few minutes. Let's just relax." Sam sits next to Ann on the couch waiting for Max to come over.

Sam hears a knock on the door. He opens it and two

men storm in with guns blazing. He sees Don Cresto jerk from the bullets hitting and drop to the floor. Then Sam feels a sharp pain in his chest. *Good grief Cresto shot me!*

Ann is screaming, "Oh no! Oh no!"

Sam feels her cradle his head in her hands as he sinks to the floor. As his eyes close, he hears one of the gunmen talking.

"This guy is dead too. Let's throw them both over-board."

"I'm not dead!" Sam shouts. He feels someone shake him.

"Wake up love. I know you're not dead!"

Chapter Forty-Nine

"I hate this! I dreamed I was shot on the cruise ship!"

"I know a psychiatrist friend…" Ann pauses then continues. "I think you should see him tomorrow."

"There's nothing wrong with me! I only have these crazy dreams when I have death looming over me. It's just this Don Cresto thing now. It's bothering me a lot."

"But Sam, none of us have these nightmares. Not yet anyhow."

"I should call Gustavo. I want to know if he's found Cresto."

"Maybe you should, but wait until morning. Six o'clock here is midnight there."

"Right! I guess there's nothing I can do until morning."

They settle together on the couch and watch some news. Max calls Sam at six forty-five reminding him of their dinner date.

"It's time to go my love." Sam tells Ann and slips into his shoes. Driving a few minutes later, he calls Max when he is a few blocks away from the house. When Sam pulls into the carport, he sees Max and Peggy sitting in lounge chairs in the carport. Max opens the rear door of the minivan.

"I would have rung the doorbell. You didn't have to sit outside."

"Peggy had trouble staying inside, even with me here."

"Sorry… Let's forget about all this for a while." Sam says.

"Yes, I don't think there's anything spooky inside

the van. Next stop is Café del Mar! Dinner is on me!" Max says as he gets in the van.

"Sounds like a lobster night!" Sam says backing up the minivan.

The meal at the Café del Mar is excellent and the service unmatched. They chat, eat and drink and by nine thirty after consuming some wine, they leave.

"I think you and Peggy should stay at our place again."

"What say Peg?"

"I think we need to settle our nerves and stay at Sam's a little longer."

"Okay lovey. Okay with you Ann?" Max asks.

"It's fun having you there. No problem Max."

Sam carefully drives back. He feels a little inebriated as he enters the apartment. He goes right to the kitchen, pours four glasses of red wine, and brings out the drinks. He makes another toast to their success. After some chitchat, they retire to the bedrooms.

It is barely eleven when Sam closes the door to his bedroom. He makes a mental note as he crawls in bed to call Gustavo in the morning. He must find out the status of Don Cresto hoping the Bellasettas have heard something by now. Thinking about that settles his mind. He sleeps quietly through the night.

Max is already in the kitchen at eight o'clock in the morning when Ann and Sam come out of the bedroom. Max has mixed up some batter and is just starting to cook pancakes. Peggy is setting the table with knives and forks. She has already set a bottle of molasses and a bottle of honey on the table.

Ann walks to the refrigerator. "I want some blueberries with the pancakes. I'll get them."

Peggy approaches Sam as he enters the kitchen.

"Have we hugged yet?" She grins at him.

"No... I don't think so." he gives her a big hug.

"Me too," Ann sets the blueberries on the table and hugs Sam.

"You guys..." Max says. "Just sit and eat!"

Sam calls Gustavo shortly after breakfast. He sees it is nearly nine o'clock so it would be about three o'clock in the afternoon in Italy. He turns on his phone speaker after he dials the number. Gustavo answers on the third ring.

"Pronto!"

"Hello Gustavo," Sam says.

"How are you Sam?"

"We are alive and kicking."

"Bene! We are also well."

"Gustavo I want to know if you found out any more about Don Cresto. Is he really coming to the USA?"

"He has bad wounds in his side and shoulder according to the nurse at the hospital. They gave him blood, antibiotics, a pain pill and patched him in the hospital but the nurse said he needs more attention. As you know, he has a factious passport. We have located the man who made it but he fails to give us Don's new name. Other than that, we have not heard from him or been able to locate him."

"This is not good that you have not heard from him."

"As I told Max, as soon as we were told he was at the hospital, we sent men to hold him but he was already gone when our men got there. He was supposed to stay in the hospital to heal. He has old friends here as well. I suspect he will travel to the USA. It is only a matter of time until we find where he is if he stays here. If we find him, we will have him arrested for something. I am not sure on what charges but he will not be going to America if we find him. I can guarantee that."

"Thank you so much Gustavo. Good luck! Please keep in touch!"

"Be careful my friends. I cannot imagine he will be sneaking back to America, but anything is possible these days. We are doing what we can here. We are on full alert. If he shows up here we will take care of him."

"If he shows up here, I hope we can do the same."

Sam says goodbye and rings off. *There's no way he could travel back to the US in his condition, could he?* The knot in Sam's stomach tightens again.

Chapter Fifty

Gustavo's two men arrive at the hospital a short while after Don and Angelino have left. One of the two men talks with the nurse who tended to Don Cresto.

"I know the man with this Don Cresto." She says. "His name is Angelino. I cannot remember his last name. He was here not long ago for a foot injury." She frowns but after looking through the files, she finds his information and gives it to one of Gustavo's men.

"Angelino Petroni. Let's go!" The two men rush to their car and race toward Angelino's house. It takes longer than it should to find the little house since they are unfamiliar with the area. Finally, they stop out front and after rapping on the door, Camilla answers.

"We must talk with Angelino Petroni." The first man says.

"He is not here. He left and I do not know where he went."

"Please have him call us." The man hands Camilla his card before the two men exit. Outside, they park a short distance from the house and wait.

Don Cresto winces with pain as he leaves the hospital and slides into the old tan truck. First Angelino drives to Kyle's and guarantees a large loan for Don. Next, he takes Don to his friend Gino who sells Don a new passport and ID. Gino fits Don with a light brown wig and takes photos for the ID's.

"Do I have to wear a wig?"

"It makes you harder to recognize." Gino says as he collects his cash.

"Yeah, yeah... Angelino, now take me to the airport!" The trip to the airport is long with an occasional bump in the road. A pothole and the lumpy seat just add to the pain in his side and in his shoulder. He swallows the last pain pill from Angelino. The temperature is cool outside but Don is sweating from the pain. He had Camilla wrap his side with several layers of gauze and two rolls of tape to cover any bleeding he may have. He still holds his side as Angelino drives toward the Reggio Calabria Airport.

"I think you are crazy to do this, less than a week since you were shot. My own wound is still heeling. Your wounds are much worse." Angelino says hearing Don groaning.

"The nurse gave me a shot to cure the infections and I will get pills for the pain. I will be fine Angie. I have my new passport and my airfare thanks to you. I must go. They must pay."

"You should leave it be, Donny. A silent divorce is sometimes better. I know we can get work for you after you recover. I have a friend here. He works a delivery business. He always can use help."

"No! You heard the recording. My last hope in Bruno failed. Now they are going on a cruise with my money!"

"So now it is your money?"

"Yours and mine Angie trust me. I will also split the money with the families of those who died. I will not forget all the help I have had. You will get much more than you make working."

"You remember the diamond was stolen Donny. It was not your father's diamond. Your health is more important old friend. I am worried you will die before you can get revenge or the money."

"I am a different man Angie. All my life I try to be the opposite of my father. Arturo was not always doing things for good but I always did. Yet look what happened. Please do not worry my friend about repaying Kyle. I have already gone online to request withdrawals from my investment accounts so Kyle will get his money and not come after you. It should be there when I get back and I will send it to you so you can pay Kyle. Once I get the money from Max and his friends, I'll repay my investment accounts."

"Don, I see a man in great pain."

"Just take me to the airport. I need to get to America. I need to get to Lauderdale in time to be on that cruise with them. I need to upset their plans permanently!"

On Thursday, Max and Peggy move back in their house. Max has done a lot. He had his doors replaced with steel doors and frames. He had someone install the paddle fan and he added a long overdue alarm system. The yellow tape is gone and no news about Cresto comes to disturb the calm. Additionally, Max contacted his realtor friend and put 812 Clifton Street up for sale. He also put a bid in to buy the house on Lux Lane.

In two days, Sam and Ann have paid off their vehicles. Sam paid off his parent's home and a small loan for Ann's church. He thinks maybe Don Cresto is stuck in Italy and probably will die there of his wounds. He still worries not knowing where Don Cresto is, but the knot in his stomach is easing up.

Eventually Friday night comes and Sam and Ann decide to meet at Max's house to play Hearts. They try to blank from their minds that Bruno died in the dining room. Peggy keeps all her clothes on. For whatever reason she seems more content not flaunting her body anymore.

"So what did you think about Brad and Casey's house?" Sam asks.

"I like it. We still have trouble sleeping here. We may become Chet's neighbor. I thought you might want to live there Sam."

"I have to get used to my new wealth. I'm still used to scrimping along. Maybe after a while I will move somewhere else."

They split the games. Max rechecks their reservations for the cruise.

"The reservations on the Conquest are in order. We depart on Sunday as scheduled."

Saturday they all stay at home packing and checking their bags in preparation for the cruise. The knot in Sam's stomach seems minor. He sleeps like a baby without any nightmare Saturday night.

Chapter Fifty-One

Sunday morning Sam and Ann are packed and ready to go on their first cruise. They check to be sure that they have their passports with them and their luggage has their room number tags firmly attached. It's a warm and rainy morning as Ann and Sam drive over to Max's house.

Sam is wearing tan shorts and a multi-colored tan shirt. Ann is wearing tan short-shorts and a light yellow halter-top. She has her blonde hair pulled back into a ponytail. Sam is happy just to glance at her as he drives. He parks the minivan in the carport to wait for Max.

Max and Peggy greet them carrying their luggage.

"I called a taxi. I think it's easier to have a cab drop us off at the dock."

"Okay. That's a good idea Max." Sam unloads their bags into the carport.

He looks at Peggy wearing about the same short-shorts and halter as Ann is except her clothes are pink.

"Have we hugged yet?" She says.

"No...I don't think so." He gives her a warm hug.

"Enough you two!" Max says shaking his head.

"Where is your laptop Max?" Sam asks.

"I'm leaving it home. The computer geek says he removed the virus, but I don't trust it now. I think I'll trade it in when we get back."

They wait a few minutes and a taxi drives by the house. Max whistles to him and waves. The taxi backs up brakes squealing and pulls alongside the carport. They barely are able to load all the bags in the trunk.

Max sits up front with the cabbie once again. Sam enjoys being sandwiched between Ann and Peggy. The girls have fun rubbing against him as they ride to the dock.

"You know I can only stand this for a few hours." Sam jests.

The taxi driver drops them off right in front of the terminal. The porters load their bags on a cart with a pile of other luggage. Max and Sam give the porter a generous amount of folding money and walk into the terminal with the girls.

Max has somehow paid someone because a woman in a Carnival uniform escorts him and the others to a special line. They have their pictures taken, register and receive their guest cards. They board the ship within twenty minutes.

The four of them go on board at the same time. According to Peggy, they have about the most expensive staterooms. After asking a crewmember what to do, they head for their rooms.

"Sam you and Ann are in 7440 port side right?"

"Yes. That's the left I think."

"Correct Sam! I'll make you a sailor one of these days. We're in 7445 on the starboard side. We just go to deck 7 and head aft."

"Right." Sam says and follows his friends into an elevator. Eventually they reach their rooms.

"Wow what a view!" Sam is in awe as he opens the door of the room. He sees a huge area with an ocean view through the glass wall that leads to a huge balcony. It is more like an open deck than a balcony. The room could easily sleep four people or more, but they have it all to themselves. It is much bigger than what Sam pictured in that bad dream he had a few days ago.

"This is lovely!" Ann says. She dances across the room and opens a glass door to the balcony.

Sam follows her onto the deck. It has a mostly glass low rail around the back, two lounge chairs and a small table waiting for them to relax in. Sam slinks into one of them. Ann sits down on the other one. He closes his eyes and listens to the sound of birds chirping and water sloshing against the ship. He hears a distant rumble of thunder.

"Ah, now this is relaxing! So this is how the rich people live. The ship sails at four. Maybe we should just lie back and enjoy the atmosphere until then." Sam is smiling as he leans back in his lounge chair. Then his phone rings.

"Hello Max."

"Hey, let's go get some chow!"

"We're relaxing on the balcony." Sam grumps.

"Aren't you hungry? Meet us up on the Lido deck... deck nine. That's where the buffet is. All the food you can eat and then some!"

"Okay, okay. See you there in ten minutes."

He sees Ann stretched out on her lounge chair, eyes closed and smiling. He touches her shoulder. She opens her eyes, yawns and smiles as he sees her flash her steel gray eyes at him.

"Max wants us to go eat."

"Um, I like it here."

"We need some lunch."

"Well, okay. Where do we go?"

"He says the Lido deck. There is a ship layout somewhere in the room. I told him we would meet him there in ten minutes."

"You guys! You spend all this money for a beautiful suite like this and all you want to do is eat."

"We have to eat my love."

"I suppose you're right." She reluctantly gets up from the lounge chair, pulls down on her short-shorts and gives him a quick kiss as she goes back into the cabin. Ten minutes later, they meet Max and Peggy.

The Lido deck is buzzing, the noise is deafening and people are everywhere all carrying plates, cups, or both. The whole area is full of occupied tables and people waiting for seats.

"This is incredible!" Sam is impressed seeing all the food and the mass of people. He searches for an empty table as Max is doing.

"You guys go get some food. I'll hold this table." Max shouts above the noise. He spots a couple leaving a window table on the port side of the ship and quickly claims it. He pulls out the black rubber spider from his back pocket and lays it on the table after pushing a used plate away.

"That will help me save the seats!"

"You brought the spider on the cruise? Nice!" Peggy frowns.

Max smiles and orders everyone to go to the buffet tables. He reexamines the fake spider lying on the table. He loves the ugly hairy spider and its beady red eyes. *I name thee Harry my spider friend. All this food is making me hungry Harry!*

"Excuse please." A crewmember says as he stacks

the used dishes to remove them and cleans the table.

"You like my spider?" Max asks but the man just smiles and leaves.

Max gets up quickly as soon as Sam returns with a plate full of food and a glass of apple juice. The girls are not back yet but Max stuffs the spider in his rear pocket and heads for the buffet line anyway.

Max quickly loads his plate full of a roasted chicken breast, mashed potatoes, a vegetable mix, a small slice of beef, and a roll. He dips out a small bowl of cream of mushroom soup before returning to the table just after the girls do. He makes idle talk between feasting.

"This whole cruise thing is a new and pleasant experience for me." Max says munching on his second plate of food.

They decide to stay on the Lido deck until sailing time. At quarter to four, Ann gets up to refill her glass of tea.

Max continues chatting. He notices the sky is dark.

"Hey, it's raining outside again."

"Oh yeah," Sam says, but he stands up when he sees Ann coming back to the table with a frightened look on her face. She barely keeps control of her shaking glass of tea holding it with both hands.

"What happened? You look like you've seen a ghost."

"I think I have! He's here! I saw him!" She sits down and nervously sets her drink on the table.

"Who did you see?" Sam asks rubbing her shoulder.

"I was filling my glass over there. He smiled at me! I saw Don Cresto!"

Chapter Fifty-Two

"I'll find him!" Sam shouts and rushes away from his seat. He zigzags his way across the room, dodging through a maze of people trying not to disturb anyone. He searches every area but sees no one resembling Don Cresto anywhere. One table near an exit has an abandoned plate of food. *Was Don Cresto there?* Sam thinks as he walks back to his table. He shrugs his shoulders.

"I didn't see him. Maybe you saw someone who looks like him."

"I think it's him but you may be right... I hope you're right!" Ann is on edge and her hand still shakes as she tries to drink her tea.

"Let's go out to the open deck area. Cresto was shot up just a few days ago. Do you really think he is here on our cruise?" Max says as he gets up.

"No, maybe you're right. Maybe I just imagined I saw him, a subconscious guilt." Ann seems to cheer up a little.

"Guilty of what? We are not the bad guys here." Sam says.

"I know but somehow I feel bad about Don Cresto."

They walk onto the open area of the Lido deck. People are already standing at the edge of the covered part of the deck leaning on the rails watching the final preparations before the ship sails.

Sam watches the birds flying around chirping over the water in a light rain that started. He hears clanging like bells on a lower deck. Being on board a cruise ship with several thousand other strangers is a very different experience for him.

Max goes to the bar and brings back four Budweiser beers. The foursome stand around chatting with other passengers watching the shore hands release the moorings.

A foghorn blasts exactly at four o'clock and the ship begins moving sideways. After sidling a safe distance from the dock, the ship moves forward away from Port Everglades. An announcement says their next stop will be the island of St. Maarten.

Sam turns to go back inside. He catches a glimpse of what looks like Don Cresto walking along the inside wall. The man walks around the edge of a wall and disappears before Sam can make a positive identification. Sam tilts over to Max's ear away from Ann.

"I think I just saw Don Cresto too!" Sam whispers.

Max continues to stare out at the ocean.

"How could that be? Even if he came back to America, how would he book on the same cruise as we did?" Max whispers back.

"I thought about that, just some assumptions you know." He whispers as quietly as he can with all the surrounding noises from the ship and other passengers.

"He knows his friend is dead, killed in your house! I think he still has Arturo's computer and he can hear what went on from your laptop. He heard of the cruise from your laptop so he came back to get the money in person. I think he booked whatever he could get on our cruise and wants the money or revenge for his brother's death."

"All possible I guess." Max whispers and feels Peggy nudge him.

"What are you two up to now? Are you planning some prank on the trip? The captain will have you thrown overboard!"

"It's nothing honey." Max squeezes Peggy and feels her shiver.

"This rainy wind is making me cold. I'm going to our cabin."

"I'll go with you Peg."

"Something's bothering you Max. What is it?" Peggy senses a problem as they walk away.

Sam knows Max will tell Peggy about his sighting so he decides to tell Ann. After Max and Peggy leave, he puts his arm around Ann. She snuggles up against him and smiles.

"I love you Ann. I need to tell you something."

"What is it? I'm getting cold here too." She still smiles at Sam.

"I think I saw Don Cresto too. I saw him a moment ago."

"Oh no! Then it is true! He is here!"

"I am almost sure it was Cresto but not positive. I think we need to go everywhere in pairs until we are sure it is not him on board."

"I can't believe this! How could he be on the same cruise with us?" Ann says. She listens to Sam's theory.

"My God! What do we do now?"

"Just stay close." The knot in his stomach tightens.

"Let's go stay in our room." Ann sobs.

Sam is on alert, his muscles are tense and his eyes examine everything along the way to their room. He expects to see Don Cresto somewhere but he sees no sign of him. He opens the stateroom door and sees their luggage neatly placed in their room.

"Good!" Sam locks the door before he unlocks his roll-around suitcase. He retrieves a bottle of Zinfandel wine.

"Let's have a drink and try to relax for now." He can tell Ann is overly worried as he opens the bottle and pours two glasses of wine.

"I can't relax right now." Ann says. Her sparkly gray eyes have dark shadows under them.

"It looks like the rain stopped. Let's go out on the balcony and sip wine for a while. It could take some of the tension away." Sam grabs a big towel and heads for the balcony. He waves a hand for her to follow and she reluctantly goes with him.

After Sam dries off the lounge chairs, Ann sets her glass on the table next to her and sits down on the edge of the chair. She cups her face with her hands and begins to weep. She feels Sam sit down beside her on the lounge chair and put his arm around her.

"It'll be alright. He will not ruin our cruise."

"He already has! He's going to kill us!"

"I hardly think so, but we'll think of some way to thwart him if he tries." Sam sounds confident but he has no idea of what to do next. He isn't completely sure Don Cresto is on the ship.

He sits with Ann for a while his arm on her back to comfort her. He feels her arm go around him and her kiss on his cheek. Cupping her face in his hands, he kisses her on the lips. He wraps his arms around her kissing her on the lips again and then on her neck.

Their passion grows as they work their way back into the room and onto the bed. Perhaps it is the feeling they may not live through the cruise and the danger that spurs them on. There in the semidarkness of the rainy afternoon they make love in Suite 7440.

Chapter Fifty-Three

Sam has never experienced a woman quite like Ann. He never truly was in love with any of the women he dated before Ann came into his life. Never before has he said to himself, "This person is different; special!" As he stretches out on the bed staring at the ceiling, he cannot imagine his life without Ann. For the moment, he thinks of nothing but Ann lying beside him. He turns his eyes toward Ann and sees her looking at him with her steel gray eyes.

"I love you." Ann whispers. She swings herself across him before getting up to shower off. Even though they are in one of the biggest suites, the shower stall is not big. They shower separately.

Sam sees rain pouring down on the deck area again as he walks out of the shower. He begins to towel off and sits down on the bed next to Ann. The phone rings. He looks at it for a couple rings wondering if this is Max or Don Cresto calling. Finally, he gives the phone a macho grab and says hello.

"Sam I have an idea." Hearing Max, Sam blows a sigh of relief.

"You think you have an answer to our problem?"

"Yeah, come to my room and we will discuss it."

"You can't tell me on the phone?"

"No, dumb ass, just come over here!"

The words hit like an uppercut to Sam's stomach. He feels his knees give out as the meaning of the words sink in. After a long pause, he responds.

"Okay Max, but the dumb ass just got out of the shower. We'll be over in a few minutes."

"Who is that on the phone?" Ann asks as she stands up combing her hair. She sees Sam's ashen face and losses her smile.

"That was dumb ass Max." He says. This time she recognizes the code words right away.

"Oh my God! He's really here! What are we going to do?"

"I don't know. I have to think. I said we were just out of the shower, which is true. We have a few minutes to plan something."

"Plan what?"

"I want to call the purser and maybe have the ship security show up with us. We need a plan of how to go in there with an element of surprise." He starts to reach for the phone but it rings again. Sam is puzzled as he answers it.

"Hello Sam... This is Don Cresto. The house cleaner is so kind. She let me in your room earlier. I am monitoring what you say. Do not call anyone or your friends die! I want you to know I let you have your fun time and your weak hope of calling the crew. Now that your fun time is over, you must come to Max's room right now. You and Ann come right now or I kill Peggy or maybe Max and then Peggy."

"You've been listening to us!"

"Oh yes. I enjoy just listening sometimes, thank you very much."

"That's creepy Cresto."

"You would be amazed at what I hear."

"Can I leave Ann here? She has nothing to do with this."

"You are both guilty! Come now or someone dies!"

"We will be over in a minute." He hangs up the phone.

"Well we aren't surprising him." Sam says aloud but then he whispers.

"We're bugged! Don Cresto obviously is using some of his brother's equipment to spy on us... or everyone."

"You mean he heard us..." Ann's face flushes as Sam nods.

"We'll have to face the man and see if we can reason with him. Perhaps all he wants is the money." Sam says aloud.

Sam is thinking, *everything is about the money, isn't it? He just wants the money. That should appease him if we all wire the money to him. That should go a long way to forgiving us for the loss of his brother.* He whispers his thoughts to Ann but she shakes her head.

Sam puts on a flowery T-shirt and laces up his sneakers before leaving the suite. He looks at Ann and kisses her as he closes the door and bows his head.

"I'm sorry Ann." He clings to her desperately.

"It's okay Sam. At least I'm with you. I never want to be anywhere else." She holds Sam tightly too.

"We will make it through this... Well, we'd better go." He embraces Ann a few more seconds not wanting to stop, but knows he must go face the man.

They leave the room on unsteady legs clinging to each other for support. It is not the gentle rock of the boat causing them to stumble along the passageways. Sam keeps one arm around Ann as he raps on the door of Suite 7445. The door opens almost immediately and Sam tenses up seeing Max's solemn face.

Sam looks beyond Max. Although the rain has

stopped apparently as quickly as it started, the deck is wet again. He guesses the rain quit while he and Ann were walking to Max's suite. He sees Don Cresto on the balcony holding a gun to Peggy's head as he follows Max onto the balcony.

Sam is surprised at what Don Cresto is wearing. He has on a heavy jacket over a long sleeve white shirt and dark gray long pants. The jacket is wide open exposing a white bandage under Don's shirt with bloodstains. His shoes look like Bruno Magli leathers that he knew Max once had. Sam thinks, *He is obviously not dressed for a cruise!* He sees Don swing the .38-caliber revolver away from Peggy's head and aim it at him!

Don grimaces with pain. A gentle breeze whips around the balcony disturbing Don's hair as the ship rocks slightly from side to side. The musky cologne Don is wearing overpowers the smell of rain in the air. Don's voice strains when he finally talks.

"So here we are. You can't believe how much I paid for a crummy inside room and look where you are staying. My brother Arturo and my friends Carl, Albert and Bruno are all dead you know, and my father too. You have caused me much pain!"

Sam feels his body on alert. His muscles are tense and his eyes watch for any opportunity to take charge of the situation. He tries to move closer to Don.

"Stay back!" Don's leather shoes slip a little as he moves to the side of the balcony dragging Peggy with him.

"I remember what you did to us on the highway. If you try kicking at me she will be the first to die!"

Sam steps back still watching Don for any opening

to kick at the gun or jump him. There is no opportunity. Sam tries talking to Don.

"Mister Cresto, we are all very sorry for what happened to you and your friends. This has all happened beyond our control. It was a pure accident that we found the diamond."

"Many people have died because of what you did."

"I'm curious. How on earth did you get back here and how did you get a gun on board?"

"You are still curious when you are about to die?" Don Cresto manages to smile at Sam though obviously in pain.

"Yes curious, but we thought your wounds would keep you in Italy. I figure you really just want the money, right?" Sam's mind is racing. He is thinking of anything to stall whatever evil plan Cresto has for them.

"The money would be nice and I did want it. I had to return to America for my own sake. My friend helped me return so I could complete my mission before I die too. I had to come on this cruise because it is so convenient having you all here together."

"How... I mean I thought the screening would catch any attempt to bring a gun onboard." Sam stalls thinking of how to disarm Cresto. After a long silent stare from Cresto, he speaks.

"Okay, I broke it down and wrapped it in aluminum foil to look like a DVD Player in my suitcase. Ingenious, no?"

"They obviously didn't catch that, wow." Sam's eyes sadden. "I'm truly sorry for the death of your brother and your friends, but we had no control over that. We merely returned the diamond to the rightful owners."

"You took the diamond that is rightfully my diamond! Arturo was murdered because we did not get the diamond to sell. He needed money to pay his debts." Don grimaces again and looks at his side. He releases Peggy and she darts over to Max. Don's leather shoes slip again on the wet deck but he catches his balance.

Sam watches the tall man slip. *If those leather shoes slip again, maybe I can jump him!*

Chapter Fifty-Four

Sam sees fresh blood oozing onto Don's shirt and Don holds his free hand to his abdomen.

"You look like you are in pain."

"Not that I care if you know, but I got sewed up by a veterinarian friend of Arturo's. I think I was about to die before I called him. He said just take a lot of Tylenol for pain. I took a lot so I could be here to see you die!"

"We think the diamond rightfully belongs to the Bellasettas. After your friend told us why your father stole the diamond, we thought it really should have gone to your dad's friend Tony Albero, or maybe his relatives since your father killed Tony! So where does that leave us? We just did what we thought was right. I guess we really are dumb asses."

"You fooled Bruno with your 'dumb ass' thing but not me. Now it is time to pay. Who will go overboard first? Sam! Climb up on the rail, or do I have to shoot all of you?" Don's face is crazy with hatred. All of Don's frustrations over years of always doing the right thing blow away his normally sensible mind.

"You can't be serious! What about the money, don't you want the money?" Sam shouts.

"Money will not bring my brother back or my friends. I have lost everything, my brother, my friends, my job, my health. This is the perfect way for you all to die. You go into the ocean by falling off the ship and unless someone sees you, the ship just sails away from you. I may shoot each of you just as you go over to ensure your death!" He leans against the railing and looks over it, keeping his distance from Sam.

"Look down there Sam. It is a long way to the ocean. It is getting dark. The fish will soon be hunting for food!" He motions for Sam to peer over the rail. His foot slips again but he regains his footing. He turns his head toward the ocean for a second.

"A little blood will help attract predators too." Don looks back toward Sam but something catches his eye.

Sam watches as if in slow motion as a large black object with legs flies at Don. He hears Don scream.

"Argh!"

Pop! Don fires a shot at the object. The recoil of the gun and his slick leather shoes cause him to lose his footing and tip over the rail. Don screams as he falls out of sight.

"Aaaaah!"

Sam turns back to look over the stern. All he sees is the churning wake of the ship and a brief sight of Don Cresto before he disappears under the churning water.

"What the Hell just happened!" Sam looks back at Max dumfounded and shaking uncontrollably.

"I threw my spider friend Harry at him!" Max says as he crumbles onto a lounge chair.

"Harry? You named the spider Harry?"

"I thought 'What the Hell'. We're going to die anyway. Maybe he slips with those shoes and you can jump him." Max clasps his hands together. Peggy sits down next to him. They embrace each other shaken by what happened.

"We have to call. We have to tell someone what happened!" Ann begins weeping clutching on to Sam.

"Do we really want to rescue him?" Peggy blurts

still shaking.

"Yes Peggy, please go call the purser! Tell him there is a man overboard! This must be the bad omen I felt." Max lifts his head up.

Peggy separates from Max and runs into the cabin without saying a word. Ann walks with shaky legs to the edge of another wet lounge chair and sits down not caring about the water seeping into her shorts.

Sam sits down next to her hearing the muffled voice of Peggy talking.

"You had a bad omen?" Sam questions Max.

"Well, yes. I have felt uneasy since the first gun battle in Italy. I just feel things. You know, like I knew Gustavo was on our side."

"So all this time, you have been worrying about what would happen?"

"Yes. I could just feel something bad was going to happen. I thought the plane failing was it. Then I thought the Bruno attack was it. But I still had a bad feeling."

"How do you feel now Max?"

"It's over. The feeling is gone. Hey, I think Cresto hit my spider. Did you see what happened to it? Where is it?"

"Here's your spider, behind this lounge chair." Peggy says walking back out on the deck. She feels the ship lurch as it begins slowing down. She looks next to the divider panel. She picks up the spider sticking her finger in a small hole.

Max can see the hole is almost dead center. One eye is missing too. He stares at the damaged toy, then looks at the divider panel, and sees a bullet hole just above the middle. Peggy tosses the spider to Max.

"Thank you Harry! You saved our lives!" Max says.

"You know the purser says the ship will be pretty far away before it can stop! He is sending a tender out to search. He is contacting the coast guard too with hopes they can find Cresto, but he says the chances of finding him alive are slim. At least there is still some daylight. The ship will wait for the tender to get back." She sees Max looking sad at the spider.

"Harry went all the way to Italy and back without a scratch. Now look at him. I'll need to buy another one."

Sam is dizzy from what just happened. His life for the past few months is like a rollercoaster ride switching from elation to fear and back to elation again. *Peaks and valleys*, he thinks. *Maybe this ride is finally over now.*

Two officers in white uniforms come into the suite. They question everyone. Sam explains that apparently the force from the gunshot caused Don Cresto to slip on the wet deck and go over the railing. The gun apparently went overboard with him. There is really no evidence of him even being in Max's suite except for the bullet hole in the middle of the divider panel and the wounded rubber spider. Max is the last one questioned.

"Actually we do not even know what name he was using to get onboard, sir. We were told he had a fake passport." Max tells the officer. By the time the officer finishes questioning Max, it is eight o'clock in the evening.

"Well, that's about it. This explains the gunshot a man reported hearing. Imagine someone wearing leather soles here." The officer reaches for his beeping radiophone.

"Yes?" He listens and then disconnects the call. He turns to Max.

"The crewmen have not found the victim. We will continue the search until dark. We have alerted the coast guard."

"Wow! What a horrible way to go!" Max says.

"Yes. The poor man has little chance of surviving without a life jacket. It's been nearly an hour now and still we have not found him. There is a chance he just sank below the surface." The officer answers his radiophone again.

"We are calling our crewmen back to the ship. The Coast Guard is in the area and will continue the search."

"Could he survive this long?" Max asks.

"We have three foot swells and waves, which is fairly calm. However, with no life jacket in the open ocean he will either die of fright or drown. I suspect it will just be a recovery search."

Max stares at the man trying to believe what he said.

"Unless you have another question I'll be leaving." Seeing them look numbly at him the officer tips his hat, and exits with the other officer.

Chapter Fifty-Five

Max stands around for a minute after the door closes looking at his friends. Finally, he breaks the silence.

"Well guys, I know you are all upset about someone going overboard, but tonight we should celebrate. Unless we hear of some miraculous rescue in the morning, I will call Gustavo when we get into port and give him the good news. Let's go to the fancy dining I read about."

Max exits the suite and as he walks, he is still somewhat dazed. People along the way are laughing and acting normal as if nothing unusual has happened. He finally smiles as he sees the restaurant.

"The Steakhouse!" He shouts.

"What a lovely name!" Peggy says.

"We can have that big thick juicy steak we want now." Sam says.

Max suddenly comes to reality and stops. He is thinking about the two helpings of roast beef, the chicken, a plate full of mashed potatoes, various vegetables, a bowl of cream of mushroom soup, and some dessert treats coupled with a quart or so of iced tea that keeps him from being hungry. He looks at the others for a second.

"Are you guys really hungry?"

"I say no, as much as I want a thick juicy steak." Peggy admits.

"Yeah, maybe that steak can wait a day or so." Sam agrees.

"Okay, let's find a bar instead." Max says.

They wander around until they find a piano bar

near the middle of the ship. They relax on a circular sofa listening to the gentle melody from the piano player dressed in a blue suit white shirt and tie. A fancy barmaid takes their order.

"Well here we are. We are finally on our cruise. Let's have a toast to that deadly diamond and the internet and the Bellasettas and..." Max gives a giant sigh raising his drink, but Sam interrupts.

"Enough Max! Let's just say thanks for our good fortune just to have each other. Here's to our family!" Sam clinks glasses with the other three. He feels humble, proud and warm all at the same time.

They relax listening to the piano for a while. Later Max checks with the purser but there is no news about Cresto. At midnight, they walk along the deck heading for the elevator and their rooms. As they come to where they part for their separate suites, they join in a group hug, a rare moment. They stay together for perhaps a minute holding on to their family before they separate. It is one of those warm and fuzzy feelings, they will never forget. Finally as they separate Max speaks.

"Sam, are you happy you moved back to Fort Lauderdale?" Max watches Sam smile.

"Even with all the scary things happening, it is the best thing that ever happened to me. Thank you, Max, and I think you must continue doing pranks. You're definitely the king of pranks!" Sam pats Max on the back.

"Amen! Your Harry saved us!" Ann nods and smiles.

"Well, I never thought anyone would go overboard for it!"

"Oh that's bad!" Peggy laughs.

"I'll call Gustavo with the good news when we get cell service again." Max grins and waves good night.

Ann and Sam smile as they walk to their room holding hands. Sam goes in and grabs their glasses of wine and the bottle and steps back out onto the balcony. He pours more wine.

"It's funny how things turn out. For lack of a fake spider we could have been fish bait like Don Cresto." Ann trembles from her own words. She sips some wine seeing her hand still shaking a little.

"That's a gruesome way to die. Thank God it wasn't any of us!"

Sam sits on a lounge chair for a while sipping wine and enjoying the view of Ann and the ocean rushing by. He relaxes so much he dozes off. The excitement of the past few days and nearly being fish bait today has drained his energy completely. He wakes to hear Ann.

"I think we should go to bed. It's been a long terrifying day and evening." She walks into the suite setting her glass on the small writing table.

Sam decides to hunt for the bug Cresto planted and finds a small transmitter stuck to the smoke detector. He takes it down and crushes it under his foot. Ann gives Sam an all clear sign. It seems like a sign to Sam that all is well. The knot in his stomach is nearly gone. They brush their teeth and shut off all the lights. The clouds are gone and there is a full moon shining in through the glass doors of the balcony. They slip out of their clothes and snuggle together under the covers.

Even with all the trouble Don Cresto and Arturo caused Sam, he feels a twinge of sorrow for them. He gives Ann a gentle squeeze.

"You know Don and Arturo were just normal guys trying to eke out a living. Their father forced a diamond to die for on them. I think if Sal Cresto had died before he told Don about that diamond Don and Arturo would still be alive and happy. It's sad in a way."

"Well I'm glad it's over. Let's hope for a less terrifying day tomorrow. Hey Sam did you know you're the first millionaire I've ever slept with?"

"Yes and I hope I'm the only one you ever do."

"Oh you!" Ann grabs his face and kisses Sam.

Although Sam is not sitting back on his balcony at home, he feels the danger is finally over. Content and feeling the gentle motion of the ship he kisses Ann again.

"I have to admit, our first cruise is more exciting than I ever thought it would be. Max always says enjoy the journey." Sam says.

"It's definitely not blah." Ann says snuggling against Sam.

Sam feels her warm body caress him. He closes his eyes and smiles. *Life is good!*

-0-

About the Author

Living through many adventures in his life, from hurricanes to sink holes, oak trees falling on his house to amazing rescues, has given Rob a wealth of stories to tell. He now enjoys writing adventure-mystery books that include some of his exciting life events.

Ever since he can remember, Rob wanted to write stories. He did a lot of non-fiction writing in the real estate business, eventually writing an eBook on property management called *The Landlord Way.* He finally began adapting stories based loosely on his early experiences visualizing many more adventures happening in in future stories to come.

His first fiction novel *Deadly Plans* was inspired by a visit to an orange bauxite lake in Jamaica. His Jamaican guide said nothing grows or lives in the lakes and are a dumping place for the byproduct of Jamaica's Bauxite industry. Sometimes the littlest thing can have a lasting effect. Deadly Plans became much more than a tale about the orange lakes it evolved to a tale of two friends Max and Sam who try to stop a shipment of deadly chemical bombs made from the toxic lake mud. Max convinces Sam to travel to Jamaica with him where Sam where Max inadvertently causes a series of deadly plans in his desire to right wrongs.

Follow me at www.facebook.com/Author.Rob.Davis, www.authorrobdavis.com or email me at: author.rob.davis@gmail.com

www.ingramcontent.com/pod-product-compliance
Lightning Source LLC
Chambersburg PA
CBHW061011120726
47910CB00006B/1873